What This Story is About

It was Sam Marlowe's fate to fall in love with a girl on the R.M.S. "Atlantic" (New York to Southampton) who had ideals. She was looking for a man just like Sir Galahad, and refused to be put off with any inferior substitute. A lucky accident on the first day of the voyage placed Sam for the moment in the Galahad class, but he could not stay the pace.

He follows Billie Bennett "around," scheming, blundering and hoping, so does the parrot faced young man Bream Mortimer, Sam's rival.

There is a somewhat hectic series of events at Windles, a country house in Hampshire, where Billie's ideals still block the way and Sam comes on in spite of everything.

Then comes the moment when Billie.... It is a Wodehouse novel in every sense of the term.

ONE MOMENT!

Before my friend Mr. Jenkins—wait a minute, Herbert—before my friend Mr. Jenkins formally throws this book open to the public, I should like to say a few words. You, sir, and you, and you at the back, if you will kindly restrain your impatience.... There is no need to jostle. There will be copies for all. Thank you. I shall not detain you long.

I wish to clear myself of a possible charge of plagiarism. You smile. Ah! but you don't know. You don't realise how careful even a splendid fellow like myself has to be. You wouldn't have me go down to posterity as Pelham the Pincher, would you? No! Very well, then. By the time this volume is in the hands of the customers, everybody will, of course, have read Mr. J. Storer Clouston's "The Lunatic at Large Again." (Those who are chumps enough to miss it deserve no consideration.) Well, both the hero of "The Lunatic" and my "Sam Marlowe" try to get out of a tight corner by hiding in a suit of armour in the hall

The Girl on the Boat

Pelham Grenville Wodehouse

TUTIS Digital Publishing Pvt Ltd

ISBN 978-81-89952-91-4

THE GIRL ON THE BOAT

This impression 2007

Published by
TUTIS Digital Publishing Pvt Ltd.
26 Ramasamy Street
T. Nagar, Chennai 600 017

of a country-house. Looks fishy, yes? And yet I call on Heaven to witness that I am innocent, innocent. And, if the word of Northumberland Avenue Wodehouse is not sufficient, let me point out that this story and Mr. Clouston's appeared simultaneously in serial form in their respective magazines. This proves, I think, that at these cross-roads, at any rate, there has been no dirty work. All right, Herb., you can let 'em in now.

P. G. WODEHOUSE.

Constitutional Club,
Northumberland Avenue.

CONTENTS

CHAPTER I

A Disturbing Morning

Through the curtained windows of the furnished flat which Mrs. Horace Hignett had rented for her stay in New York, rays of golden sunlight peeped in like the foremost spies of some advancing army. It was a fine summer morning. The hands of the Dutch clock in the hall pointed to thirteen minutes past nine; those of the ormolu clock in the sitting-room to eleven minutes past ten; those of the carriage clock on the bookshelf to fourteen minutes to six. In other words, it was exactly eight; and Mrs. Hignett acknowledged the fact by moving her head on the pillow, opening her eyes, and sitting up in bed. She always woke at eight precisely.

Was this Mrs. Hignett *the* Mrs. Hignett, the world-famous writer on Theosophy, the author of "The Spreading Light," "What of the Morrow," and all the rest of that well-known series? I'm glad you

1

asked me. Yes, she was. She had come over to America on a lecturing tour.

About this time there was a good deal of suffering in the United States, for nearly every boat that arrived from England was bringing a fresh swarm of British lecturers to the country. Novelists, poets, scientists, philosophers, and plain, ordinary bores; some herd instinct seemed to affect them all simultaneously. It was like one of those great race movements of the Middle Ages. Men and women of widely differing views on religion, art, politics, and almost every other subject; on this one point the intellectuals of Great Britain were single-minded, that there was easy money to be picked up on the lecture-platforms of America, and that they might just as well grab it as the next person.

Mrs. Hignett had come over with the first batch of immigrants; for, spiritual as her writings were, there was a solid streak of business sense in this woman, and she meant to get hers while the getting was good. She was half way across the Atlantic with a complete itinerary booked, before ninety per cent. of the poets and philosophers had finished sorting out their clean collars and getting their photographs taken for the passport.

She had not left England without a pang, for departure had involved sacrifices. More than anything else in the world she loved her charming home, Windles, in the county of Hampshire, for so many years the seat of the Hignett family. Windles was as the breath of life to her. Its shady walks, its silver lake, its noble elms, the old grey stone of its walls— these were bound up with her very being. She felt that she belonged to Windles, and Windles to her. Unfortunately, as a matter of cold, legal accuracy, it did not. She did but hold it in trust for her son, Eustace, until such time as he should marry and take possession of it himself. There were times when the thought of Eustace marrying and bringing a strange woman to Windles chilled Mrs. Hignett to her very marrow. Happily, her firm policy of keeping her son permanently under her eye at home and never permitting him to have speech with a female below the age of fifty, had averted the peril up till now.

Eustace had accompanied his mother to America. It was his faint snores which she could hear in the adjoining room as, having bathed and dressed, she went down the hall to where breakfast awaited her. She smiled tolerantly. She had never desired to convert her son to her own early-rising habits, for, apart from not allowing him to call his soul his own, she was an indulgent mother. Eustace would get up at half-past nine, long after she had finished breakfast, read her correspondence, and started her duties for the day.

Breakfast was on the table in the sitting-room, a modest meal of rolls, porridge, and imitation coffee. Beside the pot containing this hell-brew, was a little pile of letters. Mrs. Hignett opened them as she ate. The majority were from disciples and dealt with matters of purely theosophical interest. There was an invitation from the Butterfly Club, asking her to be the guest of honour at their weekly dinner. There was a letter from her brother Mallaby—Sir Mallaby Marlowe, the eminent London lawyer—saying that his son Sam, of whom she had never approved, would be in New York shortly, passing through on his way back to England, and hoping that she would see something of him. Altogether a dull mail. Mrs. Hignett skimmed through it without interest, setting aside one or two of the letters for Eustace, who acted as her unpaid secretary, to answer later in the day.

She had just risen from the table, when there was a sound of voices in the hall, and presently the domestic staff, a gaunt Irish lady of advanced years, entered the room.

"Ma'am, there was a gentleman."

Mrs. Hignett was annoyed. Her mornings were sacred.

"Didn't you tell him I was not to be disturbed?"

"I did not. I loosed him into the parlour." The staff remained for a moment in melancholy silence, then resumed. "He says he's your nephew. His name's Marlowe."

Mrs. Hignett experienced no diminution of her annoyance. She had not seen her nephew Sam for ten years, and would have been willing to extend the period. She remembered him as an untidy small boy who once or twice, during his school holidays, had disturbed the cloistral peace of Windles with his beastly presence. However, blood being thicker than water, and all that sort of thing, she supposed she would have to give him five minutes. She went into the sitting-room, and found there a young man who looked more or less like all other young men, though perhaps rather fitter than most. He had grown a good deal since she had last met him, as men so often do between the ages of fifteen and twenty-five, and was now about six feet in height, about forty inches round the chest, and in weight about thirteen stone. He had a brown and amiable face, marred at the moment by an expression of discomfort somewhat akin to that of a cat in a strange alley.

"Hullo, Aunt Adeline!" he said awkwardly.

"Well, Samuel!" said Mrs. Hignett.

There was a pause. Mrs. Hignett, who was not fond of young men and disliked having her mornings broken into, was thinking that he had not improved in the slightest degree since their last meeting; and Sam, who imagined that he had long since grown to man's estate and put off childish things, was embarrassed to discover that his aunt still affected him as of old. That is to say, she made him feel as if he had omitted to shave and, in addition to that, had swallowed some drug which had caused him to swell unpleasantly, particularly about the hands and feet.

"Jolly morning," said Sam, perseveringly.

"So I imagine. I have not yet been out."

"Thought I'd look in and see how you were."

"That was very kind of you. The morning is my busy time, but ... yes, that was very kind of you!"

There was another pause.

"How do you like America?" said Sam.

"I dislike it exceedingly."

"Yes? Well, of course, some people do. Prohibition and all that. Personally, it doesn't affect me. I can take it or leave it alone. I like America myself," said Sam. "I've had a wonderful time. Everybody's treated me like a rich uncle. I've been in Detroit, you know, and they practically gave me the city and asked me if I'd like another to take home in my pocket. Never saw anything like it. I might have been the missing heir! I think America's the greatest invention on record."

"And what brought you to America?" said Mrs. Hignett, unmoved by this rhapsody.

"Oh, I came over to play golf. In a tournament, you know."

"Surely at your age," said Mrs. Hignett, disapprovingly, "you could be better occupied. Do you spend your whole time playing golf?"

"Oh, no! I play cricket a bit and shoot a bit and I swim a good lot and I still play football occasionally."

"I wonder your father does not insist on your doing some useful work."

"He is beginning to harp on the subject rather. I suppose I shall take a stab at it sooner or later. Father says I ought to get married, too."

"He is perfectly right."

"I suppose old Eustace will be getting hitched up one of these days?" said Sam.

Mrs. Hignett started violently.

"Why do you say that?"

"Eh?"

"What makes you say that?"

"Oh, well, he's a romantic sort of fellow. Writes poetry, and all that."

"There is no likelihood at all of Eustace marrying. He is of a shy and retiring temperament, and sees few women. He is almost a recluse."

Sam was aware of this, and had frequently regretted it. He had always been fond of his cousin in that half-amused and rather patronising way in which men of thews and sinews are fond of the weaker brethren who run more to pallor and intellect; and he had always felt that if Eustace had not had to retire to Windles to spend his life with a woman whom from his earliest years he had always considered the Empress of the Washouts, much might have been made of him. Both at school and at Oxford, Eustace had been—if not a sport—at least a decidedly cheery old bean. Sam remembered Eustace at school, breaking gas globes with a slipper in a positively rollicking manner. He remembered him at Oxford playing up to him manfully at the piano on the occasion when he had done that imitation of Frank Tinney which had been such a hit at the Trinity smoker. Yes, Eustace had had the makings of a pretty sound egg, and it was too bad that he had allowed his mother to coop him up down in the country, miles away from anywhere.

"Eustace is returning to England on Saturday," said Mrs. Hignett. She spoke a little wistfully. She had not been parted from her son since he had come down from Oxford; and she would have liked to keep him with her till the end of her lecturing tour. That, however, was out of the question. It was imperative that, while she was away, he should be at Windles. Nothing would have induced her to leave the place at the mercy of servants who might trample over the flowerbeds, scratch the polished floors, and forget to cover up the canary at night. "He sails on the 'Atlantic.'"

"That's splendid!" said Sam. "I'm sailing on the 'Atlantic' myself. I'll go down to the office and see if we can't have a stateroom together. But where is he going to live when he gets to England?"

"Where is he going to live? Why, at Windles, of course. Where else?"

"But I thought you were letting Windles for the summer?"

Mrs. Hignett stared.

"Letting Windles!" She spoke as one might address a lunatic. "What put that extraordinary idea into your head?"

"I thought father said something about your letting the place to some American."

"Nothing of the kind!"

It seemed to Sam that his aunt spoke somewhat vehemently, even snappishly, in correcting what was a perfectly natural mistake. He could not know that the subject of letting Windles for the summer was one which had long since begun to infuriate Mrs. Hignett. People had certainly asked her to let Windles. In fact, people had pestered her. There was a rich, fat man, an American named Bennett, whom she had met just before sailing at her brother's house in London. Invited down to Windles for the day, Mr. Bennett had fallen in love with the place, and had begged her to name her own price. Not content with this, he had pursued her with his pleadings by means of the wireless telegraph while she was on the ocean, and had not given up the struggle even when she reached New York. She had not been in America two days when there had arrived a Mr. Mortimer, bosom friend of Mr. Bennett, carrying on the matter where the other had left off. For a whole week Mr. Mortimer had tried to induce her to reconsider her decision, and had only stopped because he had had to leave for England himself, to join his friend. And even then the thing had gone on. Indeed, this very morning, among the letters on Mrs. Hignett's table, the buff envelope of a cable from Mr. Bennett had peeped out, nearly spoiling her breakfast. No wonder, then, that Sam's allusion to the affair had caused the authoress of "The Spreading Light" momentarily to lose her customary calm.

"Nothing will induce me ever to let Windles," she said with finality, and rose significantly. Sam, perceiving that the audience was at an end—and glad of it—also got up.

"Well, I think I'll be going down and seeing about that state-room" he said.

"Certainly. I am a little busy just now, preparing notes for my next lecture."

"Of course, yes. Mustn't interrupt you. I suppose you're having a great time, gassing away—I mean—well, good-bye!"

"Good-bye!"

Mrs. Hignett, frowning, for the interview had ruffled her and disturbed that equable frame of mind which is so vital to the preparation of lectures on Theosophy, sat down at the writing-table and began to go through the notes which she had made overnight. She had hardly succeeded in concentrating herself when the door opened to admit the daughter of Erin once more.

"Ma'am, there was a gentleman."

"This is intolerable!" cried Mrs. Hignett. "Did you tell him that I was busy?"

"I did not. I loosed him into the dining-room."

"Is he a reporter from one of the newspapers?"

"He is not. He has spats and a tall-shaped hat. His name is Bream Mortimer."

"Bream Mortimer!"

"Yes, ma'am. He handed me a bit of a kyard, but I dropped it, being slippy from the dishes."

Mrs. Hignett strode to the door with a forbidding expression. This, as she had justly remarked, was intolerable. She remembered Bream Mortimer. He was the son of the Mr. Mortimer who wanted Windles. This visit could only have to do with the subject of Windles, and she went into the dining-room in a state of cold fury, determined to squash the

Mortimer family, in the person of their New York representative, once and for all.

"Good morning, Mr. Mortimer."

Bream Mortimer was tall and thin. He had small bright eyes and a sharply curving nose. He looked much more like a parrot than most parrots do. It gave strangers a momentary shock of surprise when they saw Bream Mortimer in restaurants, eating roast beef. They had the feeling that he would have preferred sunflower seeds.

"Morning, Mrs. Hignett."

"Please sit down."

Bream Mortimer looked as though he would rather have hopped on to a perch, but he sat down. He glanced about the room with gleaming, excited eyes.

"Mrs. Hignett, I must have a word with you alone!"

"You *are* having a word with me alone."

"I hardly know how to begin."

"Then let me help you. It is quite impossible. I will never consent."

Bream Mortimer started.

"Then you have heard about it?"

"I have heard about nothing else since I met Mr. Bennett in London. Mr. Bennett talked about nothing else. Your father talked about nothing else. And now," cried Mrs. Hignett, fiercely, "you come and try to re-open the subject. Once and for all, nothing will alter my decision. No money will induce me to let my house."

"But I didn't come about that!"

"You did not come about Windles?"

"Good Lord, no!"

"Then will you kindly tell me why you have come?"

Bream Mortimer seemed embarrassed. He wriggled a little, and moved his arms as if he were trying to flap them.

"You know," he said, "I'm not a man who butts into other people's affairs...." He stopped.

"No?" said Mrs. Hignett.

Bream began again.

"I'm not a man who gossips with valets...."

"No?"

"I'm not a man who...."

Mrs. Hignett was never a very patient woman.

"Let us take all your negative qualities for granted," she said curtly. "I have no doubt that there are many things which you do not do. Let us confine ourselves to issues of definite importance. What is it, if you have no objection to concentrating your attention on that for a moment, that you wish to see me about?"

"This marriage."

"What marriage?"

"Your son's marriage."

"My son is not married."

"No, but he's going to be. At eleven o'clock this morning at the Little Church Round the Corner!"

Mrs. Hignett stared.

"Are you mad?"

"Well, I'm not any too well pleased, I'm bound to say," admitted Mr. Mortimer. "You see, darn it all, I'm in love with the girl myself!"

"Who is this girl?"

"Have been for years. I'm one of those silent, patient fellows who hang around and look a lot but never tell their love...."

"Who is this girl who has entrapped my son?"

"I've always been one of those men who...."

"Mr. Mortimer! With your permission we will take your positive qualities, also, for granted. In fact, we will not discuss you at all. You come to me with this absurd story...."

"Not absurd. Honest fact. I had it from my valet who had it from her maid."

"Will you please tell me who is the girl my misguided son wishes to marry?"

"I don't know that I'd call him misguided," said Mr. Mortimer, as one desiring to be fair. "I think he's a right smart picker! She's such a corking girl, you know. We were children together, and I've loved her for years. Ten years at least. But you know how it is—somehow one never seems to get in line for a proposal. I thought I saw an opening in the summer of nineteen-twelve, but it blew over. I'm not one of these smooth, dashing chaps, you see, with a great line of talk. I'm not...."

"If you will kindly," said Mrs. Hignett impatiently, "postpone this essay in psycho-analysis to some future occasion, I shall be greatly obliged. I am waiting to hear the name of the girl my son wishes to marry."

"Haven't I told you?" said Mr. Mortimer, surprised. "That's odd. I haven't. It's funny how one doesn't do the things one thinks one does. I'm the sort of man...."

"What is her name?"

"... the sort of man who...."

"What is her name?"

"Bennett."

"Bennett? Wilhelmina Bennett? The daughter of Mr. Rufus Bennett? The red-haired girl I met at lunch one day at your father's house?"

"That's it. You're a great guesser. I think you ought to stop the thing."

"I intend to."

"Fine!"

"The marriage would be unsuitable in every way. Miss Bennett and my son do not vibrate on the same plane."

"That's right. I've noticed it myself."

"Their auras are not the same colour."

"If I've thought that once," said Bream Mortimer, "I've thought it a hundred times. I wish I had a dollar for every time I've thought it. Not the same colour. That's the whole thing in a nutshell."

"I am much obliged to you for coming and telling me of this. I shall take immediate steps."

"That's good. But what's the procedure? It's getting late. She'll be waiting at the church at eleven."

"Eustace will not be there."

"You think you can fix it?"

"Eustace will not be there," repeated Mrs. Hignett.

Bream Mortimer hopped down from his chair.

"Well, you've taken a weight off my mind."

"A mind, I should imagine, scarcely constructed to bear great weights."

"I'll be going. Haven't had breakfast yet. Too worried to eat breakfast. Relieved now. This is where three eggs and a rasher of ham get cut off in their prime. I feel I can rely on you."

"You can!"

"Then I'll say good-bye."

"Good-bye."

"I mean really good-bye. I'm sailing for England on Saturday on the 'Atlantic.'"

"Indeed? My son will be your fellow-traveller."

Bream Mortimer looked somewhat apprehensive.

"You won't tell him that I was the one who spilled the beans?"

"I beg your pardon?"

"You won't wise him up that I threw a spanner into the machinery?"

"I do not understand you."

"You won't tell him that I crabbed his act … gave the thing away … gummed the game?"

"I shall not mention your chivalrous intervention."

"Chivalrous?" said Bream Mortimer a little doubtfully. "I don't know that I'd call it absolutely chivalrous. Of course, all's fair in love and war. Well, I'm glad you're going to keep my share in the business under your hat. It might have been awkward meeting him on board."

"You are not likely to meet Eustace on board. He is a very indifferent sailor and spends most of his time in his cabin."

"That's good! Saves a lot of awkward-ness. Well, good-bye."

"Good-bye. When you reach England, remember me to your father."

"He won't have forgotten you," said Bream Mortimer, confidently. He did not see how it was humanly possible for anyone to forget this woman. She was like a celebrated chewing-gum. The taste lingered.

Mrs. Hignett was a woman of instant and decisive action. Even while her late visitor was speaking, schemes had begun to form in her mind like bubbles rising to the surface of a rushing river. By the time the door had closed behind Bream Mortimer she had at her disposal no fewer than seven, all good. It took her but a moment to select the best and simplest. She tiptoed softly to her son's room. Rhythmic snores greeted her listening ears. She opened the door and went noiselessly in.

CHAPTER II

Gallant Rescue by Well-Dressed Young Man

§ 1

The White Star liner "Atlantic" lay at her pier with steam up and gangway down, ready for her trip to Southampton. The hour of departure was near, and there was a good deal of mixed activity going on. Sailors fiddled about with ropes. Junior officers flitted to and fro. White-jacketed stewards wrestled with trunks. Probably the captain, though not visible, was also employed on some useful work of a nautical nature and not wasting his time. Men, women, boxes, rugs, dogs, flowers, and baskets of fruits were flowing on board in a steady stream.

The usual drove of citizens had come to see the travellers off. There were men on the passenger-list who were being seen off by fathers, by mothers, by sisters, by cousins, and by aunts. In the steerage, there was an elderly

Jewish lady who was being seen off by exactly thirty-seven of her late neighbours in Rivington Street. And two men in the second cabin were being seen off by detectives, surely the crowning compliment a great nation can bestow. The cavernous Customs sheds were congested with friends and relatives, and Sam Marlowe, heading for the gang-plank, was only able to make progress by employing all the muscle and energy which Nature had bestowed upon him, and which during the greater part of his life he had developed by athletic exercise. However, after some minutes of silent endeavour, now driving his shoulder into the midriff of some obstructing male, now courteously lifting some stout female off his feet, he had succeeded in struggling to within a few yards of his goal, when suddenly a sharp pain shot through his right arm, and he spun round with a cry.

It seemed to Sam that he had been bitten, and this puzzled him, for New York crowds, though they may shove and jostle, rarely bite.

He found himself face to face with an extraordinarily pretty girl.

She was a red-haired girl, with the beautiful ivory skin which goes with red hair. Her eyes, though they were under the shadow of her hat, and he could not be certain, he diagnosed as green, or may be blue, or possibly grey. Not that it mattered, for he had a catholic taste in feminine eyes. So long as they were large and bright, as were the specimens under his immediate notice, he was not the man to quibble about a point of colour. Her nose was small, and on the very tip of it there was a tiny freckle. Her mouth was nice and wide, her chin soft and round. She was just about the height which every girl ought to be. Her figure was trim, her feet tiny, and she wore one of those dresses of which a man can say no more than that they look pretty well all right.

Nature abhors a vacuum. Samuel Marlowe was a susceptible young man, and for many a long month his heart had been lying empty, all swept and garnished, with "Welcome" on the mat.

This girl seemed to rush in and fill it. She was not the prettiest girl he had ever seen. She was the third prettiest. He had an orderly mind, one capable of classifying and docketing girls. But there was a subtle something about her, a sort of how-shall-one-put-it, which he had never encountered before. He swallowed convulsively. His well-developed chest swelled beneath its covering of blue flannel and invisible stripe. At last, he told himself, he was in love, really in love, and at first sight, too, which made it all the more impressive. He doubted whether in the whole course of history anything like this had ever happened before to anybody. Oh, to clasp this girl to him and....

But she had bitten him in the arm. That was hardly the right spirit. That, he felt, constituted an obstacle.

"Oh, I'm so sorry!" she cried.

Well, of course, if she regretted her rash act.... After all, an impulsive girl might bite a man in the arm in the excitement of the moment and still have a sweet, womanly nature....

"The crowd seems to make Pinky-Boodles so nervous."

Sam might have remained mystified, but at this juncture there proceeded from a bundle of rugs in the neighbourhood of the girl's lower ribs, a sharp yapping sound, of such a calibre as to be plainly audible over the confused noise of Mamies who were telling Sadies to be sure and write, of Bills who were instructing Dicks to look up old Joe in Paris and give him their best, and of all the fruit-boys, candy-boys, magazine-boys, American-flag-boys, and telegraph boys who were honking their wares on every side.

"I hope he didn't hurt you much. You're the third person he's bitten to-day." She kissed the animal in a loving and congratulatory way on the tip of his black nose. "Not counting waiters at the hotel, of course," she added. And then she was swept from him in the crowd, and he was left thinking of all the things he might have said—all those graceful, witty, ingratiating things which just make a bit of difference on these occasions.

He had said nothing. Not a sound, exclusive of the first sharp yowl of pain, had proceeded from him. He had just goggled. A rotten exhibition! Perhaps he would never see this girl again. She looked the sort of girl who comes to see friends off and doesn't sail herself. And what memory of him would she retain? She would mix him up with the time when she went to visit the deaf-and-dumb hospital.

§ 2

Sam reached the gang-plank, showed his ticket, and made his way through the crowd of passengers, passengers' friends, stewards, junior officers, and sailors who infested the deck. He proceeded down the main companion-way, through a rich smell of india-rubber and mixed pickles, as far as the dining saloon; then turned down the narrow passage leading to his state-room.

State-rooms on ocean liners are curious things. When you see them on the chart in the passenger-office, with the gentlemanly clerk drawing rings round them in pencil, they seem so vast that you get the impression that, after stowing away all your trunks, you will have room left over to do a bit of entertaining— possibly an informal dance or something. When you go on board, you find that the place has shrunk to the dimensions of an undersized cupboard in which it would be impossible to swing a cat. And then, about the second day out, it suddenly expands again. For one reason or another the necessity for swinging cats does not arise, and you find yourself quite comfortable.

Sam, balancing himself on the narrow, projecting ledge which the chart in the passenger-office had grandiloquently described as a lounge, began to feel the depression which marks the second phase. He almost wished now that he had not been so energetic in having his room changed in order to enjoy the company of his cousin Eustace. It was going to be a tight fit. Eustace's bag was already in the cabin, and it seemed to take up the entire fairway. Still, after all, Eustace was a good sort, and would be a cheerful companion. And Sam realised that if the girl with the red hair was not a passenger on the boat, he was going to have need of diverting society.

A footstep sounded in the passage outside. The door opened.

"Hullo, Eustace!" said Sam.

Eustace Hignett nodded listlessly, sat down on his bag, and emitted a deep sigh. He was a small, fragile-looking young man with a pale, intellectual face. Dark hair fell in a sweep over his forehead. He looked like a man who would write *vers libre*, as indeed he did.

"Hullo!" he said, in a hollow voice.

Sam regarded him blankly. He had not seen him for some years, but, going by his recollections of him at the University, he had expected something cheerier than this. In fact, he had rather been relying on Eustace to be the life and soul of the party. The man sitting on the bag before him could hardly have filled that role at a gathering of Russian novelists.

"What on earth's the matter?" said Sam.

"The matter?" Eustace Hignett laughed mirthlessly. "Oh, nothing. Nothing much. Nothing to signify. Only my heart's broken." He eyed with considerable malignity the bottle of water in the rack above his head, a harmless object provided by the White Star Company for clients who might desire to clean their teeth during the voyage.

"If you would care to hear the story...?" he said.

"Go ahead."

"It is quite short."

"That's good."

"Soon after I arrived in America, I met a girl...."

"Talking of girls," said Sam with enthusiasm, "I've just seen the only one in the world that really amounts to anything. It was like this. I was shoving my way through the mob on the dock, when suddenly...."

"Shall I tell you my story, or will you tell yours?"

"Oh, sorry! Go ahead."

Eustace Hignett scowled at the printed notice on the wall, informing occupants of the state-room that the name of their steward was J. B. Midgeley.

"She was an extraordinarily pretty girl...."

"So was mine! I give you my honest word I never in all my life saw such...."

"Of course, if you prefer that I postponed my narrative?" said Eustace coldly.

"Oh, sorry! Carry on."

"She was an extraordinarily pretty girl...."

"What was her name?"

"Wilhelmina Bennett. She was an extraordinarily pretty girl, and highly intelligent. I read her all my poems, and she appreciated them immensely. She enjoyed my singing. My conversation appeared to interest her. She admired my...."

"I see. You made a hit. Now get on with the story."

"Don't bustle me," said Eustace querulously.

"Well, you know, the voyage only takes eight days."

"I've forgotten where I was."

"You were saying what a devil of a chap she thought you. What happened? I suppose, when you actually came to propose, you found she was engaged to some other johnny?"

"Not at all! I asked her to be my wife and she consented. We both agreed that a quiet wedding was what we wanted—she thought her father might stop the thing if he knew, and I was dashed sure my mother would—so we decided to get married without telling anybody. By now," said Eustace, with a morose glance at the porthole, "I ought to have been on my honeymoon. Everything was settled. I had the licence and the parson's fee. I had been breaking in a new tie for the wedding."

"And then you quarrelled?"

"Nothing of the kind. I wish you would stop trying to tell me the story. I'm telling *you*. What happened was this: somehow—I can't make out how—mother found out. And then, of course, it was all over. She stopped the thing."

Sam was indignant. He thoroughly disliked his Aunt Adeline, and his cousin's meek subservience to her revolted him.

"Stopped it? I suppose she said 'Now, Eustace, you mustn't!' and you said 'Very well, mother!' and scratched the fixture?"

"She didn't say a word. She never has said a word. As far as that goes, she might never have heard anything about the marriage."

"Then how do you mean she stopped it?"

"She pinched my trousers!"

"Pinched your trousers!"

Eustace groaned. "All of them! The whole bally lot! She gets up long before I do, and she must have come into my room and cleaned it out while I was asleep. When I woke up and started to dress, I couldn't find a single damned pair of bags in the whole place. I looked everywhere. Finally, I went into the sitting-room where she was writing letters and asked if she had happened to see any anywhere. She said she had sent them all to be pressed. She said she knew I never went out in the mornings—I don't as a rule—and they would be back at lunch-time. A fat lot of use that was! I had to be at the church at eleven. Well, I told her I had a most important engagement with a man at eleven, and she wanted to know what it was, and I tried to think of something, but it sounded pretty feeble, and she said I had better telephone to the man and put it off. I did it, too. Rang up the first number in the book and told some fellow I had never seen in my life that I couldn't meet him because I hadn't any trousers! He was pretty peeved, judging from what he said about my being on the wrong number. And mother, listening all the time, and I knowing that she knew— something told me that she knew—and she knowing that I knew she knew.... I tell you, it was awful!"

"And the girl?"

"She broke off the engagement. Apparently she waited at the church from eleven till one-thirty, and then began to get impatient. She wouldn't see me when I called in the afternoon, but I got a letter from her saying that what had happened was all for the best, as she had been thinking it over and had come to the conclusion that she had made a mistake. She said something about my not being as dynamic as she had thought

I was. She said that what she wanted was something more like Lancelot or Sir Galahad, and would I look on the episode as closed."

"Did you explain about the trousers?"

"Yes. It seemed to make things worse. She said that she could forgive a man anything except being ridiculous."

"I think you're well out of it," said Sam, judicially. "She can't have been much of a girl."

"I feel that now. But it doesn't alter the fact that my life is ruined. I have become a woman-hater. It's an infernal nuisance, because practically all the poetry I have ever written rather went out of its way to boost women, and now I'll have to start all over again and approach the subject from another angle. Women! When I think how mother behaved and how Wilhelmina treated me, I wonder there isn't a law against them. 'What mighty ills have not been done by Woman! Who was't betrayed the Capitol....'"

"In Washington?" said Sam, puzzled. He had heard nothing of this. But then he generally confined his reading of the papers to the sporting page.

"In Rome, you ass! Ancient Rome."

"Oh, as long ago as that?"

"I was quoting from Thomas Otway's 'Orphan.' I wish I could write like Otway. He knew what he was talking about. 'Who was't betrayed the Capitol? A woman. Who lost Marc Anthony the world? A woman. Who was the cause of a long ten years' war and laid at last old Troy in ashes? Woman! Destructive, damnable, deceitful woman!'"

"Well, of course, he may be right in a way. As regards some women, I mean. But the girl I met on the dock...."

"Don't!" said Eustace Hignett. "If you have anything bitter and derogatory to say about women, say it and I will listen eagerly. But if you merely wish to gibber about the ornamental exterior of some dashed girl you have been fool enough to get attracted by, go and tell it to the captain or the ship's cat or J. B. Midgeley. Do try to realise that I am a soul in torment. I am a ruin, a spent force, a man without a future. What does life hold for me? Love? I shall never love again. My work? I haven't any. I think I shall take to drink."

"Talking of that," said Sam, "I suppose they open the bar directly we pass the three-mile limit. How about a small one?"

Eustace shook his head gloomily.

"Do you suppose I pass my time on board ship in gadding about and feasting? Directly the vessel begins to move, I go to bed and stay there. As a matter of fact, I think it would be wisest to go to bed now. Don't let me keep you if you want to go on deck."

"It looks to me," said Sam, "as if I had been mistaken in thinking that you were going to be a ray of sunshine on the voyage."

"Ray of sunshine!" said Eustace Hignett, pulling a pair of mauve pyjamas out of the kit-bag. "I'm going to be a volcano!"

Sam left the state-room and headed for the companion. He wanted to get on deck and ascertain if that girl was still on board. About now, the sheep would be separating from the goats; the passengers would be on deck and their friends returning to the shore. A slight tremor in the boards on which he trod told him that this separation must have already taken place. The ship was moving. He ran lightly up the companion. Was she on board or was she not? The next few minutes would decide. He reached the top of the stairs, and passed out on to the crowded deck. And, as he did so, a scream, followed by confused shouting, came from the rail nearest the shore. He perceived that the rail was black with people hanging over it. They were all looking into the water.

Samuel Marlowe was not one of those who pass aloofly by when there is excitement toward. If a horse fell down in the street, he was always among those present: and he was never too busy to stop and stare at a blank window on which were inscribed the words, "Watch this space!" In short, he was one of Nature's rubbernecks, and to dash to the rail and shove a fat man in a tweed cap to one side was with him the work of a moment. He had thus an excellent view of what was going on—a view which he improved the next instant by climbing up and kneeling on the rail.

There was a man in the water, a man whose upper section, the only one visible, was clad in a blue jersey. He wore a bowler hat, and from time to time, as he battled with the waves, he would put up a hand and adjust this more firmly on his head. A dressy swimmer.

Scarcely had he taken in this spectacle when Marlowe became aware of the girl he had met on the dock. She was standing a few feet away, leaning out over the rail with wide eyes and parted lips. Like everybody else, she was staring into the water.

As Sam looked at her, the thought crossed his mind that here was a wonderful chance of making the most tremendous impression on this girl. What would she not think of a man who, reckless of his own safety, dived in and went boldly to the rescue? And there were men, no doubt, who would be chumps enough to do it, he thought, as he prepared to shift back to a position of greater safety.

At this moment, the fat man in the tweed cap, incensed at having been jostled out of the front row, made his charge. He had but been crouching, the better to spring. Now he sprang. His full weight took Sam squarely in the spine. There was an instant in which that young man hung, as it were, between sea and sky: then he shot down over the rail to join the man in the blue jersey, who had just discovered that his hat was not on straight and had paused to adjust it once more with a few skilful touches of the finger.

§ 3

In the brief interval of time which Marlowe had spent in the state-room chatting with Eustace about the latter's bruised soul, some rather curious things had been happening above. Not extraordinary, perhaps, but curious. These must now be related. A story, if it is to grip the reader, should, I am aware, go always forward. It should march. It should leap from crag to crag like the chamois of the Alps. If there is one thing I hate, it is a novel which gets you interested in the hero in chapter one and then cuts back in chapter two to tell you all about his grandfather. Nevertheless, at this point we must go back a space. We must return to the moment when, having deposited her Pekinese dog in her state-room, the girl with the red hair came out again on deck. This happened just about the time when Eustace Hignett was beginning his narrative.

The girl went to the rail and gazed earnestly at the shore. There was a rattle, as the gang-plank moved inboard and was deposited on the deck. The girl uttered a little cry of dismay. Then suddenly her face brightened, and she began to wave her arm to attract the attention of an elderly man with a red face made redder by exertion, who had just forced his way to the edge of the dock and was peering up at the passenger-lined rail.

The boat had now begun to move slowly out of its slip, backing into the river. It was now that the man on the dock sighted the girl. She gesticulated at him. He gesticulated at her. He produced a handkerchief, swiftly tied up a bundle of currency bills in it, backed to give himself room, and then, with all the strength of his arm, hurled the bills in the direction of the deck. The handkerchief with its precious contents shot in a graceful arc towards the deck, fell short by a good six feet, and dropped into the water, where it unfolded like a lily, sending twenty-dollar bills, ten-dollar bills, five-dollar bills, and an assortment of ones floating out over the wavelets.

It was at this moment that Mr. Oscar Swenson, one of the thriftiest souls who ever came out of Sweden, perceived that the chance of a lifetime had arrived for adding substantially to his little savings.

By profession he was one of those men who eke out a precarious livelihood by rowing dreamily about the water-front in skiffs. He was doing so now: and, as he sat meditatively in his skiff, having done his best to give the liner a good send off by paddling round her in circles, the pleading face of a twenty-dollar bill peered up at him. Mr. Swenson was not the man to resist the appeal. He uttered a sharp bark of ecstasy, pressed his bowler hat firmly upon his brow, and dived in. A moment later he had risen to the surface, and was gathering up money with both hands.

He was still busy with this congenial task when a tremendous splash at his side sent him under again: and, rising for a second time, he observed with not a little chagrin that he had been joined by a young man in a blue flannel suit with an invisible stripe.

"Svensk!" exclaimed Mr. Swenson, or whatever it is that natives of Sweden exclaim in moments of justifiable annoyance. He resented the advent of this newcomer. He had been getting along fine and had had the situation well in hand. To him Sam Marlowe represented Competition, and Mr. Swenson desired no competitors in his treasure-seeking enterprise. He travels, thought Mr. Swenson, the fastest who travels alone.

Sam Marlowe had a touch of the philosopher in him. He had the ability to adapt himself to circumstances. It had been no part of his plans to come whizzing down off the rail into this singularly soup-like water which tasted in equal parts of oil and dead rats; but, now that he was here he was prepared to make the best of the situation. Swimming, it happened, was one of the things he did best, and somewhere among his belongings at home was a tarnished pewter cup which he had won at school in the "Saving Life" competition. He knew exactly what to do. You get behind the victim and grab him firmly under his arms, and then you start swimming on your back. A moment later, the astonished Mr. Swenson who, being practically amphibious, had not anticipated that anyone would have the cool impertinence to try to save him from drowning, found himself seized from behind and towed vigorously away from a ten-dollar bill which he had almost succeeded in grasping. The spiritual agony caused by this assault rendered him mercifully dumb; though, even had he contrived to utter the rich Swedish oaths which occurred to him, his remarks could scarcely have been heard, for the crowd on the dock was cheering as one man. They had often paid good money to see far less gripping sights in the movies. They roared applause. The liner, meanwhile, continued to move stodgily out into mid-river.

The only drawback to these life-saving competitions at school, considered from the standpoint of fitting the competitors for the problems of afterlife, is that the object saved on such occasions is a leather dummy, and of all things in this world a leather dummy is perhaps the most placid and phlegmatic. It differs in many respects from an emotional Swedish gentleman, six foot high and constructed throughout of steel and india-rubber, who is being lugged away from cash which he has been regarding in the light of a legacy. Indeed, it would be hard to find a respect in which it does not differ. So far from lying inert in Sam's arms and allowing himself to be saved in a quiet and orderly manner, Mr. Swenson betrayed all the symptoms of one who feels that he has fallen among murderers. Mr. Swenson, much as he disliked competition, was ready to put up with it, provided that it was fair competition. This pulling your rival away from the loot so that you could grab it yourself—thus shockingly had the man misinterpreted Sam's motives—was another thing altogether, and his stout soul would have none of it. He began immediately to struggle with all the violence at his disposal. His large, hairy hands came out of the water and swung hopefully in the direction where he assumed his assailant's face to be.

Sam was not unprepared for this display. His researches in the art of life-saving had taught him that your drowning man frequently struggles against his best interests. In which case, cruel to be kind, one simply stunned the blighter. He decided to stun Mr. Swenson, though, if he had known that gentleman more intimately and had been aware that he had the reputation of possessing the thickest head on the water-front, he would have realised the magnitude of the task. Friends of Mr. Swenson, in convivial moments, had frequently endeavoured to stun him with bottles, boots and bits of lead piping and had gone away depressed by failure. Sam, ignorant of this, attempted to do the job with clenched fist, which he brought down as smartly as possible on the crown of the other's bowler hat.

It was the worst thing he could have done. Mr. Swenson thought highly of his hat and this brutal attack upon it confirmed his gloomiest apprehensions. Now thoroughly convinced that the only thing to do was to sell his life dearly, he wrenched himself round, seized his assailant by the neck, twined his arms about his middle, and accompanied him below the surface.

By the time he had swallowed his first pint and was beginning his second, Sam was reluctantly compelled to come to the conclusion that this was the end. The thought irritated him unspeakably. This, he felt, was just the silly, contrary way things always happened. Why should it be he who was perishing like this? Why not Eustace Hignett? Now there was a fellow whom this sort of thing would just have suited. Broken-hearted Eustace Hignett would have looked on all this as a merciful release.

He paused in his reflections to try to disentangle the more prominent of Mr. Swenson's limbs from about him. By this time he was sure that he had never met anyone he disliked so intensely as Mr. Swenson—not even his Aunt Adeline. The man was a human octopus. Sam could count seven distinct legs twined round him and at least as many arms. It seemed to him that he was being done to death in his prime by a solid platoon of Swedes. He put his whole soul into one last effort ... something seemed to give ... he was free. Pausing only to try to kick Mr. Swenson in the face, Sam shot to the surface. Something hard and sharp prodded him in the head. Then something caught the collar of his coat; and, finally, spouting like a whale, he found himself dragged upwards and over the side of a boat.

The time which Sam had spent with Mr. Swenson below the surface had been brief, but it had been long enough to enable the whole floating population of the North River to converge on the scene in scows, skiffs, launches, tugs, and other vessels. The fact that the water in that vicinity was crested with currency had not escaped the notice of these navigators, and they had gone to it as one man. First in the race came the tug "Reuben S. Watson," the skipper of which, following a famous precedent, had taken his little daughter to bear him company. It was to this fact that Marlowe really owed his rescue. Women often have a vein of sentiment in them where men can only see the hard business side of a situation; and it was the skipper's daughter who insisted that the family boat-hook, then in use as a harpoon for spearing dollar bills, should be devoted to the less profitable but humaner end of extricating the young man from a watery grave.

The skipper had grumbled a bit at first but had given way—he always spoiled the girl—with the result that Sam found himself sitting on the deck of the tug, engaged in the complicated process of restoring his faculties to the normal. In a sort of dream he perceived Mr. Swenson rise to the surface some feet away, adjust his bowler hat, and, after one long look of dislike in his direction, swim off rapidly to intercept a five which was floating under the stern of a near-by skiff.

Sam sat on the deck and panted. He played on the boards like a public fountain. At the back of his mind there was a flickering thought that he wanted to do something, a vague feeling that he had some sort of an appointment which he must keep; but he was unable to think what it was. Meanwhile, he conducted tentative experiments with his breath. It was so long since he had last breathed that he had lost the knack of it.

"Well, aincher wet?" said a voice.

The skipper's daughter was standing beside him, looking down commiseratingly. Of the rest of the family all he could see was the broad blue seats of their trousers as they leaned hopefully over the side in the quest for wealth.

"Yes, sir! You sure are wet! Gee! I never seen anyone so wet! I seen wet guys but I never seen anyone so wet as you. Yessir, you're certainly *wet*!"

"I *am* wet," admitted Sam.

"Yessir, you're wet! Wet's the word all right. Good and wet, that's what you are!"

"It's the water," said Sam. His brain was still clouded; he wished he could remember what that appointment was. "That's what has made me wet."

"It's sure made you wet all right," agreed the girl. She looked at him interestedly. "Wotcha do it for?" she asked.

"Do it for?"

"Yes, wotcha do it for? Wotcha do a Brodie for off'n that ship? I didn't see it myself, but pa says you come walloping down off'n the deck like a sack of potatoes."

Sam uttered a sharp cry. He had remembered.

"Where is she?"

"Where's who?"

"The liner."

"She's off down the river, I guess. She was swinging round, the last I seen of her."

"She's not gone!"

"Sure she's gone. Wotcha expect her to do? She's gotta get over to the other side, ain't she? Cert'nly nly she's gone." She looked at him interested. "Do you want to be on board her?"

"Of course I do."

"Then, for the love of Pete, wotcha doin' walloping off'n her like a sack of potatoes?"

"I slipped. I was pushed or something." Sam sprang to his feet and looked wildly about him. "I must get back. Isn't there any way of getting back?"

"Well, you could ketch up with her at quarantine out in the bay. She'll stop to let the pilot off."

"Can you take me to quarantine?"

The girl glanced doubtfully at the seat of the nearest pair of trousers.

"Well, we *could*," she said. "But pa's kind of set in his ways, and right now he's fishing for dollar bills with the boat hook. He's apt to get sorta mad if he's interrupted."

"I'll give him fifty dollars if he'll put me on board."

"Got it on you?" inquired the nymph coyly. She had her share of sentiment, but she was her father's daughter and inherited from him the business sense.

"Here it is." He pulled out his pocket book. The book was dripping, but the contents were only fairly moist.

"Pa!" said the girl.

The trouser-seat remained where it was, deaf to its child's cry.

"Pa! Cummere! Wantcha!"

The trousers did not even quiver. But this girl was a girl of decision. There was some nautical implement resting in a rack convenient to her hand. It was long, solid, and constructed of one of the harder forms of wood. Deftly extracting this from its place, she smote her inattentive parent on the only visible portion of him. He turned sharply, exhibiting a red, bearded face.

"Pa, this gen'man wants to be took aboard the boat at quarantine. He'll give you fifty berries."

The wrath died out of the skipper's face like the slow turning down of a lamp. The fishing had been poor, and so far he had only managed to secure a single two-dollar bill. In a crisis like the one which had so suddenly arisen you cannot do yourself justice with a boat-hook.

"Fifty berries!"

"Fifty seeds!" the girl assured him. "Are you on?"

"Queen," said the skipper simply, "you said a mouthful!"

Twenty minutes later Sam was climbing up the side of the liner as it lay towering over the tug like a mountain. His clothes hung about him clammily. He squelched as he walked.

A kindly-looking old gentleman who was smoking a cigar by the rail regarded him with open eyes.

"My dear sir, you're very wet," he said.

Sam passed him with a cold face and hurried through the door leading to the companion way.

"Mummie, why is that man wet?" cried the clear voice of a little child.

Sam whizzed by, leaping down the stairs.

"Good Lord, sir! You're very wet!" said a steward in the doorway of the dining saloon.

"You *are* wet," said a stewardess in the passage.

Sam raced for his state-room. He bolted in and sank on the lounge. In the lower berth Eustace Hignett was lying with closed eyes. He opened them languidly, then stared.

"Hullo!" he said. "I say! You're wet!"

§ 4

Sam removed his clinging garments and hurried into a new suit. He was in no mood for conversation and Eustace Hignett's frank curiosity jarred upon him. Happily, at this point, a sudden shivering of the floor and a creaking of woodwork proclaimed the fact that the vessel was under way again, and his cousin, turning pea-green, rolled over on his side with a hollow moan. Sam finished buttoning his waistcoat and went out.

He was passing the inquiry bureau on the C-deck, striding along with bent head and scowling brow, when a sudden exclamation caused him to look up, and the scowl was wiped from his brow as with a sponge. For there stood the girl he had met on the dock. With her was a superfluous young man who looked like a parrot.

"Oh, *how* are you?" asked the girl breathlessly.

"Splendid, thanks," said Sam.

"Didn't you get very wet?"

"I did get a little damp."

"I thought you would," said the young man who looked like a parrot. "Directly I saw you go over the side I said to myself: 'That fellow's going to get wet!'"

There was a pause.

"Oh!" said the girl. "May I—Mr.——?"

"Marlowe."

"Mr. Marlowe. Mr. Bream Mortimer."

Sam smirked at the young man. The young man smirked at Sam.

"Nearly got left behind," said Bream Mortimer.

"Yes, nearly."

"No joke getting left behind."

"No."

"Have to take the next boat. Lose a lot of time," said Mr. Mortimer, driving home his point.

The girl had listened to these intellectual exchanges with impatience. She now spoke again.

"Oh, Bream!"

"Hello?"

"Do be a dear and run down to the saloon and see if it's all right about our places for lunch."

"It is all right. The table steward said so."

"Yes, but go and make certain."

"All right."

He hopped away and the girl turned to Sam with shining eyes.

"Oh, Mr. Marlowe, you oughtn't to have done it! Really, you oughtn't! You might have been drowned! But I never saw anything so wonderful. It was like the stories of knights who used to jump into lions' dens after gloves!"

"Yes?" said Sam a little vaguely. The resemblance had not struck him. It seemed a silly hobby, and rough on the lions, too.

"It was the sort of thing Sir Lancelot or Sir Galahad would have done! But you shouldn't have bothered, really! It's all right, now."

"Oh, it's all right now?"

"Yes. I'd quite forgotten that Mr. Mortimer was to be on board. He has given me all the money I shall need. You see it was this way. I had to sail on this boat in rather a hurry. Father's head clerk was to have gone to the bank and got some money and met me on board and given it to me, but the silly old man was late and when he got to the dock they had just pulled in the gang-plank. So he tried to throw the money to me in a handkerchief and it fell into the water. But you shouldn't have dived in after it."

"Oh, well!" said Sam, straightening his tie, with a quiet, brave smile. He had never expected to feel grateful to that obese bounder who had shoved him off the rail, but now he would have liked to seek him out and shake him by the hand.

"You really are the bravest man I ever met!"

"Oh, no!"

"How modest you are! But I suppose all brave men are modest!"

"I was only too delighted at what looked like a chance of doing you a service."

"It was the extraordinary quickness of it that was so wonderful. I do admire presence of mind. You didn't hesitate for a second. You just shot over the side as though propelled by some irresistible force!"

"It was nothing, nothing really. One just happens to have the knack of keeping one's head and acting quickly on the spur of the moment. Some people have it, some haven't."

"And just think! As Bream was saying...."

"It *is* all right," said Mr. Mortimer, reappearing suddenly. "I saw a couple of the stewards and they both said it was all right. So it's all right."

"Splendid," said the girl. "Oh, Bream!"

"Hello?"

"Do be an angel and run along to my state-room and see if Pinky-Boodles is quite comfortable."

"Bound to be."

"Yes. But do go. He may be feeling lonely. Chirrup to him a little."

"Chirrup?"

"Yes, to cheer him up."

"Oh, all right."

"Run along!"

Mr. Mortimer ran along. He had the air of one who feels that he only needs a peaked cap and a uniform two sizes too small for him to be a properly equipped messenger boy.

"And, as Bream was saying," resumed the girl, "you might have been left behind."

"That," said Sam, edging a step closer, "was the thought that tortured me, the thought that a friendship so delightfully begun...."

"But it hadn't begun. We have never spoken to each other before now."

"Have you forgotten? On the dock...."

Sudden enlightenment came into her eyes.

"Oh, you are the man poor Pinky-Boodles bit!"

"The lucky man!"

Her face clouded.

"Poor Pinky is feeling the motion of the boat a little. It's his first voyage."

"I shall always remember that it was Pinky who first brought us together. Would you care for a stroll on deck?"

"Not just now, thanks. I must be getting back to my room to finish unpacking. After lunch, perhaps."

"I will be there. By the way, you know my name, but...."

"Oh, mine?" She smiled brightly. "It's funny that a person's name is the last thing one thinks of asking. Mine is Bennett."

"Bennett!"

"Wilhelmina Bennett. My friends," she said softly as she turned away, "call me Billie!"

CHAPTER III

Sam Paves the Way

For some moments Sam remained where he was, staring after the girl as she flitted down the passage. He felt dizzy. Mental acrobatics always have an unsettling effect, and a young man may be excused for feeling a little dizzy when he is called upon suddenly and without any warning to re-adjust all his preconceived views on any subject. Listening to Eustace Hignett's story of his blighted romance, Sam had formed an unflattering opinion of this Wilhelmina Bennett who had broken off her engagement simply because on the day of the marriage his cousin had been short of the necessary wedding garment. He had, indeed, thought a little smugly how different his goddess of the red hair was from the object of Eustace Hignett's affections. And now they had proved to be one and the same. It was disturbing. It was like suddenly finding the vampire of a five-reel feature film turn into the heroine.

Some men, on making the discovery of this girl's identity, might have felt that Providence had intervened to save them from a disastrous entanglement. This point of view never occurred to Samuel Marlowe. The way he looked at it was that he had been all wrong about Wilhelmina Bennett. Eustace, he felt, had been to blame throughout. If this girl had maltreated Eustace's finer feelings, then her reason for doing so must have been excellent and praiseworthy.

After all ... poor old Eustace ... quite a good fellow, no doubt in many ways ... but, coming down to brass tacks, what was there about Eustace that gave him any claim to monopolise the affections of a wonderful girl? Where, in a word, did Eustace Hignett get off? He made a tremendous grievance of the fact that she had broken off the engagement, but what right had he to go about the place expecting her to be engaged to him? Eustace Hignett, no doubt, looked upon the poor girl as utterly heartless. Marlowe regarded her behaviour as thoroughly sensible. She had made a mistake, and, realising this at the eleventh hour, she had had the force of character to correct it. He was sorry for poor old Eustace, but he really could not permit the suggestion that Wilhelmina Bennett—her friends called her Billie—had not behaved in a perfectly splendid way throughout. It was women like Wilhelmina Bennett—Billie to her intimates—who made the world worth living in.

Her friends called her Billie. He did not blame them. It was a delightful name and suited her to perfection. He practised it a few times. "Billie ... Billie ... Billie...." It certainly ran pleasantly off the tongue. "Billie Bennett." Very musical. "Billie Marlowe." Still better. "We noticed among those present the charming and popular Mrs. 'Billie' Marlowe...."

A consuming desire came over him to talk about the girl to someone. Obviously indicated as the party of the second part was Eustace Hignett. If Eustace was still capable of speech—and after all the boat was hardly rolling at all—he would enjoy a further chat about his ruined life. Besides, he had another reason for seeking Eustace's society. As a man who had been actually engaged to marry this supreme girl, Eustace Hignett had an attraction for Sam akin to that of some great public monument. He had become a sort of shrine. He had taken on a glamour. Sam entered the state-room almost reverentially, with something of the emotions of a boy going into his first dime museum.

The exhibit was lying on his back, staring at the roof of the berth. By lying absolutely still and forcing himself to think of purely inland scenes and objects, he had contrived to reduce the green in his complexion to a mere tinge. But it would be paltering with the truth to say that he felt debonair. He received Sam with a wan austerity.

"Sit down!" he said. "Don't stand there swaying like that. I can't bear it."

"Why, we aren't out of the harbour yet. Surely you aren't going to be sea-sick already."

"I can issue no positive guarantee. Perhaps if I can keep my mind off it....

I have had good results for the last ten minutes by thinking steadily of the Sahara. There," said Eustace Hignett with enthusiasm, "is a place for you! That is something like a spot. Miles and miles of sand and not a drop of water anywhere!"

Sam sat down on the lounge.

"You're quite right. The great thing is to concentrate your mind on other topics. Why not, for instance, tell me some more about your unfortunate affair with that girl—Billie Bennett I think you said her name was."

"Wilhelmina Bennett. Where on earth did you get the idea that her name was Billie?"

"I had a notion that girls called Wilhelmina were sometimes Billie to their friends."

"I never called her anything but Wilhelmina. But I really cannot talk about it. The recollection tortures me."

"That's just what you want. It's the counter-irritation principle. Persevere, and you'll soon forget that you're on board ship at all."

"There's something in that," admitted Eustace reflectively. "It's very good of you to be so sympathetic and interested."

"My dear fellow ... anything that I can do ... where did you meet her first, for instance?"

"At a dinner...." Eustace Hignett broke off abruptly. He had a good memory and he had just recollected the fish they had served at that dinner—a flabby and exhausted looking fish half sunk beneath the surface of a thick white sauce.

"And what struck you most forcibly about her at first? Her lovely hair, I suppose?"

"How did you know she had lovely hair?"

"My dear chap, I naturally assumed that any girl with whom you fell in love would have nice hair."

"Well, you are perfectly right, as it happens. Her hair was remarkably beautiful. It was red...."

"Like autumn leaves with the sun on them!" said Marlowe ecstatically.

Hignett started.

"What an extraordinary thing! That is an absolutely exact description. Her eyes were a deep blue...."

"Or, rather, green."

"Blue."

"Green. There is a shade of green that looks blue."

"What the devil do you know about the colour of her eyes?" demanded Eustace heatedly. "Am I telling you about her, or are you telling me?"

"My dear old man, don't get excited. Don't you see I am trying to construct this girl in my imagination, to visualise her? I don't pretend to doubt your special knowledge, but after all green eyes generally do go with red hair and there are all shades of green. There is the bright green of meadow grass, the dull green of the uncut emerald, the faint yellowish green of your face at the present moment...."

"Don't talk about the colour of my face! Now you've gone and reminded me just when I was beginning to forget."

"Awfully sorry. Stupid of me. Get your mind off it again—quick. What were we saying? Oh, yes, this girl. I always think it helps one to form a mental picture of people if one knows something about their tastes—what sort of things they are interested in, their favourite topics of conversation, and so on. This Miss Bennett now, what did she like talking about?"

"Oh, all sorts of things."

"Yes, but what?"

"Well, for one thing she was very fond of poetry. It was that which first drew us together."

"Poetry!" Sam's heart sank a little. He had read a certain amount of poetry at school, and once he had won a prize of three shillings and sixpence for the last line of a Limerick in a competition in a weekly paper; but he was self-critic enough to know that poetry was not his long suit. Still there was a library on board the ship, and no doubt it would be possible to borrow the works of some standard bard and bone them up from time to time. "Any special poet?"

"Well, she seemed to like my stuff. You never read my sonnet-sequence on Spring, did you?"

"No. What other poets did she like besides you?"

"Tennyson principally," said Eustace Hignett with a reminiscent quiver in his voice. "The hours we have spent together reading the Idylls of the King!"

"The which of what?" inquired Sam, taking a pencil from his pocket and shooting out a cuff.

"'The Idylls of the King.' My good man, I know you have a soul which would be considered inadequate by a common earthworm but you have surely heard of Tennyson's 'Idylls of the King?'"

"Oh, *those*! Why, my dear old chap! Tennyson's 'Idylls of the King?' Well, I should say! Have I heard of Tennyson's 'Idylls of the King?' Well, really? I suppose you haven't a copy with you on board by any chance?"

"There is a copy in my kit bag. The very one we used to read together. Take it and keep it or throw it overboard. I don't want to see it again."

Sam prospected among the shirts, collars, and trousers in the bag and presently came upon a morocco-bound volume. He laid it beside him on the lounge.

"Little by little, bit by bit," he said, "I am beginning to form a sort of picture of this girl, this—what was her name again? Bennett—this Miss Bennett. You have a wonderful knack of description. You make her seem so real and vivid. Tell me some more about her. She wasn't keen on golf, by any chance, I suppose?"

"I believe she did play. The subject came up once and she seemed rather enthusiastic. Why?"

"Well, I'd much sooner talk to a girl about golf than poetry."

"You are hardly likely to be in a position to have to talk to Wilhelmina Bennett about either, I should imagine."

"No, there's that, of course. I was thinking of girls in general. Some girls bar golf, and then it's rather difficult to know how to start the conversation. But, tell me, were there any topics which got on this Miss Bennett's nerves, if you know what I mean? It seems to me that at one time or another you may have said something that offended her. I mean, it seems curious that she should have broken off the engagement if you had never disagreed or quarrelled about anything."

"Well, of course, there was always the matter of that dog of hers. She had a dog, you know, a snappy brute of a Pekinese. If there was ever any shadow of disagreement between us, it had to do with that dog. I made rather a point of it that I would not have it about the home after we were married."

"I see!" said Sam. He shot his cuff once more and wrote on it: "Dog—conciliate." "Yes, of course, that must have wounded her."

"Not half so much as he wounded me. He pinned me by the ankle the day before we—Wilhelmina and I, I mean—were to have been married. It is some satisfaction to me in my broken state to remember that I got home on the little beast with considerable juiciness and lifted him clean over the Chesterfield."

Sam shook his head reprovingly.

"You shouldn't have done that," he said. He extended his cuff and added the words "Vitally Important" to what he had just written. "It was probably that which decided her."

"Well, I hate dogs," said Eustace Hignett querulously. "I remember Wilhelmina once getting quite annoyed with me because I refused to step in and separate a couple of the brutes, absolute strangers to me, who were fighting in the street. I reminded her that we were all fighters nowadays, that life itself was in a sense a fight; but she wouldn't be reasonable about it. She said that Sir Galahad would have done it like a shot. I thought not. We have no evidence whatsoever that Sir Galahad was ever called upon to do anything half as dangerous. And, anyway, he wore armour. Give me a suit of mail, reaching well down over the ankles, and I will willingly intervene in a hundred dog fights. But in thin flannel trousers, no!"

Sam rose. His heart was light. He had never, of course, supposed that the girl was anything but perfect; but it was nice to find his high opinion of her corroborated by one who had no reason to exhibit her in a favourable light. He understood her point of view and sympathised with it. An idealist, how could she trust herself to Eustace Hignett? How could she be content with a craven who, instead of scouring the world in the quest for deeds of derring-do, had fallen down so lamentably on his first assignment? There was a specious attractiveness about poor old Eustace which might conceivably win a girl's heart for a time; he wrote poetry, talked well, and had a nice singing voice; but, as a partner for life ... well, he simply wouldn't do. That was all there was to it. He simply didn't add up right. The man a girl like Wilhelmina Bennett required for a husband was somebody entirely different ... somebody, felt Samuel Marlowe, much more like Samuel Marlowe.

Swelled almost to bursting point with these reflections, he went on deck to join the ante-luncheon promenade. He saw Billie almost at once. She had put on one of those nice sacky sport-coats which so enhance feminine charms, and was striding along the deck with the breeze playing in her vivid hair like the female equivalent of a Viking. Beside her walked young Mr. Bream Mortimer.

Sam had been feeling a good deal of a fellow already, but at the sight of her welcoming smile his self-esteem almost caused him to explode. What magic there is in a girl's smile! It is the raisin which, dropped in the yeast of male complacency, induces fermentation.

"Oh, there you are, Mr. Marlowe!"

"Oh, *there* you are," said Bream Mortimer with a slightly different inflection.

"I thought I'd like a breath of fresh air before lunch," said Sam.

"Oh, Bream!" said the girl.

"Hello?"

"Do be a darling and take this great heavy coat of mine down to my state-room, will you? I had no idea it was so warm."

"I'll carry it," said Bream.

"Nonsense! I wouldn't dream of burdening you with it. Trot along and put it on the berth. It doesn't matter about folding it up."

"All right," said Bream moodily.

He trotted along. There are moments when a man feels that all he needs in order to be a delivery wagon is a horse and a driver. Bream Mortimer was experiencing such a moment.

"He had better chirrup to the dog while he's there, don't you think?" suggested Sam. He felt that a resolute man with legs as long as Bream's might well deposit a cloak on a berth and be back under the half-minute.

"Oh yes! Bream!"

"Hello?"

"While you're down there, just chirrup a little more to poor Pinky. He does appreciate it so!"

Bream disappeared. It is not always easy to interpret emotion from a glance at a man's back; but Bream's back looked like that of a man to whom the thought has occurred that, given a couple of fiddles and a piano, he would have made a good hired orchestra.

"How is your dear little dog, by the way?" inquired Sam solicitously, as he fell into step by her side.

"Much better now, thanks. I've made friends with a girl on board—did you ever hear her name—Jane Hubbard—she's a rather well-known big-game hunter, and she fixed up some sort of a mixture for Pinky which did him a world of good. I don't know what was in it except Worcester Sauce, but she said she always gave it to her mules in Africa when they had the botts ... it's very nice of you to speak so affectionately of poor Pinky when he bit you."

"Animal spirits!" said Sam tolerantly. "Pure animal spirits. I like to see them. But, of course, I love all dogs."

"Oh, do you? So do I!"

"I only wish they didn't fight so much. I'm always stopping dog-fights."

"I do admire a man who knows what to do at a dog-fight. I'm afraid I'm rather helpless myself. There never seems anything to catch hold of." She looked down. "Have you been reading? What is the book?"

"The book? Oh, this. It's a volume of Tennyson."

"Are you fond of Tennyson?"

"I worship him," said Sam reverently.

"Those——" he glanced at his cuff— "those 'Idylls of the King!' I do not like to think what an ocean voyage would be if I had not my Tennyson with me."

"We must read him together. He is my favourite poet!"

"We will! There is something about Tennyson...."

"Yes, isn't there! I've felt that myself so often."

"Some poets are whales at epics and all that sort of thing, while others call it a day when they've written something that runs to a couple of verses, but where Tennyson had the bulge was that his long game was just as good as his short. He was great off the tee and a marvel with his chip-shots."

"That sounds as though you play golf."

"When I am not reading Tennyson, you can generally find me out on the links. Do you play?"

"I love it. How extraordinary that we should have so much in common. You seem to like all the things I like. We really ought to be great friends."

He was pausing to select the best of three replies when the lunch bugle sounded.

"Oh dear!" she cried. "I must rush. But we shall see one another again up here afterwards?"

"We will," said Sam.

"We'll sit and read Tennyson."

"Fine! Er—you and I and Mortimer?"

"Oh no, Bream is going to sit down below and look after poor Pinky."

"Does he—does he know he is?"

"Not yet," said Billie. "I'm going to tell him at lunch."

CHAPTER IV

Sam Clicks

§ 1

It was the fourth morning of the voyage. Of course, when this story is done in the movies they won't be satisfied with a bald statement like that; they will have a Spoken Title or a Cut-Back Sub-Caption or whatever they call the thing in the low dens where motion-picture scenario-lizards do their dark work, which will run:—

AND SO, CALM AND GOLDEN,
THE DAYS WENT BY, EACH
FRAUGHT WITH HOPE AND
YOUTH AND SWEETNESS,
LINKING TWO YOUNG HEARTS
IN SILKEN FETTERS FORGED BY
THE LAUGHING LOVE-GOD.

and the males in the audience will shift their chewing gum to the other cheek and take a firmer grip of their companion's hands and the man at the piano will play

"Everybody wants a key to my cellar," or something equally appropriate, very soulfully and slowly, with a wistful eye on the half-smoked cigarette which he has parked on the lowest octave and intends finishing as soon as the picture is over. But I prefer the plain frank statement that it was the fourth day of the voyage. That is my story and I mean to stick to it.

Samuel Marlowe, muffled in a bathrobe, came back to the state-room from his tub. His manner had the offensive jauntiness of the man who has had a cold bath when he might just as easily have had a hot one. He looked out of the porthole at the shimmering sea. He felt strong and happy and exuberant.

It was not merely the spiritual pride induced by a cold bath that was uplifting this young man. The fact was that, as he towelled his glowing back, he had suddenly come to the decision that this very day he would propose to Wilhelmina Bennett. Yes, he would put his fortune to the test, to win or lose it all. True, he had only known her for four days, but what of that?

Nothing in the way of modern progress is more remarkable than the manner in which the attitude of your lover has changed concerning proposals of marriage. When Samuel Marlowe's grandfather had convinced himself, after about a year and a half of respectful aloofness, that the emotion which he felt towards Samuel Marlowe's grandmother-to-be was love, the fashion of the period compelled him to approach the matter in a roundabout way. First, he spent an evening or two singing sentimental ballads, she accompanying him on the piano and the rest of the family sitting on the side-lines to see that no rough stuff was pulled. Having noted that she drooped her eyelashes and turned faintly pink when he came to the "Thee—only thee!" bit, he felt a mild sense of encouragement, strong enough to justify him in taking her sister aside next day and asking if the object of his affections ever happened to mention his name in the course of conversation. Further *pour-parlers* having passed with her aunt, two more sisters, and her little brother, he felt that the moment had arrived when he might send her a volume of Shelley, with some of the passages

93

marked in pencil. A few weeks later, he interviewed her father and obtained his consent to the paying of his addresses. And finally, after writing her a letter which began "Madam, you will not have been insensible to the fact that for some time past you have inspired in my bosom feelings deeper than those of ordinary friendship...." he waylaid her in the rose-garden and brought the thing off.

How different is the behaviour of the modern young man. His courtship can hardly be called a courtship at all. His methods are those of Sir W. S. Gilbert's Alphonso.

> "Alphonso, who for cool assurance
>   all creation licks,
> He up and said to Emily who has
>   cheek enough for six:
> 'Miss Emily, I love you. Will you
>   marry? Say the word!'
> And Emily said: 'Certainly, Alphonso,
>   like a bird!'"

Sam Marlowe was a warm supporter of the Alphonso method. He was a bright young man and did not require a year to make up his mind that Wilhelmina Bennett had been set apart by Fate from the beginning of time to be his bride. He had known it from the moment he saw her on the dock, and all the subsequent strolling, reading, talking, soup-drinking, tea-drinking, and shuffle-board-playing which they had done together had merely solidified his original impression. He loved this girl with all the force of a fiery nature—the fiery nature of the Marlowes was a by-word in Bruton Street, Berkeley Square—and something seemed to whisper that she loved him. At any rate she wanted somebody like Sir Galahad, and, without wishing to hurl bouquets at himself, he could not see where she could possibly get anyone liker Sir Galahad than himself. So, wind and weather permitting, Samuel Marlowe intended to propose to Wilhelmina Bennett this very day.

He let down the trick basin which hung beneath the mirror and, collecting his shaving materials, began to lather his face.

"I am the Bandolero!" sang Sam blithely through the soap. "I am, I am the Bandolero! Yes, yes, I am the Bandolero!"

The untidy heap of bedclothes in the lower berth stirred restlessly.

"Oh, God!" said Eustace Hignett thrusting out a tousled head.

Sam regarded his cousin with commiseration. Horrid things had been happening to Eustace during the last few days, and it was quite a pleasant surprise each morning to find that he was still alive.

"Feeling bad again, old man?"

"I was feeling all right," replied Hignett churlishly, "until you began the farmyard imitations. What sort of a day is it?"

"Glorious! The sea...."

"Don't talk about the sea!"

"Sorry! The sun is shining brighter than it has ever shone in the history of the race. Why don't you get up?"

"Nothing will induce me to get up."

"Well, go a regular buster and have an egg for breakfast."

Eustace Hignett shuddered. He eyed Sam sourly. "You seem devilish pleased with yourself this morning!" he said censoriously.

Sam dried the razor carefully and put it away. He hesitated. Then the desire to confide in somebody got the better of him.

"The fact is," he said apologetically, "I'm in love!"

"In love!" Eustace Hignett sat up and bumped his head sharply against the berth above him. "Has this been going on long?"

"Ever since the voyage started."

"I think you might have told me," said Eustace reproachfully. "I told you my troubles. Why did you not let me know that this awful thing had come upon you?"

"Well, as a matter of fact, old man, during these last few days I had a notion that your mind was, so to speak, occupied elsewhere."

"Who is she?"

"Oh, a girl I met on board."

"Don't do it!" said Eustace Hignett solemnly. "As a friend I entreat you not to do it. Take my advice, as a man who knows women, and don't do it!"

"Don't do what?"

"Propose to her. I can tell by the glitter in your eye that you are intending to propose to this girl—probably this morning."

"Not this morning—after lunch. I always think one can do oneself more justice after lunch."

"Don't do it. Women are the devil, whether they marry you or jilt you. Do you realise that women wear black evening dresses that have to be hooked up in a hurry when you are late for the theatre, and that, out of sheer wanton malignity, the hooks and eyes on those dresses are also made black? Do you realise...?"

"Oh, I've thought it all out."

"And take the matter of children. How would you like to become the father—and a mere glance around you will show you that the chances are enormously in favour of such a thing happening—of a boy with spectacles and protruding front teeth who asks questions all the time? Out of six small boys whom I saw when I came on board, four wore spectacles and had teeth like rabbits. The other two were equally revolting in different styles. How would you like to become the father...?"

"There is no need to be indelicate," said Sam stiffly. "A man must take these chances."

"Give her the miss in baulk," pleaded Hignett. "Stay down here for the rest of the voyage. You can easily dodge her when you get to Southampton. And, if she sends messages, say you're ill and can't be disturbed."

Sam gazed at him, revolted. More than ever he began to understand how it was that a girl with ideals had broken off her engagement with this man. He finished dressing, and, after a satisfying breakfast, went on deck.

§ 2

It was, as he had said, a glorious morning. The sample which he had had through the porthole had not prepared him for the magic of it. The ship swam in a vast bowl of the purest blue on an azure carpet flecked with silver. It was a morning which impelled a man to great deeds, a morning which shouted to him to chuck his chest out and be romantic. The sight of Billie Bennett, trim and gleaming in a pale green sweater and white skirt had the effect of causing Marlowe to alter the programme which he had sketched out. Proposing to this girl was not a thing to be put off till after lunch. It was a thing to be done now and at once. The finest efforts of the finest cooks in the world could not put him in better form than he felt at present.

"Good morning, Miss Bennett."

"Good morning, Mr. Marlowe."

"Isn't it a perfect day?"

"Wonderful!"

"It makes all the difference on board ship if the weather is fine."

"Yes, doesn't it?"

How strange it is that the great emotional scenes of history, one of which is coming along almost immediately, always begin in this prosaic way Shakespeare tries to conceal the fact, but there can be little doubt that Romeo and Juliet edged into their balcony scene with a few remarks on the pleasantness of the morning.

"Shall we walk round?" said Billie.

Sam glanced about him. It was the time of day when the promenade deck was always full. Passengers in cocoons of rugs lay on chairs, waiting in a dull trance till the steward should arrive with the eleven o'clock soup. Others, more energetic, strode up and down. From the point of view of a man who wished to reveal his most sacred feelings to a beautiful girl, the place was practically a tube station during the rush hour.

"It's so crowded," he said. "Let's go on to the upper deck."

"All right. You can read to me. Go and fetch your Tennyson."

Sam felt that fortune was playing into his hands. His four-days' acquaintance with the bard had been sufficient to show him that the man was there forty ways when it came to writing about love. You could open his collected works almost anywhere and shut your eyes and dab down your finger on some red-hot passage. A proposal of marriage is a thing which it is rather difficult to bring neatly into the ordinary run of conversation. It wants leading up to. But, if you once start reading poetry, especially Tennyson's, almost anything is apt to give you your cue. He bounded light-heartedly into the state-room, waking Eustace Hignett from an uneasy dose.

"Now what?" said Eustace.

"Where's that copy of Tennyson you gave me? I left it—ah, here it is. Well, see you later!"

"Wait! What are you going to do?"

"Oh, that girl I told you about," said Sam making for the door. "She wants me to read Tennyson to her on the upper deck."

"Tennyson?"

"Yes."

"On the upper deck?"

"Yes."

"This is the end," said Eustace Hignett, turning his face to the wall.

Sam raced up the companion-way as far as it went; then, going out on deck, climbed a flight of steps and found himself in the only part of the ship which was ever even comparatively private. The main herd of passengers preferred the promenade deck, two layers below.

He threaded his way through a maze of boats, ropes, and curious-shaped steel structures which the architect of the ship seemed to have tacked on at the last moment in a spirit of sheer exuberance. Above him towered one of the funnels, before him a long, slender mast. He hurried on, and presently came upon Billie sitting on a garden seat, backed by the white roof of the smoke-room; beside this was a small deck which seemed to have lost its way and strayed up here all by itself. It was the deck on which one could occasionally see the patients playing an odd game with long sticks and bits of wood—not shuffleboard but something even lower in the mental scale. This morning, however, the devotees of this pastime were apparently under proper restraint, for the deck was empty.

"This is jolly," he said sitting down beside the girl and drawing a deep breath of satisfaction.

"Yes, I love this deck. It's so peaceful."

"It's the only part of the ship where you can be reasonably sure of not meeting stout men in flannels and nautical caps. An ocean voyage always makes me wish that I had a private yacht."

"It would be nice."

"A private yacht," repeated Sam, sliding a trifle closer. "We would sail about, visiting desert islands which lay like jewels in the heart of tropic seas."

"We?"

"Most certainly we. It wouldn't be any fun if you were not there."

"That's very complimentary."

"Well, it wouldn't. I'm not fond of girls as a rule...."

"Oh, aren't you?"

"No!" said Sam decidedly. It was a point which he wished to make clear at the outset. "Not at all fond. My friends have often remarked upon it. A palmist once told me that I had one of those rare spiritual natures which cannot be satisfied with substitutes but must seek and seek till they find their soul-mate. When other men all round me were frittering away their emotions in idle flirtations which did not touch their deeper natures, I was ... I was ... well, I wasn't, if you see what I mean."

"Oh, you wasn't ... weren't?"

"No. Some day I knew I should meet the only girl I could possibly love, and then I would pour out upon her the stored-up devotion of a lifetime, lay an unblemished heart at her feet, fold her in my arms and say 'At last!'"

"How jolly for her. Like having a circus all to oneself."

"Well, yes," said Sam after a momentary pause.

"When I was a child I always thought that that would be the most wonderful thing in the world."

"The most wonderful thing in the world is love, a pure and consuming love, a love which...."

"Oh, hello!" said a voice.

All through this scene, right from the very beginning of it, Sam had not been able to rid himself of a feeling that there was something missing. The time and the place and the girl—they were all present and correct; nevertheless there was something missing, some familiar object which seemed to leave a gap. He now perceived that what had caused the feeling was the complete absence of Bream Mortimer. He was absent no longer. He was standing in front of them with one leg, his head lowered as if he were waiting for someone to scratch it. Sam's primary impulse was to offer him a nut.

"Oh, hello, Bream!" said Billie.

"Hullo!" said Sam.

"Hello!" said Bream Mortimer. "Here you are!"

There was a pause.

"I thought you might be here," said Bream.

"Yes, here we are," said Billie.

"Yes, we're here," said Sam.

There was another pause.

"Mind if I join you?" said Bream.

"N—no," said Billie.

"N—no," said Sam.

"No," said Billie again. "No ... that is to say ... oh no, no at all."

There was a third pause.

"On second thoughts," said Bream, "I believe I'll take a stroll on the promenade deck if you don't mind."

They said they did not mind. Bream Mortimer, having bumped his head twice against overhanging steel ropes, melted away.

"Who is that fellow?" demanded Sam wrathfully.

"He's the son of father's best friend."

Sam started. Somehow this girl had always been so individual to him that he had never thought of her having a father.

"We have known each other all our lives," continued Billie. "Father thinks a tremendous lot of Bream. I suppose it was because Bream was sailing by her that father insisted on my coming over on this boat. I'm in disgrace, you know I was cabled for and had to sail at a few days' notice. I...."

"Oh, hello!"

"Why, Bream!" said Billie looking at him as he stood on the old spot in the same familiar attitude with rather less affection than the son of her father's best friend might have expected. "I thought you said you were going down to the promenade deck.

"I did go down to the promenade deck. And I'd hardly got there when a fellow who's getting up the ship's concert to-morrow night nobbled me to do something for it. I said I could only do conjuring tricks and juggling and so on, and he said all right, do conjuring tricks and juggling, then. He wanted to know if I knew anyone else who would help. I came up to ask you," he said to Sam, "if you would do something."

"No," said Sam. "I won't."

"He's got a man who's going to lecture on deep-sea fish and a couple of women who both want to sing 'The Rosary' but he's still a turn or two short. Sure you won't rally round?"

"Quite sure."

"Oh, all right." Bream Mortimer hovered wistfully above them. "It's a great morning, isn't it?"

"Yes," said Sam.

"Oh, Bream!" said Billie.

"Hello?"

"Do be a pet and go and talk to Jane Hubbard. I'm sure she must be feeling lonely. I left her all by herself down on the next deck."

A look of alarm spread itself over Bream's face.

"Jane Hubbard! Oh, say, have a heart!"

"She's a very nice girl."

"She's so darned dynamic. She looks at you as if you were a giraffe or something and she would like to take a pot at you with a rifle."

"Nonsense! Run along. Get her to tell you some of her big-game hunting experiences. They are most interesting."

Bream drifted sadly away.

"I don't blame Miss Hubbard," said Sam.

"What do you mean?"

"Looking at him as if she wanted to pot at him with a rifle. I should like to do it myself."

"Oh, don't let's talk about Bream. Read me some Tennyson."

Sam opened the book very willingly. Infernal Bream Mortimer had absolutely shot to pieces the spell which had begun to fall on them at the beginning of their conversation. Only by reading poetry, it seemed to him, could it be recovered. And when he saw the passage at which the volume had opened he realised that his luck was in. Good old Tennyson! He was all right. He had the stuff. You could rely on him every time.

He cleared his throat.

"Oh let the solid ground
    Not fail beneath my feet
Before my life has found
    What some have found so sweet;
Then let come what come may,
    What matter if I go mad,
I shall have had my day.

Let the sweet heavens endure,
    Not close and darken above me
Before I am quite quite sure
    That there is one to love me...."

This was absolutely topping. It was like diving off a spring-board. He could see the girl sitting with a soft smile on her face, her eyes, big and dreamy, gazing out over the sunlit sea. He laid down the book and took her hand.

"There is something," he began in a low voice, "which I have been trying to say ever since we met, something which I think you must have read in my eyes."

Her head was bent. She did not withdraw her hand.

"Until this voyage began," he went on, "I did not know what life meant. And then I saw you! It was like the gate of heaven opening. You're the dearest girl I ever met, and you can bet I'll never forget...." He stopped. "I'm not trying to make it rhyme," he said apologetically. "Billie, don't think me silly ... I mean ... if you had the merest notion, dearest ... I don't know what's the matter with me ... Billie, darling, you are the only girl in the world! I have been looking for you for years and years and I have found you at last, my soul-mate. Surely this does not come as a surprise to you? That is, I mean, you must have seen that I've been keen.... There's that damned Walt Mason stuff again!" His eyes fell on the volume beside him and he uttered an exclamation of enlightenment. "It's those poems!" he cried. "I've been boning them up to such an extent that they've got me doing it too. What I'm trying to say is, Will you marry me?"

She was drooping towards him. Her face was very sweet and tender, her eyes misty. He slid an arm about her waist. She raised her lips to his.

§ 3

Suddenly she drew herself away, a cloud on her face.

"Darling," she said, "I've a confession to make."

"A confession? You? Nonsense!"

"I can't get rid of a horrible thought. I was wondering if this will last."

"Our love? Don't be afraid that it will fade ... I mean ... why, it's so vast, it's bound to last ... that is to say, of course it will."

She traced a pattern on the deck with her shoe.

"I'm afraid of myself. You see, once before—and it was not so very long ago,— I thought I had met my ideal, but...."

Sam laughed heartily.

"Are you worrying about that absurd business of poor old Eustace Hignett?"

She started violently.

"You know!"

"Of course! He told me himself."

"Do you know him? Where did you meet him?"

"I've known him all my life. He's my cousin. As a matter of fact, we are sharing a state-room on board now."

"Eustace is on board! Oh, this is awful! What shall I do when I meet him?"

"Oh, pass it off with a light laugh and a genial quip. Just say: 'Oh, here you are!' or something. You know the sort of thing."

"It will be terrible."

"Not a bit of it. Why should you feel embarrassed? He must have realised by now that you acted in the only possible way. It was absurd his ever expecting you to marry him. I mean to say, just look at it dispassionately ... Eustace ... poor old Eustace ... and *you*! The Princess and the Swineherd!"

"Does Mr. Hignett keep pigs?" she asked, surprised.

"I mean that poor old Eustace is so far below you, darling, that, with the most charitable intentions, one can only look on his asking you to marry him in the light of a record exhibition of pure nerve. A dear, good fellow, of course, but hopeless where the sterner realities of life are concerned. A man who can't even stop a dog-fight! In a world which is practically one seething mass of fighting dogs, how could you trust yourself to such a one? Nobody is fonder of Eustace Hignett than I am, but ... well, I mean to say!"

"I see what you mean. He really wasn't my ideal."

"Not by a mile!"

She mused, her chin in her hand.

"Of course, he was quite a dear in a lot of ways."

"Oh, a splendid chap," said Sam tolerantly.

"Have you ever heard him sing? I think what first attracted me to him was his beautiful voice. He really sings extraordinarily well."

A slight but definite spasm of jealousy afflicted Sam. He had no objection to praising poor old Eustace within decent limits, but the conversation seemed to him to be confining itself too exclusively to one subject.

"Yes?" he said. "Oh yes, I've heard him sing. Not lately. He does drawing-room ballads and all that sort of thing still, I suppose?"

"Have you ever heard him sing 'My love is like a glowing tulip that in an old-world garden grows'?"

"I have not had that advantage," replied Sam stiffly. "But anyone can sing a drawing-room ballad. Now something funny, something that will make people laugh, something that really needs putting across ... that's a different thing altogether."

"Do you sing that sort of thing?"

"People have been good enough to say...."

"Then," said Billie decidedly, "you must certainly do something at the ship's concert to-morrow! The idea of your trying to hide your light under a bushel! I will tell Bream to count on you. He is an excellent accompanist. He can accompany you."

"Yes, but ... well, I don't know," said Sam doubtfully. He could not help remembering that the last time he had sung in public had been at a house-supper at school, seven years before, and that on that occasion somebody whom it was a lasting grief to him that he had been unable to identify had thrown a pat of butter at him.

"Of course you must sing," said Billie. "I'll tell Bream when I go down to lunch. What will you sing?"

"Well—er—"

"Well, I'm sure it will be wonderful whatever it is. You are so wonderful in every way. You remind me of one of the heroes of old!"

Sam's discomposure vanished. In the first place, this was much more the sort of conversation which he felt the situation indicated. In the second place he had remembered that there was no need for him to sing at all. He could do that imitation of Frank Tinney which had been such a hit at the Trinity smoker. He was on safe ground there. He knew he was good. He clasped the girl to him and kissed her sixteen times.

§ 4

Billie Bennett stood in front of the mirror in her state-room dreamily brushing the glorious red hair that fell in a tumbled mass about her shoulders. On the lounge beside her, swathed in a business-like grey kimono, Jane Hubbard watched her, smoking a cigarette.

Jane Hubbard was a splendid specimen of bronzed, strapping womanhood. Her whole appearance spoke of the open air and the great wide spaces and all that sort of thing. She was a thoroughly wholesome, manly girl, about the same age as Billie, with a strong chin and an eye that had looked leopards squarely in the face and caused them to withdraw abashed into the undergrowth, or where-ever it is that leopards withdraw when abashed. One could not picture Jane Hubbard flirting lightly at garden parties, but one could picture her very readily arguing with a mutinous native bearer, or with a firm touch putting sweetness and light into the soul of a refractory mule. Boadicea in her girlhood must have been rather like Jane Hubbard.

She smoked contentedly. She had rolled her cigarette herself with one hand, a feat beyond the powers of all but the very greatest. She was pleasantly tired after walking eighty-five times round the promenade deck. Soon she would go to bed and fall asleep the moment her head touched the pillow. But meanwhile she lingered here, for she felt that Billie had something to confide in her.

"Jane," said Billie, "have you ever been in love?"

Jane Hubbard knocked the ash off her cigarette.

"Not since I was eleven," she said in her deep musical voice. "He was my music-master. He was forty-seven and completely bald, but there was an appealing weakness in him which won my heart. He was afraid of cats, I remember."

Billie gathered her hair into a molten bundle and let it run through her fingers.

"Oh, Jane!" she exclaimed. "Surely you don't like weak men. I like a man who is strong and brave and wonderful."

"I can't stand brave men," said Jane, "it makes them so independent. I could only love a man who would depend on me in everything. Sometimes, when I have been roughing it out in the jungle," she went on rather wistfully, "I have had my dreams of some gentle clinging man who would put his hand in mine and tell me all his poor little troubles and let me pet and comfort him and bring the smiles back to his face. I'm beginning to want to settle down. After all there are other things for a woman to do in this life besides travelling and big-game hunting. I should like to go into Parliament. And, if I did that, I should practically have to marry. I mean, I should have to have a man to look after the social end of life and arrange parties and receptions and so on, and sit ornamentally at the head of my table. I can't imagine anything jollier than marriage under conditions like that. When I came back a bit done up after a long sitting at the House, he would mix me a whisky-and-soda and read poetry to me or prattle about all the things he had been doing during the day.... Why, it would be ideal!"

Jane Hubbard gave a little sigh. Her fine eyes gazed dreamily at a smoke ring which she had sent floating towards the ceiling.

"Jane," said Billie. "I believe you're thinking of somebody definite. Who is he?"

The big-game huntress blushed. The embarrassment which she exhibited made her look manlier than ever.

"I don't know his name."

"But there is really someone?"

"Yes."

"How splendid! Tell me about him."

Jane Hubbard clasped her strong hands and looked down at the floor.

"I met him on the Subway a couple of days before I left New York. You know how crowded the Subway is at the rush hour. I had a seat, of course, but this poor little fellow—*so* good-looking, my dear! he reminded me of the pictures of Lord Byron—was hanging from a strap and being jerked about till I thought his poor little arms would be wrenched out of their sockets. And he looked so unhappy, as though he had some secret sorrow. I offered him my seat, but he wouldn't take it. A couple of stations later, however, the man next to me got out and he sat down and we got into conversation. There wasn't time to talk much. I told him I had been down-town fetching an elephant-gun which I had left to be mended. He was so prettily interested when I showed him the mechanism. We got along famously. But—oh, well, it was just another case of ships that pass in the night—I'm afraid I've been boring you."

"Oh, Jane! You haven't! You see ... you see, I'm in love myself."

"I had an idea you were," said her friend looking at her critically. "You've been refusing your oats the last few days, and that's a sure sign. Is he that fellow that's always around with you and who looks like a parrot?"

"Bream Mortimer? Good gracious, no!" cried Billie indignantly. "As if I should fall in love with Bream!"

"When I was out in British East Africa," said Miss Hubbard, "I had a bird that was the living image of Bream Mortimer. I taught him to whistle 'Annie Laurie' and to ask for his supper in three native dialects. Eventually he died of the pip, poor fellow. Well, if it isn't Bream Mortimer, who is it?"

"His name is Marlowe. He's tall and handsome and very strong-looking. He reminds me of a Greek god."

"Ugh!" said Miss Hubbard.

"Jane, we're engaged."

"No!" said the huntress, interested. "When can I meet him?"

"I'll introduce you to-morrow I'm so happy."

"That's fine!"

"And yet, somehow," said Billie, plaiting her hair, "do you ever have presentiments? I can't get rid of an awful feeling that something's going to happen to spoil everything."

"What could spoil everything?"

"Well, I think him so wonderful, you know. Suppose he were to do anything to blur the image I have formed of him."

"Oh, he won't. You said he was one of those strong men, didn't you? They always run true to form. They never do anything except be strong."

Billie looked meditatively at her reflection in the glass.

"You know I thought I was in love once before, Jane."

"Yes?"

"We were going to be married and I had actually gone to the church. And I waited and waited and he didn't come; and what do you think had happened?"

"What?"

"His mother had stolen his trousers."

Jane Hubbard laughed heartily.

"It's nothing to laugh at," said Billie seriously "It was a tragedy. I had always thought him romantic, and when this happened the scales seemed to fall from my eyes. I saw that I had made a mistake."

"And you broke off the engagement?"

"Of course!"

"I think you were hard on him. A man can't help his mother stealing his trousers."

"No. But when he finds they're gone, he can 'phone to the tailor for some more or borrow the janitor's or do *something*. But he simply stayed where he was and didn't do a thing. Just because he was too much afraid of his mother to tell her straight out that he meant to be married that day."

"Now that," said Miss Hubbard, "is just the sort of trait in a man which would appeal to me. I like a nervous, shrinking man."

"I don't. Besides, it made him seem so ridiculous, and—I don't know why it is—I can't forgive a man for looking ridiculous. Thank goodness, my darling Sam couldn't look ridiculous, even if he tried. He's wonderful, Jane. He reminds me of a knight of the Round Table. You ought to see his eyes flash."

Miss Hubbard got up and stretched herself with a yawn.

"Well, I'll be on the promenade deck after breakfast to-morrow. If you can arrange to have him flash his eyes then—say between nine-thirty and ten—I shall be delighted to watch them."

CHAPTER V

Persecution of Eustace

"Good God!" cried Eustace Hignett.

He stared at the figure which loomed above him in the fading light which came through the porthole of the stateroom. The hour was seven-thirty, and he had just woken from a troubled doze, full of strange nightmares, and for the moment he thought that he must still be dreaming, for the figure before him could have walked straight into any nightmare and no questions asked. Then suddenly he became aware that it was his cousin, Samuel Marlowe. As in the historic case of father in the pigstye, he could tell him by his hat. But why was he looking like that? Was it simply some trick of the uncertain light, or was his face really black and had his mouth suddenly grown to six times its normal size and become a vivid crimson?

Sam turned. He had been looking at himself in the mirror with a satisfaction which, to the casual observer, his appearance would not have seemed to justify. Hignett had not been suffering from a delusion. His cousin's face was black; and, even as he turned, he gave it a dab with a piece of burnt cork and made it blacker.

"Hullo! You awake?" he said, and switched on the light.

Eustace Hignett shied like a startled horse. His friend's profile, seen dimly, had been disconcerting enough. Full face, he was a revolting object. Nothing that Eustace Hignett had encountered in his recent dreams—and they had included such unusual fauna as elephants in top hats and running shorts—had affected him so profoundly. Sam's appearance smote him like a blow. It seemed to take him straight into a different and a dreadful world.

"What ... what ... what...?" he gurgled.

Sam squinted at himself in the glass and added a touch of black to his nose.

"How do I look?"

Eustace Hignett began to fear that his cousin's reason must have become unseated. He could not conceive of any really sane man, looking like that, being anxious to be told how he looked.

"Are my lips red enough? It's for the ship's concert, you know. It starts in half-an-hour, though I believe I'm not on till the second part. Speaking as a friend, would you put a touch more black round the ears, or are they all right?"

Curiosity replaced apprehension in Hignett's mind.

"What on earth are you doing performing at the ship's concert?"

"Oh, they roped me in. It got about somehow that I was a valuable man, and they wouldn't take no." Sam deepened the colour of his ears. "As a matter of fact," he said casually, "my fiancée made rather a point of my doing something."

A sharp yelp from the lower berth proclaimed the fact that the significance of the remark had not been lost on Eustace.

"Your fiancée?"

"The girl I'm engaged to. Didn't I tell you about that? Yes, I'm engaged."

Eustace sighed heavily.

"I feared the worst. Tell me, who is she?"

"Didn't I tell you her name?"

"No."

"Curious! I must have forgotten." He hummed an airy strain as he blackened the tip of his nose. "It's rather a curious coincidence, really. Her name is Bennett."

"She may be a relation."

"That's true. Of course, girls do have relations."

"What is her first name?"

"That is another rather remarkable thing. It's Wilhelmina."

"Wilhelmina!"

"Of course, there must be hundreds of girls in the world called Wilhelmina Bennett, but still it is a coincidence."

"What colour is her hair?" demanded Eustace Hignett in a hollow voice. "Her hair! What colour is it?"

"Her hair? Now, let me see. You ask me what colour is her hair. Well, you might call it auburn ... or russet ... or you might call it Titian...."

"Never mind what I might call it. Is it red?"

"Red? Why, yes. That is a very good description of it. Now that you put it to me like that, it *is* red."

"Has she a trick of grabbing at you suddenly, when she gets excited, like a kitten with a ball of wool?"

"Yes. Yes, she has."

Eustace Hignett uttered a sharp cry.

"Sam," he said, "can you bear a shock?"

"I'll have a dash at it."

"Brace up!"

"I'm ready."

"The girl you are engaged to is the same girl who promised to marry *me*."

"Well, well!" said Sam.

There was a silence.

"Awfully sorry, of course, and all that," said Sam.

"Don't apologise to *me*!" said Eustace. "My poor old chap, my only feeling towards you is one of the purest and profoundest pity." He reached out and pressed Sam's hand. "I regard you as a toad beneath the harrow!"

"Well, I suppose that's one way of offering congratulations and cheery good wishes."

"And on top of that," went on Eustace, deeply moved, "you have got to sing at the ship's concert."

"Why shouldn't I sing at the ship's concert?"

"My dear old man, you have many worthy qualities, but you must know that you can't sing. You can't sing for nuts! I don't want to discourage you, but, long ago as it is, you can't have forgotten what an ass you made of yourself at that house-supper at school. Seeing you up against it like this, I regret that I threw a lump of butter at you on that occasion, though at the time it seemed the only course to pursue."

Sam started.

"Was it you who threw that bit of butter?"

"It was."

"I wish I'd known! You silly chump, you ruined my collar."

"Ah, well, it's seven years ago. You would have had to send it to the wash anyhow by this time. But don't let us brood on the past. Let us put our heads together and think how we can get you out of this terrible situation."

"I don't want to get out of it. I confidently expect to be the hit of the evening."

"The hit of the evening! You! Singing!"

"I'm not going to sing. I'm going to do that imitation of Frank Tinney which I did at the Trinity smoker. You haven't forgotten that? You were at the piano taking the part of the conductor of the orchestra. What a riot I was— we were! I say, Eustace, old man, I suppose you don't feel well enough to come up now and take your old part? You could do it without a rehearsal. You remember how it went.... 'Hullo, Ernest!' 'Hullo, Frank!' Why not come along?"

"The only piano I will ever sit at will be one firmly fixed on a floor that does not heave and wobble under me."

"Nonsense! The boat's as steady as a rock now. The sea's like a mill-pond."

"Nevertheless, thanking you for your suggestion, no!"

"Oh, well, then I shall have to get on as best I can with that fellow Mortimer. We've been rehearsing all the afternoon, and he seems to have the hang of the thing. But he won't be really right. He has no pep, no vim. Still, if you won't ... well, I think I'll be getting along to his state-room. I told him I would look in for a last rehearsal."

The door closed behind Sam, and Eustace Hignett, lying on his back, gave himself up to melancholy meditation. He was deeply disturbed by his cousin's sad story. He knew what it meant being engaged to Wilhelmina Bennett. It was like being taken aloft in a balloon and dropped with a thud on the rocks.

His reflections were broken by the abrupt opening of the door. Sam rushed in. Eustace peered anxiously out of his berth. There was too much burnt cork on his cousin's face to allow of any real registering of emotion, but he could tell from his manner that all was not well.

"What's the matter?"

Sam sank down on the lounge.

"The bounder has quit!"

"The bounder? What bounder?"

"There is only one! Bream Mortimer, curse him! There may be others whom thoughtless critics rank as bounders, but he is the only man really deserving of the title. He refuses to appear! He has walked out on the act! He has left me flat! I went into his state-room just now, as arranged, and the man was lying on his bunk, groaning."

"I thought you said the sea was like a mill-pond."

"It wasn't that! He's perfectly fit. But it seems that the silly ass took it into his head to propose to Billie just before dinner—apparently he's loved her for years in a silent, self-effacing way—and of course she told him that she was engaged to me, and the thing upset him to such an extent that he says the idea of sitting down at a piano and helping me give an imitation of Frank Tinney revolts him. He says he intends to spend the evening in bed, reading Schopenhauer I hope it chokes him!"

"But this is splendid! This lets you out."

"What do you mean? Lets me out?"

"Why, now you won't be able to appear. Oh, you will be thankful for this in years to come."

"Won't I appear! Won't I dashed well appear! Do you think I'm going to disappoint that dear girl when she is relying on me? I would rather die."

"But you can't appear without a pianist."

"I've got a pianist."

"You have?"

"Yes. A little undersized shrimp of a fellow with a green face and ears like water-wings."

"I don't think I know him."

"Yes, you do. He's you!"

"Me!"

"Yes, you. You are going to sit at the piano to-night."

"I'm sorry to disappoint you, but it's impossible. I gave you my views on the subject just now."

"You've altered them."

"I haven't."

"Well, you soon will, and I'll tell you why. If you don't get up out of that damned berth you've been roosting in all your life, I'm going to ring for J. B. Midgeley and I'm going to tell him to bring me a bit of dinner in here and I'm going to eat it before your eyes."

"But you've had dinner."

"Well, I'll have another. I feel just ready for a nice fat pork chop...."

"Stop! Stop!"

"A nice fat pork chop with potatoes and lots of cabbage," repeated Sam firmly. "And I shall eat it here on this very lounge. Now how do we go?"

"You wouldn't do that!" said Eustace piteously.

"I would and will."

"But I shouldn't be any good at the piano. I've forgotten how the thing used to go."

"You haven't done anything of the kind. I come in and say 'Hullo, Ernest!' and you say 'Hullo, Frank!' and then you help me tell the story about the

Pullman car. A child could do your part of it."

"Perhaps there is some child on board...."

"No. I want you. I shall feel safe with you. We've done it together before."

"But, honestly, I really don't think ... it isn't as if...."

Sam rose and extended a finger towards the bell.

"Stop! Stop!" cried Eustace Hignett. "I'll do it!"

Sam withdrew his finger.

"Good!" he said. "We've just got time for a rehearsal while you're dressing. 'Hullo, Ernest!'"

"'Hullo, Frank,'" said Eustace Hignett brokenly as he searched for his unfamiliar trousers.

CHAPTER VI

Scene at a Ship's Concert

Ships' concerts are given in aid of the Seamen's Orphans and Widows, and, after one has been present at a few of them, one seems to feel that any right-thinking orphan or widow would rather jog along and take a chance of starvation than be the innocent cause of such things. They open with a long speech from the master of the ceremonies—so long, as a rule, that it is only the thought of what is going to happen afterwards that enables the audience to bear it with fortitude. This done, the amateur talent is unleashed, and the grim work begins.

It was not till after the all too brief intermission for rest and recuperation that the newly-formed team of Marlowe and Hignett was scheduled to appear. Previous to this there had been dark deeds done in the quiet saloon. The lecturer on deep-sea fish had fulfilled his threat and spoken at great length on a subject which, treated by a master of oratory, would have palled on the audience after ten or fifteen minutes; and at the end of fifteen minutes this speaker had only just got past the haddocks and was feeling his way tentatively through the shrimps. "The Rosary" had been sung and there was an uneasy doubt as to whether it was not going to be sung again after the interval—the latest rumour being that the second of the rival lady singers had proved adamant to all appeals and intended to fight the thing out on the lines she had originally chosen if they put her in irons.

A young man had recited "Gunga Din" and, wilfully misinterpreting the gratitude of the audience that it was over for a desire for more, had followed it with "Fuzzy-Wuzzy." His sister—these things run in families—had sung "My Little Gray Home in the West"—rather sombrely, for she had wanted to sing "The Rosary," and, with the same obtuseness which characterised her brother, had come back and rendered plantation songs. The audience was now examining its programmes in the interval of silence in order to ascertain the duration of the sentence still remaining unexpired.

It was shocked to read the following:—

7. A Little Imitation......S. Marlowe.

All over the saloon you could see fair women and brave men wilting in their seats. Imitation...! The word, as Keats would have said, was like a knell! Many of these people were old travellers and their minds went back wincingly, as one recalls forgotten wounds, to occasions when performers at ships' concerts had imitated whole strings of Dickens' characters or, with the assistance of a few hats and a little false hair, had endeavoured to portray Napoleon, Bismarck, Shakespeare, and other of the famous dead. In this printed line on the programme there was nothing to indicate the nature or scope of the imitation which this S. Marlowe proposed to inflict upon them. They could only sit and wait and hope that it would be short.

There was a sinking of hearts as Eustace Hignett moved down the room and took his place at the piano. A pianist! This argued more singing. The more pessimistic began to fear that the imitation was going to be one of those imitations of well-known opera artistes which, though rare, do occasionally add to the horrors of ships' concerts. They stared at Hignett apprehensively. There seemed to be something ominous in the man's very aspect. His face was very pale and set, the face of one approaching a task at which his humanity shudders. They could not know that the pallor of Eustace Hignett was due entirely to the slight tremor which, even on the calmest nights, the engines of an ocean liner produce in the flooring of a dining saloon, and to that faint, yet well-defined, smell of cooked meats which clings to a room where a great many people have recently been eating a great many meals. A few beads of cold perspiration were clinging to Eustace Hignett's brow. He looked straight before him with unseeing eyes. He was thinking hard of the Sahara.

So tense was Eustace's concentration that he did not see Billie Bennett, seated in the front row. Billie had watched him enter with a little thrill of embarrassment. She wished that she had been content with one of the seats at the back. But Jane Hubbard had insisted on the front row. She always had a front-row seat at witch dances in Africa, and the thing had become a habit.

In order to avoid recognition for as long as possible, Billie now put up her fan and turned to Jane. She was surprised to see that her friend was staring eagerly before her with a fixity almost equal to that of Eustace. Under her breath she muttered an exclamation of surprise in one of the lesser-known dialects of Northern Nigeria.

"Billie!" she whispered sharply.

"What *is* the matter, Jane?"

"Who is that man at the piano? Do you know him?"

"As a matter of fact, I do," said Billie. "His name is Hignett. Why?"

"It's the man I met on the Subway!" She breathed a sigh. "Poor little fellow, how miserable he looks!"

At this moment their conversation was interrupted. Eustace Hignett, pulling himself together with a painful effort, raised his hands and struck a crashing chord, and, as he did so, there appeared through the door at the far end of the saloon a figure at the sight of which the entire audience started convulsively with the feeling that a worse thing had befallen them than even they had looked for.

The figure was richly clad in some scarlet material. Its face was a grisly black and below the nose appeared what seemed a horrible gash. It advanced towards them, smoking a cigar.

"Hullo, Ernest," it said.

And then it seemed to pause expectantly, as though desiring some reply. Dead silence reigned in the saloon.

"Hullo, Ernest!"

Those nearest the piano—and nobody more quickly than Jane Hubbard—now observed that the white face of the man on the stool had grown whiter still. His eyes gazed out glassily from under his damp brow. He looked like a man who was seeing some ghastly sight. The audience sympathised with him. They felt like that, too.

In all human plans there is ever some slight hitch, some little miscalculation which just makes all the difference. A moment's thought should have told Eustace Hignett that a half-smoked cigar was one of the essential properties to any imitation of the eminent Mr. Tinney; but he had completely overlooked the fact. The cigar came as an absolute surprise to him and it could not have affected him more powerfully if it had been a voice from the tomb. He stared at it pallidly, like Macbeth at the ghost of Banquo. It was a strong, lively young cigar, and its curling smoke played lightly about his nostrils. His jaw fell. His eyes protruded. He looked for a long moment like one of those deep-sea fishes concerning which the recent lecturer had spoken so searchingly. Then with the cry of a stricken animal, he bounded from his seat and fled for the deck.

There was a rustle at Billie's side as Jane Hubbard rose and followed him. Jane was deeply stirred. Even as he sat, looking so pale and piteous, at the piano, her big heart had gone out to him, and now, in his moment of anguish, he seemed to bring to the surface everything that was best and manliest in her nature. Thrusting aside with one sweep of her powerful arm a steward who happened to be between her and the door, she raced in pursuit.

Sam Marlowe had watched his cousin's dash for the open with a consternation so complete that his senses seemed to have left him. A general, deserted by his men on some stricken field, might have felt something akin to his emotion. Of all the learned professions, the imitation of Mr. Frank Tinney is the one which can least easily be carried through single-handed. The man at the piano, the leader of the orchestra, is essential. He is the life-blood of the entertainment. Without him, nothing can be done.

For an instant Sam stood there, gaping blankly. Then the open door of the saloon seemed to beckon an invitation. He made for it, reached it, passed through it. That concluded his efforts in aid of the Seamen's Orphans and Widows.

The spell which had lain on the audience broke. This imitation seemed to them to possess in an extraordinary measure the one quality which renders amateur imitations tolerable, that of brevity. They had seen many amateur imitations, but never one as short as this. The saloon echoed with their applause.

It brought no balm to Samuel Marlowe. He did not hear it. He had fled for refuge to his state-room and was lying in the lower berth, chewing the pillow, a soul in torment.

CHAPTER VII

Sundered Hearts

There was a tap at the door. Sam sat up dizzily. He had lost all count of time.

"Who's that?"

"I have a note for you, sir."

It was the level voice of J. B. Midgeley, the steward. The stewards of the White Star Line, besides being the civillest and most obliging body of men in the world, all have soft and pleasant voices. A White Star steward, waking you up at six-thirty, to tell you that your bath is ready, when you wanted to sleep on till twelve, is the nearest human approach to the nightingale.

"A what?"

"A note, sir."

Sam jumped up and switched on the light. He went to the door and took the note from J. B. Midgeley, who, his mission accomplished, retired in an orderly manner down the passage. Sam looked at the letter with a thrill. He had never seen the handwriting before, but, with the eye of love, he recognised it. It was just the sort of hand he would have expected Billie to write, round and smooth and flowing, the writing of a warm-hearted girl. He tore open the envelope.

"Please come up to the top deck. I want to speak to you."

Sam could not disguise it from himself that he was a little disappointed. I don't know if you see anything wrong with the letter, but the way Sam looked at it was that, for a first love-letter, it might have been longer and perhaps a shade warmer. And, without running any risk of writer's cramp, she might have signed it.

However, these were small matters. No doubt the dear girl had been in a hurry and so forth. The important point was that he was going to see her. When a man's afraid, sings the bard, a beautiful

maid is a cheering sight to see; and the
same truth holds good when a man has
made an exhibition of himself at a ship's
concert. A woman's gentle sympathy,
that was what Samuel Marlowe wanted
more than anything else at the moment.
That, he felt, was what the doctor
ordered. He scrubbed the burnt cork
off his face with all possible speed and
changed his clothes and made his way
to the upper deck. It was like Billie, he
felt, to have chosen this spot for their
meeting. It would be deserted and it
was hallowed for them both by sacred
associations.

She was standing at the rail, looking
out over the water. The moon was
quite full. Out on the horizon to the
south its light shone on the sea,
making it look like the silver beach
of some distant fairy island. The girl
appeared to be wrapped in thought
and it was not till the sharp crack of
Sam's head against an overhanging
stanchion announced his approach,
that she turned.

"Oh, is that you?"

"Yes."

"You've been a long time."

"It wasn't an easy job," explained Sam, "getting all that burnt cork off. You've no notion how the stuff sticks. You have to use butter...."

She shuddered.

"Don't!"

"But I did. You have to with burnt cork."

"Don't tell me these horrible things." Her voice rose almost hysterically. "I never want to hear the words burnt cork mentioned again as long as I live."

"I feel exactly the same." Sam moved to her side. "Darling," he said in a low voice, "it was like you to ask me to meet you here. I know what you were thinking. You thought that I should need sympathy. You wanted to pet me, to smooth my wounded feelings, to hold me in your arms and tell me that, as we loved each other, what did anything else matter?"

"I didn't."

"You didn't?"

"No, I didn't."

"Oh, you didn't? I thought you did!" He looked at her wistfully. "I thought," he said, "that possibly you might have wished to comfort me. I have been through a great strain. I have had a shock...."

"And what about me?" she demanded passionately. "Haven't I had a shock?"

He melted at once.

"Have you had a shock too? Poor little thing! Sit down and tell me all about it."

She looked away from him, her face working.

"Can't you understand what a shock I have had? I thought you were the perfect knight."

"Yes, isn't it?"

"Isn't what?"

"I thought you said it was a perfect night."

"I said I thought *you* were the perfect knight."

"Oh, ah!"

A sailor crossed the deck, a dim figure in the shadows, went over to a sort of raised summerhouse with a brass thingummy in it, fooled about for a moment, and went away again. Sailors earn their money easily.

"Yes?" said Sam when he had gone.

"I forget what I was saying."

"Something about my being the perfect knight."

"Yes. I thought you were."

"That's good."

"But you're not!"

"No?"

"No!"

"Oh!"

Silence fell. Sam was feeling hurt and bewildered. He could not understand her mood. He had come up expecting to be soothed and comforted and she was like a petulant iceberg. Cynically, he recalled some lines of poetry which he had had to write out a hundred times on one occasion at school as a punishment for having introduced a white mouse into chapel.

"Oh, woman, in our hours of ease,
Un-something, something,
    something, please.
When tiddly-umpty umpty brow,
A something something something
    thou!"

He had forgotten the exact words, but the gist of it had been that Woman, however she might treat a man in times of prosperity, could be relied on to rally round and do the right thing when he was in trouble. How little the poet had known woman.

"Why not?" he said huffily.

She gave a little sob.

"I put you on a pedestal and I find you have feet of clay. You have blurred the image which I formed of you. I can never think of you again without picturing you as you stood in that saloon, stammering and helpless...."

"Well, what can you do when your pianist runs out on you?"

"You could have done *something*!" The words she had spoken only yesterday to Jane Hubbard came back to her. "I can't forgive a man for looking ridiculous. Oh, what, what," she cried, "induced you to try to give an imitation of Bert Williams?"

Sam started, stung to the quick.

"It wasn't Bert Williams. It was Frank Tinney!"

"Well, how was I to know?"

"I did my best," said Sam sullenly.

"That is the awful thought."

"I did it for your sake."

"I know. It gives me a horrible sense of guilt." She shuddered again. Then suddenly, with the nervous quickness of a woman unstrung, thrust a small black golliwog into his hand. "Take it!"

"What's this?"

"You bought it for me yesterday at the barber's shop. It is the only present which you have given me. Take it back."

"I don't want it. I shouldn't know what to do with it."

"You must take it," she said in a low voice. "It is a symbol."

"A what?"

"A symbol of our broken love."

"I don't see how you make that out. It's a golliwog."

"I can never marry you now."

"What! Good heavens! Don't be absurd."

"I can't!"

"Oh, go on, have a dash at it," he said encouragingly, though his heart was sinking.

She shook her head.

"No, I couldn't."

"Oh, hang it all!"

"I couldn't. I'm a very strange girl...."

"You're a very silly girl...."

"I don't see what right you have to say that," she flared.

"I don't see what right you have to say you can't marry me and try to load me up with golliwogs," he retorted with equal heat.

"Oh, can't you understand?"

"No, I'm dashed if I can."

She looked at him despondently.

"When I said I would marry you, you were a hero to me. You stood to me for everything that was noble and brave and wonderful. I had only to shut my eyes to conjure up the picture of you as you dived off the rail that morning. Now—" her voice trembled "—if I shut my eyes now, I can only see a man with a hideous black face making himself the laughing stock of the ship. How could I marry you, haunted by that picture?"

"But, good heavens, you talk as though I made a habit of blacking up! You talk as though you expected me to come to the altar smothered in burnt cork."

"I shall always think of you as I saw you to-night." She looked at him sadly. "There's a bit of black still on your left ear."

He tried to take her hand. But she drew it away. He fell back as if struck.

"So this is the end," he muttered.

"Yes. It's partly on your ear and partly on your cheek."

"So this is the end," he repeated.

"You had better go below and ask your steward to give you some more butter."

He laughed bitterly.

"Well, I might have expected it. I might have known what would happen! Eustace warned me. Eustace was right. He knows women—as I do now. Women! What mighty ills have not been done by woman? Who was't betrayed the what's-its-name? A woman! Who lost ... lost ... who lost ... who—er—and so on? A woman....

So all is over! There is nothing to be said but good-bye?"

"No."

"Good-bye, then, Miss Bennett!"

"Good-bye," said Billie sadly. "I—I'm sorry."

"Don't mention it!"

"You do understand, don't you?"

"You have made everything perfectly clear."

"I hope—I hope you won't be unhappy."

"Unhappy!" Sam produced a strangled noise from his larynx like the cry of a shrimp in pain. "Unhappy! Ha! ha! I'm not unhappy! Whatever gave you that idea? I'm smiling! I'm laughing! I feel I've had a merciful escape. Oh, ha, ha!"

"It's very unkind and rude of you to say that."

"It reminds me of a moving picture I saw in New York. It was called 'Saved from the Scaffold.'"

"Oh!"

"I'm not unhappy! What have I got to be unhappy about? What on earth does any man want to get married for? I don't. Give me my gay bachelor life! My Uncle Charlie used to say 'It's better luck to get married than it is to be kicked in the head by a mule.' But *he* was a man who always looked on the bright side. Good-night, Miss Bennett. And good-bye—for ever."

He turned on his heel and strode across the deck. From a white heaven the moon still shone benignantly down, mocking him. He had spoken bravely; the most captious critic could not but have admitted that he had made a good exit. But already his heart was aching.

As he drew near to his state-room, he was amazed and disgusted to hear a high tenor voice raised in song proceeding from behind the closed door.

"I fee-er naw faw in shee-ining
    arr-mor,
Though his lance be sharrrp and—er
    keen;
But I fee-er, I fee-er the glah-mour
Therough thy der-rooping lashes
    seen:
I fee-er, I fee-er the glah-mour...."

Sam flung open the door wrathfully. That Eustace Hignett should still be alive was bad—he had pictured him hurling himself overboard and bobbing about, a pleasing sight in the wake of the vessel; that he should be singing was an outrage. Remorse, Sam felt, should have stricken Eustace Hignett dumb. Instead of which, here he was comporting himself like a blasted linnet. It was all wrong. The man could have no conscience whatever.

"Well," he said sternly, "so there you are!"

Eustace Hignett looked up brightly, even beamingly. In the brief interval which had elapsed since Sam had seen him last, an extraordinary transformation had taken place in this young man. His wan look had disappeared. His eyes were bright. His face wore that beastly self-satisfied smirk which you see in pictures advertising certain makes of fine-mesh underwear. If Eustace Hignett had been a full-page drawing in a magazine with "My dear fellow, I always wear Sigsbee's Super-fine Featherweight!" printed underneath him, he could not have looked more pleased with himself.

"Hullo!" he said. "I was wondering where you had got to."

"Never mind," said Sam coldly, "where I had got to! Where did you get to and why? You poor, miserable worm," he went on in a burst of generous indignation, "what have you to say for yourself? What do you mean by dashing away like that and killing my little entertainment?"

"Awfully sorry, old man. I hadn't foreseen the cigar. I was bearing up tolerably well till I began to sniff the smoke. Then everything seemed to go black—I don't mean you, of course. You were black already—and I got the feeling that I simply must get on deck and drown myself."

"Well, why didn't you?" demanded Sam with a strong sense of injury. "I might have forgiven you then. But to come down here and find you singing...."

A soft light came into Eustace Hignett's eyes.

"I want to tell you all about that," he said.

"It's the most astonishing story. A miracle, you might almost call it. Makes you believe in Fate and all that kind of thing. A week ago I was on the Subway in New York...."

He broke off while Sam cursed him, the Subway, and the city of New York in the order named.

"My dear chap, what is the matter?"

"What is the matter? Ha!"

"Something is the matter," persisted Eustace Hignett. "I can tell it by your manner. Something has happened to disturb and upset you. I know you so well that I can pierce the mask. What is it? Tell me!"

"Ha, ha!"

"You surely can't still be brooding on that concert business? Why, that's all over. I take it that after my departure you made the most colossal ass of yourself, but why let that worry you? These things cannot affect one permanently."

"Can't they? Let me tell you that, as a result of that concert, my engagement is broken off."

Eustace sprang forward with out-stretched hand.

"Not really? How splendid! Accept my congratulations! This is the finest thing that could possibly have happened. These are not idle words. As one who has been engaged to the girl himself, I speak feelingly. You are well out of it, Sam."

Sam thrust aside his hand. Had it been his neck he might have clutched it eagerly, but he drew the line at shaking hands with Eustace Hignett.

"My heart is broken," he said with dignity.

"That feeling will pass, giving way to one of devout thankfulness. I know. I've been there. After all ... Wilhelmina Bennett ... what is she? A rag and a bone and a hank of hair!"

"She is nothing of the kind," said Sam, revolted.

"Pardon me," said Eustace firmly, "I speak as an expert. I know her and I repeat, she is a rag and a bone and a hank of hair!"

"She is the only girl in the world, and, owing to your idiotic behaviour, I have lost her."

"You speak of the only girl in the world," said Eustace blithely. "If you want to hear about the only girl in the world, I will tell you. A week ago I was on the Subway in New York...."

"I'm going to bed," said Sam brusquely.

"All right. I'll tell you while you're undressing."

"I don't want to listen."

"A week ago," said Eustace Hignett, "I will ask you to picture me seated after some difficulty in a carriage in the New York Subway. I got into conversation with a girl with an elephant gun."

Sam revised his private commination service in order to include the elephant gun.

"She was my soul-mate," proceeded Eustace with quiet determination. "I didn't know it at the time, but she was. She had grave brown eyes, a wonderful personality, and this elephant gun."

"Did she shoot you with it?"

"Shoot me? What do you mean? Why, no!"

"The girl must have been a fool!" said Sam bitterly. "The chance of a lifetime and she missed it. Where are my pyjamas?"

"I haven't seen your pyjamas. She talked to me about this elephant gun, and explained its mechanism. She told me the correct part of a hippopotamus to aim at, how to make a nourishing soup out of mangoes, and what to do when bitten by a Borneo wire-snake. You can imagine how she soothed my aching heart. My heart, if you recollect, was aching at the moment—quite unnecessarily if I had only known—because it was only a couple of days since my engagement to Wilhelmina Bennett had been broken off. Well, we parted at Sixty-sixth Street, and, strange as it may seem, I forgot all about her."

"Do it again!"

"Tell it again?"

"Good heavens, no! Forget all about her again."

"Nothing," said Eustace Hignett gravely, "could make me do that. Our souls have blended. Our beings have called to one another from their deepest depths, saying.... There are your pyjamas, over in the corner ... saying 'You are mine!' How could I forget her after that? Well, as I was saying, we parted. Little did I know that she was sailing on this very boat! But just now she came to me as I writhed on the deck...."

"Did you writhe?" asked Sam with a flicker of moody interest.

"I certainly did!"

"That's good!"

"But not for long."

"That's bad!"

"She came to me and healed me. Sam, that girl is an angel."

"Switch off the light when you've finished."

"She seemed to understand without a word how I was feeling. There are some situations which do not need words. She went away and returned with a mixture of some description in a glass. I don't know what it was. It had Worcester Sauce in it. She put it to my lips. She made me drink it. She said it was what she always used in Africa for bull-calves with the staggers. Well, believe me or believe me not ... are you asleep?"

"Yes."

"Believe me or believe me not, in under two minutes I was not merely freed from the nausea caused by your cigar. I was smoking myself! I was walking the deck with her without the slightest qualm. I was even able to look over the side from time to time and comment on the beauty of the moon on the water.... I have said some mordant things about women since I came on board this boat. I withdraw them unreservedly. They still apply to girls like Wilhelmina Bennett, but I have ceased to include the whole sex in my remarks. Jane Hubbard has restored my faith in Woman. Sam! Sam!"

"What?"

"I said that Jane Hubbard had restored my faith in Woman."

"Oh, all right."

Eustace Hignett finished undressing and got into bed. With a soft smile on his face he switched off the light. There was a long silence, broken only by the distant purring of the engines.

At about twelve-thirty a voice came from the lower berth.

"Sam!"

"What is it now?"

"There is a sweet womanly strength about her, Sam. She was telling me she once killed a panther with a hat-pin."

Sam groaned and tossed on his mattress.

Silence fell again.

"At least I think it was a panther," said Eustace Hignett at a quarter past one. "Either a panther or a puma."

CHAPTER VIII

Sir Mallaby Offers
a Suggestion

§ 1

A week after the liner "Atlantic" had docked at Southampton Sam Marlowe might have been observed—and was observed by various of the residents—sitting on a bench on the esplanade of that rising watering-place, Bingley-on-the-Sea, in Sussex. All watering-places on the south coast of England are blots on the landscape, but though I am aware that by saying it I shall offend the civic pride of some of the others—none are so peculiarly foul as Bingley-on-the-Sea. The asphalte on the Bingley esplanade is several degrees more depressing than the asphalte on other esplanades. The Swiss waiters at the Hotel Magnificent, where Sam was stopping, are in a class of bungling incompetence by themselves, the envy and despair of all the other Swiss waiters at all the other Hotels Magnificent along the coast. For dreariness of aspect Bingley-on-the-Sea stands alone. The very waves that break on its shingle seem to creep up the beach reluctantly, as if it revolted them to have to come to such a place.

Why, then, was Sam Marlowe visiting this ozone-swept Gehenna? Why, with all the rest of England at his disposal, had he chosen to spend a week at breezy, blighted Bingley?

Simply because he had been disappointed in love.

Nothing is more curious than the myriad ways in which reaction from an unfortunate love-affair manifests itself in various men. No two males behave in the same way under the spur of female fickleness. *Archilochum*, for instance, according to the Roman writer, *proprio rabies armavit iambo*. It is no good pretending out of politeness that you know what that means, so I will translate. *Rabies*—his grouch—*armavit*—armed—*Archilochum*—Archilochus—*iambo*—with the iambic—*proprio*—his own invention. In other words, when the poet Archilochus was handed his hat by the lady of his affections, he consoled himself by going off and writing satirical verse about her in a new metre which he had thought up immediately after leaving the house. That was the way the thing affected him.

On the other hand, we read in a recent issue of a London daily paper that John Simmons (31), a meat-salesman, was accused of assaulting an officer while in the discharge of his duty, at the same time using profane language whereby the officer went in fear of his life. Constable Riggs deposed that on the evening of the eleventh instant while he was on his beat, prisoner accosted him and, after offering to fight him for fourpence, drew off his right boot and threw it at his head. Accused, questioned by the magistrate, admitted the charge and expressed regret, pleading that he had had words with his young woman, and it had upset him.

Neither of these courses appealed to Samuel Marlowe. He had sought relief by slinking off alone to the Hotel

Magnificent at Bingley-on-the-Sea. It was the same spirit which has often moved other men in similar circumstances to go off to the Rockies to shoot grizzlies.

To a certain extent the Hotel Magnificent had dulled the pain. At any rate, the service and cooking there had done much to take his mind off it. His heart still ached, but he felt equal to going to London and seeing his father, which of course he ought to have done seven days before.

He rose from his bench—he had sat down on it directly after breakfast—and went back to the hotel to inquire about trains. An hour later he had begun his journey and two hours after that he was at the door of his father's office.

The offices of the old-established firm of Marlowe, Thorpe, Prescott, Winslow and Appleby are in Ridgeway's Inn, not far from Fleet Street. The brass plate, let into the woodwork of the door, is misleading. Reading it, you get the impression that on the other side quite a covey of lawyers await your arrival. The name of the firm leads you to suppose that there will be barely standing-room in the office. You picture Thorpe jostling you aside as he makes for Prescott to discuss with him the latest case of demurrer, and Winslow and Appleby treading on your toes, deep in conversation on replevin. But these legal firms dwindle. The years go by and take their toll, snatching away here a Prescott, there an Appleby, till, before you know where you are, you are down to your last lawyer. The only surviving member of the firm of Marlowe, Thorpe—what I said before— was, at the time with which this story deals, Sir Mallaby Marlowe, son of the original founder of the firm and father of the celebrated black-face comedian, Samuel of that ilk; and the outer office, where callers were received and parked till Sir Mallaby could find time for them, was occupied by a single clerk.

When Sam opened the door this clerk, John Peters by name, was seated on a high stool, holding in one hand a half-eaten sausage, in the other an extraordinarily large and powerful-looking revolver. At the sight of Sam he laid down both engines of destruction and beamed. He was not a particularly successful beamer, being hampered by a cast in one eye which gave him a truculent and sinister look; but those who knew him knew that he had a heart of gold and were not intimidated by his repellent face. Between Sam and himself there had always existed terms of great cordiality, starting from the time when the former was a small boy and it had been John Peters' mission to take him now to the Zoo, now to the train back to school.

"Why, Mr. Samuel!"

"Hullo, Peters!"

"We were expecting you back a week ago."

"Oh, I had something to see to before I came to town," said Sam carelessly.

"So you got back safe!" said John Peters.

"Safe! Why, of course."

Peters shook his head.

"I confess that, when there was this delay in your coming here, I sometimes feared something might have happened to you. I recall mentioning it to the young lady who recently did me the honour to promise to become my wife."

"Ocean liners aren't often wrecked nowadays."

"I was thinking more of the brawls on shore. America's a dangerous country. But perhaps you were not in touch with the underworld?"

"I don't think I was."

"Ah!" said John Peters significantly.

He took up the revolver, gave it a fond and almost paternal look, and replaced it on the desk.

"What on earth are you doing with that thing?" asked Sam.

Mr. Peters lowered his voice.

"I'm going to America myself in a few days' time, Mr. Samuel. It's my annual holiday, and the guv'nor's sending me over with papers in connection with The People v. Schultz and Bowen. It's a big case over there. A client of ours is mixed up in it, an American gentleman. I am to take these important papers to his legal representative in New York. So I thought it best to be prepared."

The first smile that he had permitted himself for nearly two weeks flitted across Sam's face.

"What on earth sort of place do you think New York is?" he asked. "It's safer than London."

"Ah, but what about the Underworld? I've seen these American films that they send over here, Mr. Samuel. Did you ever see 'Wolves of the Bowery?' There was a man in that in just my position, carrying important papers, and what they didn't try to do to him! No, I'm taking no chances, Mr. Samuel!"

"I should have said you were, lugging that thing about with you."

Mr. Peters seemed wounded.

"Oh, I understand the mechanism perfectly, and I am becoming a very fair shot. I take my little bite of food in here early and go and practise at the Rupert Street Rifle Range during my lunch hour. You'd be surprised how quickly one picks it up. When I get home of a night I try how quickly I can draw. You have to draw like a flash of lightning, Mr. Samuel. If you'd ever seen a film called 'Two-Gun-Thomas,' you'd realise that. You haven't time to wait loitering about."

Mr. Peters picked up a speaking-tube and blew down it.

"Mr. Samuel to see you, Sir Mallaby. Yes, sir, very good. Will you go right in, Mr. Samuel?"

Sam proceeded to the inner office, and found his father dictating into the attentive ear of Miss Milliken, his elderly and respectable stenographer, replies to his morning mail.

Sir Mallaby Marlowe was a dapper little man, with a round, cheerful face and a bright eye. His morning coat had been cut by London's best tailor, and his trousers perfectly creased by a sedulous valet. A pink carnation in his buttonhole matched his healthy complexion. His golf handicap was twelve. His sister, Mrs. Horace Hignett, considered him worldly.

"Dear Sirs,—We are in receipt of your favour and in reply beg to state that nothing will induce us ... will induce us ... where did I put that letter? Ah!... nothing will induce us ... oh, tell 'em to go to blazes, Miss Milliken."

"Very well, Sir Mallaby."

"That's that. Ready? Messrs. Brigney, Goole and Butterworth. What infernal names these people have. SIRS,—On behalf of our client ... oh, hullo, Sam!"

"Good morning, father."

"Take a seat. I'm busy, but I'll be finished in a moment. Where was I, Miss Milliken?"

"'On behalf of our client....'"

"Oh, yes. On behalf of our client Mr. Wibblesley Eggshaw.... Where these people get their names I'm hanged if I know. Your poor mother wanted to call you Hyacinth, Sam. You may not know it, but in the 'nineties when you were born, children were frequently christened Hyacinth. Well, I saved you from that."

His attention now diverted to his son, Sir Mallaby seemed to remember that the latter had just returned from a long journey and that he had not seen him for many weeks. He inspected him with interest.

"Very glad you're back, Sam. So you didn't win?"

"No, I got beaten in the semi-finals."

"American amateurs are a very hot lot, the best ones. I suppose you were weak on the greens. I warned you about that. You'll have to rub up your putting before next year."

At the idea that any such mundane pursuit as practising putting could appeal to his broken spirit now, Sam uttered a bitter laugh. It was as if Dante had recommended some lost soul in the Inferno to occupy his mind by knitting jumpers.

"Well, you seem to be in great spirits," said Sir Mallaby approvingly. "It's pleasant to hear your merry laugh again. Isn't it, Miss Milliken?"

"Extremely exhilarating," agreed the stenographer, adjusting her spectacles and smiling at Sam, for whom there was a soft spot in her heart.

A sense of the futility of life oppressed Sam. As he gazed in the glass that morning, he had thought, not without a certain gloomy satisfaction, how remarkably pale and drawn his face looked. And these people seemed to imagine that he was in the highest spirits. His laughter, which had sounded to him like the wailing of a demon, struck Miss Milliken as exhilarating.

"On behalf of our client, Mr. Wibblesley Eggshaw," said Sir Mallaby, swooping back to duty once more, "we beg to state that we are prepared to accept service ... what time did you dock this morning?"

"I landed nearly a week ago."

"A week ago! Then what the deuce have you been doing with yourself? Why haven't I seen you?"

"I've been down at Bingley-on-the-Sea."

"Bingley! What on earth were you doing at that God-forsaken place?"

"Wrestling with myself," said Sam with simple dignity.

Sir Mallaby's agile mind had leaped back to the letter which he was answering.

"We should be glad to meet you.... Wrestling, eh? Well, I like a boy to be fond of manly sports. Still, life isn't all athletics. Don't forget that. Life is real! Life is ... how does it go, Miss Milliken?"

Miss Milliken folded her hands and shut her eyes, her invariable habit when called upon to recite.

"Life is real! Life is earnest! And the grave is not its goal; dust thou art to dust returnest, was not spoken of the soul. Art is long and time is fleeting, And our hearts, though stout and brave, Still like muffled drums are beating, Funeral marches to the grave. Lives of great men all remind us we can make our lives sublime, and, departing, leave behind us footsteps on the sands of Time. Let us then ..." said Miss Milliken respectfully, ... "be up and doing...."

"All right, all right, all right!" said Sir Mallaby. "I don't want it all. Life is real! Life is earnest, Sam. I want to speak to you about that when I've finished answering these letters. Where was I? 'We should be glad to meet you at any time, if you will make an appointment....'

Bingley-on-the-Sea! Good heavens! Why Bingley-on-the-Sea? Why not Margate while you were about it?"

"Margate is too bracing. I did not wish to be braced. Bingley suited my mood. It was grey and dark and it rained all the time, and the sea slunk about in the distance like some baffled beast...."

He stopped, becoming aware that his father was not listening. Sir Mallaby's attention had returned to the letter.

"Oh, what's the good of answering the dashed thing at all?" said Sir Mallaby. "Brigney, Goole and Butterworth know perfectly well that they've got us in a cleft stick. Butterworth knows it better than Goole, and Brigney knows it better than Butterworth. This young fool, Eggshaw, Sam, admits that he wrote the girl twenty-three letters, twelve of them in verse, and twenty-one specifically asking her to marry him, and he comes to me and expects me to get him out of it. The girl is suing him for ten thousand."

"How like a woman!"

Miss Milliken bridled reproachfully at this slur on her sex. Sir Mallaby took no notice of it whatever.

"... if you will make an appointment, when we can discuss the matter without prejudice. Get those typed, Miss Milliken. Have a cigar, Sam. Miss Milliken, tell Peters as you go out that I am occupied with a conference and can see nobody for half an hour."

When Miss Milliken had withdrawn Sir Mallaby occupied ten seconds of the period which he had set aside for communion with his son in staring silently at him.

"I'm glad you're back, Sam," he said at length. "I want to have a talk with you. You know, it's time you were settling down. I've been thinking about you while you were in America and I've come to the conclusion that I've been letting you drift along. Very bad for a young man. You're getting on. I don't say you're senile, but you're not twenty-one any longer, and at your age I was working like a beaver. You've got to remember that life is—dash it! I've forgotten it again." He broke off and puffed vigorously into the speaking tube. "Miss Milliken, kindly repeat what you were saying just now about life.... Yes, yes, that's enough!" He put down the instrument. "Yes, life is real, life is earnest," he said, gazing at Sam seriously, "and the grave is not our goal. Lives of great men all remind us we can make our lives sublime. In fact, it's time you took your coat off and started work."

"I am quite ready, father."

"You didn't hear what I said," exclaimed Sir Mallaby, with a look of surprise. "I said it was time you began work."

"And I said I was quite ready."

"Bless my soul! You've changed your views a trifle since I saw you last."

"I have changed them altogether."

Long hours of brooding among the red plush settees in the lounge of the Hotel Magnificent at Bingley-on-the-Sea had brought about this strange, even morbid, attitude of mind in Samuel Marlowe. Work, he had decided, was the only medicine for his sick soul. Here, he felt, in this quiet office, far from the tumult and noise of the world, in a haven of torts and misdemeanours and Vic. I. cap. 3's, and all the rest of it, he might find peace. At any rate, it was worth taking a stab at it.

"Your trip has done you good," said Sir Mallaby approvingly. "The sea air has given you some sense. I'm glad of it. It makes it easier for me to say something else that I've had on my mind for a good while. Sam, it's time you got married."

Sam barked bitterly. His father looked at him with concern.

"Swallow some smoke the wrong way?"

"I was laughing," explained Sam with dignity.

Sir Mallaby shook his head.

"I don't want to discourage your high spirits, but I must ask you to approach this matter seriously. Marriage would do you a world of good, Sam. It would brace you up. You really ought to consider the idea. I was two years younger than you are when I married your poor mother, and it was the making of me. A wife might make something of you."

"Impossible!"

"I don't see why she shouldn't. There's lots of good in you, my boy, though you may not think so."

"When I said it was impossible," said Sam coldly, "I was referring to the impossibility of the possibility.... I mean, that it was impossible that I could possibly ... in other words, father, I can never marry. My heart is dead."

"Your what?"

"My heart."

"Don't be a fool. There's nothing wrong with your heart. All our family have had hearts like steam-engines. Probably you have been feeling a sort of burning. Knock off cigars and that will soon stop."

"You don't understand me. I mean that a woman has treated me in a way that has finished her whole sex as far as I am concerned. For me, women do not exist."

"You didn't tell me about this," said Sir Mallaby, interested. "When did this happen? Did she jilt you?"

"Yes."

"In America, was it?"

"On the boat."

Sir Mallaby chuckled heartily.

"My dear boy, you don't mean to tell me that you're taking a shipboard flirtation seriously? Why, you're expected to fall in love with a different girl every time you go on a voyage. You'll get over this in a week. You'd have got over it by now if you hadn't gone and buried yourself in a depressing place like Bingley-on-the-Sea."

The whistle of the speaking-tube blew. Sir Mallaby put the instrument to his ear.

"All right," he turned to Sam. "I shall have to send you away now, Sam. Man waiting to see me. Good-bye. By the way, are you doing anything to-night?"

"No."

"Not got a wrestling match on with yourself, or anything like that? Well, come to dinner at the house. Seven-thirty. Don't be late."

Sam went out. As he passed through the outer office, Miss Milliken intercepted him.

"Oh, Mr. Sam!"

"Yes?"

"Excuse me, but will you be seeing Sir Mallaby again to-day?"

"I'm dining with him to-night."

"Then would you—I don't like to disturb him now, when he is busy—would you mind telling him that I inadvertently omitted a stanza? It runs," said Miss Milliken, closing her eyes, "'Trust no future, howe'er pleasant! Let the dead past bury its dead! Act, act, in the living present, Heart within and God o'erhead!' Thank you so much. Good afternoon."

§ 2

Sam, reaching Bruton Street at a quarter past seven, was informed by the butler who admitted him that his father was dressing and would be down in a few minutes. The butler, an old retainer of the Marlowe family, who, if he had not actually dandled Sam on his knees when an infant, had known him as a small boy, was delighted to see him again.

"Missed you very much, Mr. Samuel, we all have," he said affectionately, as he preceded him to the drawing-room.

"Yes?" said Sam absently.

"Very much indeed, sir. I happened to remark only the other day that the place didn't seem the same without your happy laugh. It's good to see you back once more, looking so well and merry."

Sam stalked into the drawing-room with the feeling that comes to all of us from time to time, that it is hopeless to struggle. The whole damned circle of his acquaintance seemed to have made up their minds that he had not a care in the world, so what was the use? He lowered himself into a deep arm-chair and lit a cigarette.

Presently the butler reappeared with a cocktail on a tray. Sam drained it, and scarcely had the door closed behind the old retainer when an abrupt change came over the whole outlook. It was as if he had been a pianola and somebody had inserted a new record. Looking well and happy! He blew a smoke ring. Well, if it came to that, why not? Why shouldn't he look well and happy? What had he got to worry about? He was a young man, fit and strong, in the springtide of life, just about to plunge into an absorbing business. Why should he brood over a sentimental episode which had ended a little unfortunately? He would never see the girl again. If anything in this world was certain, that was. She would go her way, and he his. Samuel Marlowe rose from his chair a new man, to greet his father, who came in at that moment fingering a snowy white tie.

Sam started at his parent's splendour in some consternation.

"Great Scot, father! Are you expecting a lot of people? I thought we were dining alone."

"That's all right, my boy. A dinner-jacket is perfectly in order. We shall be quite a small party. Six in all. You and I, a friend of mine and his daughter, a friend of my friend's friend and my friend's friend's son."

"Surely that's more than six!"

"No."

"It sounded more."

"Six," said Sir Mallaby firmly. He raised a shapely hand with the fingers outspread. "Count 'em for yourself." He twiddled his thumb. "Number one—Bennett."

"Who?" cried Sam.

"Bennett. Rufus Bennett. He's an American over here for the summer. Haven't I ever mentioned his name to you? He's a great fellow. Always thinking he's at death's door, but keeps up a fine appetite. I've been his legal representative in London for years. Then—" Sir Mallaby twiddled his first finger—"there's his daughter Wilhelmina, who has just arrived in England." A look of enthusiasm came into Sir Mallaby's face. "Sam, my boy, I don't intend to say a word about Miss Wilhelmina Bennett, because I think there's nothing more prejudicial than singing a person's praises in advance. I merely remark that I fancy you will appreciate her! I've only met her once, and then only for a few minutes, but what I say is, if there's a girl living who's likely to make you forget whatever fool of a woman you may be fancying yourself in love with at the moment, that girl is Wilhelmina Bennett! The others are Bennett's friend, Henry Mortimer, also an American—a big lawyer, I believe, on the other side—and his son Bream. I haven't met either of them. They ought to be here any moment now." He looked at his watch. "Ah! I think that was the front door. Yes, I can hear them on the stairs."

CHAPTER IX

Rough Work at a Dinner Table

§ 1

After the first shock of astonishment, Sam Marlowe had listened to his father's harangue with a growing indignation which, towards the end of the speech, had assumed proportions of a cold fury. If there is one thing the which your high-spirited young man resents, it is being the toy of Fate. He chafes at the idea that Fate had got it all mapped out for him. Fate, thought Sam, had constructed a cheap, mushy, sentimental, five-reel film scenario, and without consulting him had had the cool cheek to cast him for one of the puppets. He seemed to see Fate as a thin female with a soppy expression and pince-nez, sniffing a little as she worked the thing out. He could picture her glutinous satisfaction as she re-read her scenario and gloated over its sure-fire qualities. There was not a flaw in the construction. It started off splendidly with a romantic meeting, had 'em guessing half-way through when the hero and heroine quarrelled and parted—apparently for ever, and now the stage was all set for the reconciliation and the slow fade-out on the embrace. To bring this last scene about, Fate had had to permit herself a slight coincidence, but she did not jib at that. What we call coincidences are merely the occasions when Fate gets stuck in a plot and has to invent the next situation in a hurry.

Sam Marlowe felt sulky and defiant. This girl had treated him shamefully and he wanted to have nothing more to do with her. If he had had his wish, he would never have met her again. Fate, in her interfering way, had forced this meeting on him and was now complacently looking to him to behave in a suitable manner. Well, he would show her! In a few seconds now, Billie and he would be meeting. He would be distant and polite. He would be cold and aloof. He would chill her to the bone, and rip a hole in the scenario six feet wide.

The door opened, and the room became full of Bennetts and Mortimers.

§ 2

Billie, looking, as Marlowe could not but admit, particularly pretty, headed the procession. Following her came a large red-faced man whose buttons seemed to creak beneath the strain of their duties. After him trotted a small, thin, pale, semi-bald individual who wore glasses and carried his nose raised and puckered as though some faintly unpleasant smell were troubling his nostrils. The fourth member of the party was dear old Bream.

There was a confused noise of mutual greetings and introductions, and then Bream got a good sight of Sam and napped forward with his right wing outstretched.

"Why, hello!" said Bream.

"How are you, Mortimer?" said Sam coldly.

"What, do you know my son?" exclaimed Sir Mallaby.

"Came over in the boat together," said Bream.

"Capital!" said Sir Mallaby. "Old friends, eh? Miss Bennett," he turned to Billie, who had been staring wide-eyed at her late fiancé, "let me present my son, Sam. Sam, this is Miss Bennett."

"How do you do?" said Sam.

"How do you do?" said Billie.

"Bennett, you've never met my son, I think?"

Mr. Bennett peered at Sam with protruding eyes which gave him the appearance of a rather unusually stout prawn.

"How *are* you?" he asked, with such intensity that Sam unconsciously found himself replying to a question which does not as a rule call for any answer.

"Very well, thanks."

Mr. Bennett shook his head moodily. "You are lucky to be able to say so! Very few of us can assert as much. I can truthfully say that in the last fifteen years I have not known what it is to enjoy sound health for a single day. Marlowe," he proceeded, swinging ponderously round on Sir Mallaby like a liner turning in the river, "I assure you that at twenty-five minutes past four this afternoon I was very nearly convinced that I should have to call you up on the 'phone and cancel this dinner engagement. When I took my temperature at twenty minutes to six...." At this point the butler appeared at the door announcing that dinner was served.

Sir Mallaby Marlowe's dinner table, which, like most of the furniture in the house had belonged to his deceased father and had been built at a period when people liked things big and solid, was a good deal too spacious to be really ideal for a small party. A white sea of linen separated each diner from the diner opposite and created a forced intimacy with the person seated next to him. Billie Bennett and Sam Marlowe, as a consequence, found themselves, if not exactly in a solitude of their own, at least sufficiently cut off from their kind to make silence between them impossible. Westward, Mr. Mortimer had engaged Sir Mallaby in a discussion on the recent case of Ouseley *v*. Ouseley, Figg, Mountjoy, Moseby-Smith and others, which though too complicated to explain here, presented points of considerable interest to the legal mind. To the east, Mr. Bennett was relating to Bream the more striking of his recent symptoms. Billie felt constrained to make at least an attempt at conversation.

"How strange meeting you here," she said.

Sam, who had been crumbling bread in an easy and debonair manner, looked up and met her eye. Its expression was one of cheerful friendliness. He could not see his own eye, but he imagined and hoped that it was cold and forbidding, like the surface of some bottomless mountain tarn.

"I beg your pardon?"

"I said, how strange meeting you here. I never dreamed Sir Mallaby was your father."

"I knew it all along," said Sam, and there was an interval caused by the maid insinuating herself between them and collecting his soup plate. He sipped sherry and felt a sombre self-satisfaction. He had, he considered, given the conversation the right tone from the start. Cool and distant. Out of the corner of his eye he saw Billie bite her lip. He turned to her again. Now that he had definitely established the fact that he and she were strangers, meeting by chance at a dinner-party, he was in a position to go on talking.

"And how do you like England, Miss Bennett?"

Billie's eye had lost its cheerful friendliness. A somewhat feline expression had taken its place.

"Pretty well," she replied.

"You don't like it?"

"Well, the way I look at it is this. It's no use grumbling. One has got to realise that in England one is in a savage country, and one should simply be thankful one isn't eaten by the natives."

"What makes you call England a savage country?" demanded Sam, a staunch patriot, deeply stung.

"What would you call a country where you can't get ice, central heating, corn-on-the-cob, or bathrooms? My father and Mr. Mortimer have just taken a house down on the coast and there's just one niggly little bathroom in the place."

"Is that your only reason for condemning England?"

"Oh no, it has other drawbacks."

"Such as?"

"Well, Englishmen, for instance. Young Englishmen in particular. English young men are awful! Idle, rude, conceited, and ridiculous."

Marlowe refused hock with a bitter intensity which nearly startled the old retainer, who had just offered it to him, into dropping the decanter.

"How many English young men have you met?"

Billie met his eye squarely and steadily. "Well, now that I come to think of it, not many. In fact, very few. As a matter of fact, only...."

"Only?"

"Well, very few," said Billie. "Yes," she said meditatively, "I suppose I really have been rather unjust. I should not have condemned a class simply because ... I mean, I suppose there *are* young English-men who are not rude and ridiculous?"

"I suppose there are American girls who have hearts."

"Oh, plenty."

"I'll believe that when I meet one."

Sam paused. Cold aloofness was all very well, but this conversation was developing into a vulgar brawl. The ghosts of dead and gone Marlowes, all noted for their courtesy to the sex, seemed to stand beside his chair, eyeing him reprovingly. His work, they seemed to whisper, was becoming raw. It was time to jerk the interchange of thought back into the realm of distant civility.

"Are you making a long stay in London, Miss Bennett?"

"No, not long. We are going down to the country almost immediately. I told you my father and Mr. Mortimer had taken a house there."

"You will enjoy that."

"I'm sure I shall. Mr. Mortimer's son Bream will be there. That will be nice."

"Why?" said Sam, backsliding.

There was a pause.

"*He* isn't rude and ridiculous, eh?" said Sam gruffly.

"Oh, no. His manners are perfect, and he has such a natural dignity," she went on, looking affectionately across the table at the heir of the Mortimers, who, finding Mr. Bennett's medical confidences a trifle fatiguing, was yawning broadly, and absently balancing his wine glass on a fork.

"Besides," said Billie in a soft and dreamy voice, "we are engaged to be married!"

§ 3

Sam didn't care, of course. We, who have had the privilege of a glimpse into his iron soul, know that. He was not in the least upset by the news— just surprised. He happened to be raising his glass at the moment, and he registered a certain amount of restrained emotion by snapping the stem in half and shooting the contents over the tablecloth: but that was all.

"Good heavens, Sam!" ejaculated Sir Mallaby, aghast. His wine glasses were an old and valued set.

Sam blushed as red as the stain on the cloth.

"Awfully sorry, father! Don't know how it happened."

"Something must have given you a shock," suggested Billie kindly.

The old retainer rallied round with napkins, and Sir Mallaby, who was just about to dismiss the affair with the polished ease of a good host, suddenly became aware of the activities of Bream. That young man, on whose dreamy calm the accident had made no impression whatever, had successfully established the equilibrium of the glass and the fork, and was now cautiously inserting beneath the latter a section of a roll, the whole forming a charming picture in still life.

"If that glass is in your way...." said Sir Mallaby as soon as he had hitched up his drooping jaw sufficiently to enable him to speak. He was beginning to feel that he would be lucky if he came out of this dinner-party with a mere remnant of his precious set.

"Oh, Sir Mallaby," said Billie, casting an adoring glance at the juggler, "you needn't be afraid that Bream will drop it. *He* isn't clumsy! He is wonderful at that sort of thing, simply wonderful! I think it's so splendid," said Billie, "when men can do things like that. I'm always trying to get Bream to do some of his tricks for people, but he's so modest, he won't."

"Refreshingly different," Sir Mallaby considered, "from the average drawing-room entertainer."

"Yes," said Billie emphatically. "I think the most terrible thing in the world is a man who tries to entertain when he can't. Did I tell you about the man on board ship, father, at the ship's concert? Oh, it was the most awful thing you ever saw. Everybody was talking about it!" She beamed round the table, and there was a note of fresh girlish gaiety in her voice. "This man got up to do an imitation of somebody—nobody knows to this day who it was meant to be—and he came into the saloon and directly he saw the audience he got stage fright. He just stood there gurgling and not saying a word, and then suddenly his nerve failed him altogether and he turned and tore out of the room like a rabbit. He absolutely ran! And he hadn't said a word! It was the most ridiculous exhibition I've ever seen!"

The anecdote went well. Of course there will always be a small minority in any audience which does not appreciate a funny story, and there was one in the present case. But the bulk of the company roared with laughter.

"Do you mean," cried Sir Mallaby, choking, "the poor idiot just stood there dumb?"

"Well, he made a sort of yammering noise," said Billie, "but that only made him look sillier."

"Deuced good!" chuckled Sir Mallaby.

"Funniest thing I ever heard in my life!" gurgled Mr. Bennett, swallowing a digestive capsule.

"May have been half-witted," suggested Mr. Mortimer.

Sam leaned across the table with a stern set face. He meant to change the conversation if he had to do it with a crowbar.

"I hear you have taken a house in the country, Mr. Mortimer," he said.

"Yes," said Mr. Mortimer. He turned to Sir Mallaby. "We have at last succeeded in persuading your sister, Mrs. Hignett, to let us rent her house for the summer."

Sir Mallaby gasped.

"Windles! You don't mean to tell me that my sister has let you have Windles!"

Mr. Mortimer nodded triumphantly.

"Yes. I had completely resigned myself to the prospect of spending the summer in some other house, when yesterday I happened to run into your nephew, young Eustace Hignett, on the street, and he said he was just coming round to see me about that very thing. To cut a long story short, he said that it would be all right and that we could have the house." Mr. Mortimer took a sip of burgundy. "He's a curious boy, young Hignett. Very nervous in his manner."

"Chronic dyspepsia," said Mr. Bennett authoritatively, "I can tell it at a glance."

"Is Windles a very lovely place, Sir Mallaby?" asked Billie.

"Charming. Quite charming. Not large, of course, as country houses go. Not a castle, I mean, with hundreds of acres of park land. But nice and compact and comfortable and very picturesque."

"We do not require a large place," said Mr. Mortimer. "We shall be quite a small party. Bennett and myself, Wilhelmina, Bream...."

"Don't forget," said Billie, "that you have promised to invite Jane Hubbard down there."

"Ah, yes. Wilhelmina's friend, Miss Hubbard. She is coming. That will be all, except young Hignett himself."

"Hignett!" cried Mr. Bennett.

"Mr. Hignett!" exclaimed Billie.

There was an almost imperceptible pause before Mr. Mortimer spoke again, and for an instant the demon of embarrassment hovered, unseen but present, above the dinner table. Mr. Bennett looked sternly at Billie; Billie turned a shade pinker and gazed at the tablecloth; Bream started nervously. Even Mr. Mortimer seemed robbed for a moment of his legal calm.

"I forgot to tell you that," he said. "Yes, one of the stipulations—to which I personally was perfectly willing to agree—was that Eustace Hignett was to remain on the premises during our tenancy. Such a clause in the agreement was, I am quite aware, unusual, and, had the circumstances been other than they were, I would have had a good deal to say about it. But we wanted the place, and we couldn't get it except by agreeing, so I agreed. I'm sure you will think that I acted rightly, Bennett, considering the peculiar circumstances."

"Well," said Mr. Bennett reluctantly, "I certainly did want that house...."

"And we couldn't have had it otherwise," said Mr. Mortimer, "so that is all there is to it."

"Well, it need make no difference to you," said Sir Mallaby. "I am sure you will find my nephew Eustace most unobtrusive. He may even be an entertaining companion. I believe he has a nice singing voice. With that and the juggling of our friend here and my sister's late husband's orchestrion, you will have no difficulty in amusing yourselves during the evenings. You remember the orchestrion, Sam?" said Sir Mallaby, on whom his son's silence had been weighing rather heavily for some time.

"Yes," said Sam, and returned to the silence once more.

"The late Mr. Hignett had it put in. He was very fond of music. It's a thing you turn on by pressing a button in the wall," continued Sir Mallaby. "How you stop it, I don't know. When I was down there last it never seemed to stop. You mustn't miss the orchestrion!"

"I certainly shall," said Mr. Bennett decidedly. "Music of that description happens to be the one thing which jars unendurably on my nerves. My nervous system is thoroughly out of tune."

"So is the orchestrion," said Sir Mallaby. "I remember once when I was down there...."

"I hope you will come down there again, Sir Mallaby," said Mr. Mortimer, "during our occupancy of the house. And you, too," he said, addressing Sam.

"I am afraid," said Sam frigidly, "that my time will be very much occupied for the next few months. Thank you very much," he added, after a moment's pause.

"Sam's going to work," said Sir Mallaby.

"Yes," said Sam with dark determination. "Work is the only thing in life that matters!"

"Oh, come, Sam!" said Sir Mallaby. "At your age I used to think love was fairly important, too!"

"Love!" said Sam. He jabbed at his soufflé with a spoon. You could see by the scornful way he did it that he did not think much of love.

§ 4

Sir Mallaby, the last cigar of the night between his lips, broke a silence which had lasted a quarter of an hour. The guests had gone, and he and Sam were alone together.

"Sam," he said, "do you know what I think?"

"No," said Sam.

Sir Mallaby removed his cigar and spoke impressively. "I've been turning the whole thing over in my mind, and the conclusion I have come to is that there is more in this Windles business than meets the eye. I've known your Aunt Adeline all my life, and I tell you it isn't in that woman to change her infernal pig-headed mind, especially about letting her house. She is a monomaniac on that subject. If you want to know my opinion, I am quite certain that your cousin Eustace has let the place to these people without her knowledge, and intends to pocket the cheque and not say a word about it. What do you think?"

"Eh?" said Sam absently.

"I said, what do you think?"

"What do I think about what?"

"About Eustace Hignett and Windles."

"What about them?"

Sir Mallaby regarded him disprovingly. "I'm hanged if I know what's the matter with you to-night, Sam. You seem to have unhitched your brain and left it in the umbrella stand. You hadn't a word to say for yourself all through dinner. You might have been a Trappist monk. And with that delightful girl Miss Bennett, there, too. She must have thought you infernally dull."

"I'm sorry."

"It's no good being sorry now. The mischief's done. She has gone away thinking you an idiot. Do you realise," said Sir Mallaby warmly, "that when she told that extremely funny story about the man who made such a fool of himself on board the ship, you were the only person at the table who was not amused? She must have thought you had no sense of humour!"

Sam rose. "I think I'll be going," he said. "Good night!"

A man can bear just so much.

CHAPTER X

Trouble at Windles

§ 1

Mr. Rufus Bennett stood at the window of the drawing-room of Windles, looking out. From where he stood he could see all those natural and artificial charms which had made the place so desirable to him when he first beheld them. Immediately below, flower beds, bright with assorted blooms, pressed against the ivied stone wall of the house. Beyond, separated from these by a gravel pathway, a smooth lawn, whose green and silky turf rivalled the lawns of Oxford colleges, stretched to a picturesque shrubbery, not so dense as to withhold altogether from the eye of the observer an occasional silvery glimpse of the lake that lay behind it. To the left, through noble trees, appeared a white suggestion of old stable yards; while to the right, bordering on the drive as it swept round to a distant gate, nothing less than a fragment of a ruined castle reared itself against a background of firs.

It had been this sensational fragment of Old England which had definitely captured Mr. Bennett on his first visit to the place. He could not have believed that the time would ever come when he could gaze on it without any lightening of the spirits.

The explanation of his gloom was simple. In addition to looking at the flower beds, the lawn, the shrubbery, the stable yard, and the castle, Mr. Bennett was also looking at the fifth heavy shower that had fallen since breakfast. This was the third afternoon of his tenancy. The first day it had rained all the time. The second day it had rained from eight till twelve-fifteen, from twelve-thirty till four, and from five till eleven. And on this, the third day, there had been no intermission longer than ten minutes. It was a trying Summer. Even the writers in the daily papers seemed mildly surprised, and claimed that England had seen finer Julys. Mr. Bennett, who had lived his life in a country of warmth and sunshine, the thing affected in much the same way as the early days of the Flood must have affected Noah. A first startled resentment had given place to a despair too militant to be called resignation. And with the despair had come a strong distaste for his fellow human beings, notably and in particular his old friend Mr. Mortimer, who at this moment broke impatiently in on his meditations.

"Come along, Bennett. It's your deal. It's no good looking at the rain. Looking at it won't stop it."

Mr. Mortimer's nerves also had become a little frayed by the weather.

Mr. Bennett returned heavily to the table, where, with Mr. Mortimer as partner he was playing one more interminable rubber of bridge against Bream and Billie. He was sick of bridge, but there was nothing else to do.

Mr. Bennett sat down with a grunt, and started to deal. Half-way through the operation the sound of rather stertorous breathing began to proceed from beneath the table. Mr. Bennett glanced agitatedly down, and curled his legs round his chair.

"I have fourteen cards," said Mr. Mortimer. "That's the third time you've mis-dealt."

"I don't care how many cards you've got!" said Mr. Bennett with heat. "That dog of yours is sniffing at my ankles!"

He looked malignantly at a fine bulldog which now emerged from its cover and, sitting down, beamed at the company. He was a sweet-tempered dog, handicapped by the outward appearance of a canine plug-ugly. Murder seemed the mildest of the desires that lay behind that rugged countenance. As a matter of fact, what he wanted was cake. His name was Smith, and Mr. Mortimer had bought him just before leaving London to serve the establishment as a watch-dog.

"He won't hurt you," said Mr. Mortimer carelessly.

"You keep saying that!" replied Mr. Bennett pettishly. "How do you know? He's a dangerous beast, and if I had had any notion that you were buying him, I would have had something to say about it!"

"Whatever you might have said would have made no difference. I am within my legal rights in purchasing a dog. You have a dog. At least, Wilhelmina has."

"Yes, and Pinky-Boodles gets on splendidly with Smith," said Billie. "I've seen them playing together."

Mr. Bennett subsided. He was feeling thoroughly misanthropic. He disliked everybody, with perhaps the exception of Billie, for whom a faint paternal fondness still lingered. He disliked Mr. Mortimer. He disliked Bream, and regretted that Billie had become engaged to him, though for years such an engagement had been his dearest desire. He disliked Jane Hubbard, now out walking in the rain with Eustace Hignett. And he disliked Eustace.

Eustace, he told himself, he disliked rather more than any of the others. He resented the young man's presence in the house; and he resented the fact that, being in the house, he should go about, pale and haggard, as though he were sickening for something. Mr. Bennett had the most violent objection to associating with people who looked as though they were sickening for something.

He got up and went to the window. The rain leaped at the glass like a frolicking puppy. It seemed to want to get inside and play with Mr. Bennett.

§ 2

Mr. Bennett slept late on the following morning. He looked at his watch on the dressing table when he got up, and found that it was past ten. Taking a second look to assure himself that he had really slumbered to this unusual hour, he suddenly became aware of something bright and yellow resting beside the watch, and paused, transfixed, like Robinson Crusoe staring at the footprint in the sand. If he had not been in England, he would have said that it was a patch of sunshine.

Mr. Bennett stared at the yellow blob with the wistful mistrust of a traveller in a desert who has been taken in once or twice by mirages. It was not till he had pulled up the blind and was looking out on a garden full of brightness and warmth and singing birds that he definitely permitted himself to accept the situation.

It was a superb morning. It was as if some giant had uncorked a great bottle full of the distilled scent of grass, trees, flowers, and hay. Mr. Bennett rang the bell joyfully, and presently there entered a grave, thin, intellectual-looking man who looked like a duke, only more respectable. This was Webster, Mr. Bennett's valet. He carried in one hand a small mug of hot water, reverently, as if it were a present of jewellery.

"Good morning, sir."

"Morning, Webster," said Mr. Bennett. "Rather late, eh?"

"It is" replied Webster precisely, "a little late, sir. I would have awakened you at the customary hour, but it was Miss Bennett's opinion that a rest would do you good."

Mr. Bennett's sense of well-being deepened. What more could a man want in this world than fine weather and a dutiful daughter?

"She did, eh?"

"Yes, sir. She desired me to inform you that, having already breakfasted, she proposed to drive Mr. Mortimer and Mr. Bream Mortimer into Southampton in the car. Mr. Mortimer senior wished to buy a panama hat."

"A panama hat!" exclaimed Mr. Bennett.

"A panama hat, sir."

Mr. Bennett's feeling of satisfaction grew still greater. It was a fine day; he had a dutiful daughter; and he was going to see Henry Mortimer in a panama hat. Providence was spoiling him.

The valet withdrew like a duke leaving the Royal Presence, not actually walking backwards but giving the impression of doing so; and Mr. Bennett, having decanted the mug of water into the basin, began to shave himself.

Having finished shaving, he opened the drawer in the bureau where lay his white flannel trousers. Here at last was a day worthy of them. He drew them out, and as he did so, something gleamed pinkly up at him from a corner of the drawer. His salmon-coloured bathing-suit.

Mr. Bennett started. He had not contemplated such a thing, but, after all, why not? There was the lake, shining through the trees, a mere fifty yards away. What could be more refreshing? He shed his pyjamas, and climbed into the bathing-suit. And presently, looking like the sun on a foggy day, he emerged from the house and picked his way with gingerly steps across the smooth surface of the lawn.

At this moment, from behind a bush where he had been thriftily burying a yesterday's bone, Smith the bulldog waddled out on to the lawn. He drank in the exhilarating air through an upturned nose which his recent excavations had rendered somewhat muddy. Then he observed Mr. Bennett, and moved gladly towards him. He did not recognise Mr. Bennett, for he remembered his friends principally by their respective bouquets, so he cantered silently across the turf to take a sniff at him. He was half-way across the lawn when some of the mud which he had inhaled when burying the bone tickled his lungs and he paused to cough.

Mr. Bennett whirled round; and then with a sharp exclamation picked up his pink feet from the velvet turf and began to run. Smith, after a momentary pause of surprise, lumbered after him, wheezing contentedly. This man, he felt, was evidently one of the right sort, a merry playfellow.

Mr. Bennett continued to run; but already he had begun to pant and falter, when he perceived looming upon his left the ruins of that ancient castle which had so attracted him on his first visit. On that occasion, it had made merely an aesthetic appeal to Mr. Bennett; now he saw in a flash that its practical merits also were of a sterling order. He swerved sharply, took the base of the edifice in his stride, clutched at a jutting stone, flung his foot at another, and, just as his pursuer arrived and sat panting below, pulled himself on to a ledge, where he sat with his feet hanging well out of reach. The bulldog Smith, gazed up at him expectantly. The game was a new one to Smith, but it seemed to have possibilities. He was a dog who was always perfectly willing to try anything once.

Mr. Bennett now began to address himself in earnest to the task of calling for assistance. His physical discomfort was acute. Insects, some winged, some without wings but—through Nature's wonderful law of compensation—equipped with a number of extra pairs of legs, had begun to fit out exploring expeditions over his body. They roamed about him as if he were some newly opened recreation ground, strolled in couples down his neck, and made up jolly family parties on his bare feet. And then, first dropping like the gentle dew upon the place beneath, then swishing down in a steady flood, it began to rain again.

It was at this point that Mr. Bennett's manly spirit broke and time ceased to exist for him.

Aeons later, a voice spoke from below.

"Hullo!" said the voice.

Mr. Bennett looked down. The stalwart form of Jane Hubbard was standing beneath him, gazing up from under a tam o'shanter cap. Smith, the bulldog, gambolled about her shapely feet.

"Whatever are you doing up there?" said Jane. "I say, do you know if the car has come back?"

"No. It has not."

"I've got to go to the doctor's. Poor little Mr. Hignett is ill. Oh, well, I'll have to walk. Come along, Smith!" She turned towards the drive, Smith caracoling at her side.

Mr. Bennett, though free now to move, remained where he was, transfixed. That sinister word "ill" held him like a spell. Eustace Hignett was ill! He had thought all along that the fellow was sickening for something, confound him!

"What's the matter with him?" bellowed Mr. Bennett after Jane Hubbard's retreating back.

"Eh?" queried Jane, stopping.

"What's the matter with Hignett?"

"I don't know."

"Is it infectious?"

"I expect so."

"Great Heavens!" cried Mr. Bennett, and, lowering himself cautiously to the ground, squelched across the dripping grass.

In the hall, Webster the valet, dry and dignified, was tapping the barometer with the wrist action of an ambassador knocking on the door of a friendly monarch.

"A sharp downpour, sir," he remarked.

"Have you been in the house all the time?" demanded Mr. Bennett.

"Yes, sir."

"Didn't you hear me shouting?"

"I did fancy I heard something, sir."

"Then why the devil didn't you come to me?"

"I supposed it to be the owls, sir, a bird very frequent in this locality. They make a sort of harsh, hooting howl, sir. I have sometimes wondered," said Webster, pursuing a not uninteresting train of thought, "whether that might be the reason of the name."

Before Mr. Bennett could join him in the region of speculation into which he had penetrated, there was a grinding of brakes on the gravel outside, and the wettest motor car in England drew up at the front door.

§ 3

From Windles to Southampton is a distance of about twenty miles; and the rain had started to fall when the car, an open one lacking even the poor protection of a cape hood, had accomplished half the homeward journey. For the last ten miles Mr. Mortimer had been nursing a sullen hatred for all created things; and, when entering the house, he came upon Mr. Bennett hopping about in the hall, endeavouring to detain him and tell him some long and uninteresting story, his venom concentrated itself upon his erstwhile friend.

"Oh, get out of the way!" he snapped, shaking off the other's hand. "Can't you see I'm wet?"

"Wet! Wet!" Mr. Bennett's voice quivered with self-pity. "So am I wet!"

"Father dear," said Billie reprovingly, "you really oughtn't to have come into the house after bathing without drying yourself. You'll spoil the carpet."

"I've *not* been bathing! I'm trying to tell you...."

"Hullo!" said Bream, with amiable innocence, coming in at the tail-end of the party. "Been having a jolly bathe?"

Mr. Bennett danced with silent irritation, and, striking a bare toe against the leg of a chair, seized his left foot and staggered into the arms of Webster, who had been preparing to drift off to the servants' hall. Linked together, the two proceeded across the carpet in a movement which suggested in equal parts the careless vigour of the cake-walk and the grace of the old-fashioned mazurka.

"What the devil are you doing, you fool?" cried Mr. Bennett.

"Nothing, sir. And I should be glad if you would accept my week's notice," replied Webster calmly.

"What's that?"

"My notice sir, to take effect at the expiration of the current week. I cannot acquiesce in being cursed and sworn at."

"Oh, go to blazes!"

"Very good, sir." Webster withdrew like a plenipotentiary who has been handed his papers on the declaration of war, and Mr. Bennett, sprang to intercept Mr. Mortimer, who had slipped by and was making for the stairs.

"Mortimer!"

"Oh, what *is* it?"

"That infernal dog of yours. I insist on your destroying it."

"What's it been doing?"

"The savage brute chased me all over the garden and kept me sitting up on that damned castle the whole of the morning!"

"Father darling," interposed Billie, pausing on her way up the stairs, "you mustn't get excited. You know it's bad for you. I don't expect poor old Smith meant any harm," she added pacifically, as she disappeared in the direction of the landing.

"Of course he didn't," snapped Mr. Mortimer. "He's as quiet as a lamb."

"I tell you he chased me from one end of the garden to the other! I had to run like a hare!"

The unfortunate Bream, whose sense of the humorous was simple and childlike, was not proof against the picture thus conjured up.

"C'k!" giggled Bream helplessly. "C'k, c'k, c'k!"

Mr. Bennett turned on him. "Oh, it strikes you as funny, does it? Well, let me tell you that if you think you can laugh at me with—with—er—with one hand and—and—marry my daughter with the other, you're wrong! You can consider your engagement at an end."

"Oh, I say!" ejaculated Bream, abruptly sobered.

"Mortimer!" bawled Mr. Bennett, once more arresting the other as he was about to mount the stairs. "Do you or do you not intend to destroy that dog?"

"I do not."

"I insist on your doing so. He is a menace."

"He is nothing of the kind. On your own showing he didn't even bite you once. And every dog is allowed one bite by law. The case of Wilberforce v. Bayliss covers that point thoroughly."

"I don't care about the case of Wilberforce and Bayliss...."

"You will find that you have to. It is a legal precedent."

There is something about a legal precedent which gives pause to the angriest man. Mr. Bennett felt, as every layman feels when arguing with a lawyer, as if he were in the coils of a python.

"Say, Mr. Bennett...." began Bream at his elbow.

"Get out!" snarled Mr. Bennett.

"Yes, but, say...!"

The green baize door at the end of the hall opened, and Webster appeared.

"I beg your pardon, sir," said Webster, "but luncheon will be served within the next few minutes. Possibly you may wish to make some change of costume."

"Bring me my lunch on a tray in my room," said Mr. Bennett. "I am going to bed."

"Very good, sir."

"But, say, Mr. Bennett...." resumed Bream.

"Grrh!" replied his ex-prospective-father-in-law, and bounded up the stairs like a portion of the sunset which had become detached from the main body.

§ 4

Even into the blackest days there generally creeps an occasional ray of sunshine, and there are few crises of human gloom which are not lightened by a bit of luck. It was so with Mr. Bennett in his hour of travail. There were lobsters for lunch, and his passion for lobsters had made him the talk of three New York clubs. He was feeling a little happier when Billie came in to see how he was getting on.

"Hullo, father. Had a nice lunch?"

"Yes," said Mr. Bennett, cheering up a little at the recollection. "There was nothing wrong with the lunch."

How little we fallible mortals know! Even as he spoke, a tiny fragment of lobster shell, which had been working its way silently into the tip of his tongue, was settling down under the skin and getting ready to cause him the most acute mental distress which he had ever known.

"The lunch," said Mr. Bennett, "was excellent. Lobsters!" He licked his lips appreciatively.

"And, talking of lobsters," he went on, "I suppose that boy Bream has told you that I have broken off your engagement?"

"Yes."

"You don't seem very upset," said Mr. Bennett, who was in the mood for a dramatic scene and felt a little disappointed.

"Oh, I've become a fatalist on the subject of my engagements."

"I don't understand you."

"Well, I mean, they never seem to come to anything." Billie gazed wistfully at the counterpane. "Do you know, father, I'm beginning to think that I'm rather impulsive. I wish I didn't do silly things in such a hurry."

"I don't see where the hurry comes in as regards that Mortimer boy. You took ten years to make up your mind."

"I was not thinking of Bream. Another man."

"Great Heavens! Are you still imagining yourself in love with young Hignett?"

"Oh, no! I can see now that I was never in love with poor Eustace. I was thinking of a man I got engaged to on the boat!"

Mr. Bennett sat bolt upright in bed, and stared incredulously at his surprising daughter. His head was beginning to swim.

"Of course I've misunderstood you," he said. "There's a catch somewhere and I haven't seen it. But for a moment you gave me the impression that you had promised to marry some man on the boat!"

"I did!"

"But...!" Mr. Bennett was doing sums on his fingers. "Do you mean to tell me," he demanded, having brought out the answer to his satisfaction, "do you mean to tell me that you have been engaged to three men in three weeks?"

"Yes," said Billie in a small voice.

"Great Godfrey! Er——?"

"No, only three."

Mr. Bennett sank back on to his pillow with a snort.

"The trouble is," continued Billie, "one does things and doesn't know how one is going to feel about it afterwards. You can do an awful lot of thinking afterwards, father."

"I'm doing a lot of thinking now," said Mr. Bennett with austerity. "You oughtn't to be allowed to go around loose!"

"Well, it doesn't matter. I shall never get engaged again. I shall never love anyone again."

"Don't tell me you are still in love with this boat man?"

Billie nodded miserably. "I didn't realise it till we came down here. But, as I sat and watched the rain, it suddenly came over me that I had thrown away my life's happiness. It was as if I had been offered a wonderful jewel and had refused it. I seemed to hear a voice reproaching me and saying, 'You have had your chance. It will never come again!'"

"Don't talk nonsense!" said Mr. Bennett.

Billie stiffened. She had thought she had been talking rather well.

Mr. Bennett was silent for a moment. Then he started up with an exclamation. The mention of Eustace Hignett had stirred his memory. "What's young Hignett got wrong with him?" he asked.

"Mumps."

"Mumps! Good God! Not mumps!" Mr. Bennett quailed. "I've never had mumps! One of the most infectious ... this is awful!... Oh, heavens! Why did I ever come to this lazar-house!" cried Mr. Bennett, shaken to his depths.

"There isn't the slightest danger, father, dear. Don't be silly. If I were you, I should try to get a good sleep. You must be tired after this morning."

"Sleep! If I only could!" said Mr. Bennett, and did so five minutes after the door had closed.

He awoke half an hour later with a confused sense that something was wrong. He had been dreaming that he was walking down Fifth Avenue at the head of a military brass band, clad only in a bathing suit. As he sat up in bed, blinking in the dazed fashion of the half-awakened, the band seemed to be playing still. There was undeniably music in the air. The room was full of it. It seemed to be coming up through the floor and rolling about in chunks all round his bed.

Mr. Bennett blinked the last fragments of sleep out of his system, and became filled with a restless irritability. There was only one instrument in the house which could create this infernal din— the orchestrion in the drawing-room, immediately above which, he recalled, his room was situated.

He rang the bell for Webster.

"Is Mr. Mortimer playing that—that damned gas-engine in the drawing-room?"

"Yes, sir. Tosti's 'Good-bye.' A charming air, sir."

"Go and tell him to stop it!"

"Very good, sir."

Mr. Bennett lay in bed and fumed. Presently the valet returned. The music still continued to roll about the room.

"I am sorry to have to inform you, sir," said Webster, "that Mr. Mortimer declines to accede to your request."

"Oh, he said that, did he?"

"That is the gist of his remarks, sir."

"Very good! Then give me my dressing-gown!"

Webster swathed his employer in the garment indicated, and returned to the kitchen, where he informed the cook that, in his opinion, the guv'nor was not a force, and that, if he were a betting man, he would put his money in the forthcoming struggle on Consul, the Almost-Human—by which affectionate nickname Mr. Mortimer senior was generally alluded to in the servants' hall.

Mr. Bennett, meanwhile, had reached the drawing-room, and found his former friend lying at full length on a sofa, smoking a cigar, a full dozen feet away from the orchestrion, which continued to thunder out its dirge on the passing of Summer.

"Will you turn that infernal thing off!" said Mr. Bennett.

"No!" said Mr. Mortimer.

"Now, now, now!" said a voice.

Jane Hubbard was standing in the doorway with a look of calm reproof on her face.

"We can't have this, you know!" said Jane Hubbard. "You're disturbing my patient."

She strode without hesitation to the instrument, explored its ribs with a firm finger, pushed something, and the orchestrion broke off in the middle of a bar. Then, walking serenely to the door, she passed out and closed it behind her.

The baser side of his nature urged Mr. Bennett to triumph over the vanquished.

"Now, what about it!" he said, ungenerously.

"Interfering girl!" mumbled Mr. Mortimer, chafing beneath defeat. "I've a good mind to start it again."

"I dare you!" whooped Mr. Bennett, reverting to the phraseology of his vanished childhood. "Go on! I dare you!"

"I've a perfect legal right.... Oh well," he said, "there are lots of other things I can do!"

"What do you mean?" exclaimed Mr. Bennett, alarmed.

"Never mind!" said Mr. Mortimer, taking up a book.

Mr. Bennett went back to bed in an uneasy frame of mind.

He brooded for half an hour, and, at the expiration of that period, rang for Webster and requested that Billie should be sent to him.

"I want you to go to London," he said, when she appeared. "I must have legal advice. I want you to go and see Sir Mallaby Marlowe. Tell him that Henry Mortimer is annoying me in every possible way and sheltering himself behind his knowledge of the law, so that I can't get at him. Ask Sir Mallaby to come down here. And, if he can't come himself, tell him to send someone who can advise me. His son would do, if he knows anything about the business."

"Oh, I'm sure he does!"

"Eh? How do you know?"

"Well, I mean, he looks as if he does!" said Billie hastily. "He looks so clever!"

"I didn't notice it myself. Well, he'll do, if Sir Mallaby's too busy to come himself. I want you to go up to-night, so that you can see him first thing to-morrow morning. You can stop the night at the Savoy. I've sent Webster to look out a train."

"There's a splendid train in about an hour. I'll take that."

"It's giving you a lot of trouble," said Mr. Bennett, with belated consideration.

"Oh, *no!*" said Billie. "I'm only too glad to be able to do this for you, father dear!"

CHAPTER XI

Mr. Bennett has a Bad Night

The fragment of a lobster-shell which had entered Mr. Bennett's tongue at twenty minutes to two in the afternoon was still in occupation at half-past eleven that night, when that persecuted gentleman blew out his candle and endeavoured to compose himself for a night's slumber. Its unconscious host had not yet been made aware of its presence. He had a vague feeling that the tip of his tongue felt a little sore, but his mind was too engrossed with the task of keeping a look-out for the preliminary symptoms of mumps to have leisure to bestow much attention on this phenomenon. The discomfort it caused was not sufficient to keep him awake, and presently he turned on his side and began to fill the room with a rhythmical snoring.

How pleasant if one could leave him so—the good man taking his rest. Facts, however, are facts; and, having crept softly from Mr. Bennett's side with the feeling that at last everything is all right with him, we are compelled to return three hours later to discover that everything is all wrong. It is so dark in the room that our eyes can at first discern nothing; then, as we grow accustomed to the blackness, we perceive him sitting bolt upright in bed, staring glassily before him, while with the first finger of his right hand he touches apprehensively the tip of his protruding tongue.

At this point Mr. Bennett lights his candle—one of the charms of Windles was the old-world simplicity of its lighting system—and we are enabled to get a better view of him.

Mr. Bennett sat in the candlelight with his tongue out and the first beads of a chilly perspiration bedewing his forehead. It was impossible for a man of his complexion to turn pale, but he had turned as pale as he could. Panic gripped him. A man whose favourite reading was medical encyclopædias, he needed no doctor to tell him that this was the end. Fate had dealt him a knockout blow; his number was up; and in a very short while now people would be speaking of him in the past tense and saying what a pity it all was.

A man in Mr. Bennett's position experiences strange emotions, and many of them. In fact, there are scores of writers, who, reckless of the cost of white paper, would devote two chapters at this point to an analysis of the unfortunate man's reflections and be glad of the chance. It is sufficient, however, merely to set on record that there was no stint. Whatever are the emotions of a man in such a position, Mr. Bennett had them. He had them all, one after another, some of them twice. He went right through the list from soup to nuts, until finally he reached remorse. And, having reached remorse, he allowed that to monopolise him.

In his early days, when he was building up his fortune, Mr. Bennett had frequently done things to his competitors in Wall Street which would not have been tolerated in the purer atmosphere of a lumber-camp, and, if he was going to be remorseful about anything, he might well have started by being remorseful about that. But it was on his most immediate past that his wistful mind lingered. He had quarrelled with his lifelong friend, Henry Mortimer. He had broken off his daughter's engagement with a deserving young man. He had spoken harsh words to his faithful valet. The more Mr. Bennett examined his conduct, the deeper the iron entered into his soul.

Fortunately, none of his acts were irreparable. He could undo them. He could make amends. The small hours of the morning are not perhaps the most suitable time for making amends, but Mr. Bennett was too remorseful to think of that. Do It Now had ever been his motto, so he started by ringing the bell for Webster.

The same writers who would have screamed with joy at the chance of dilating on Mr. Bennett's emotions would find a congenial task in describing the valet's thought-processes when the bell roused him from a refreshing sleep at a few minutes after three a.m. However, by the time he entered his employer's room he was his own calm self again.

"Good morning, sir," he remarked equably. "I fear that it will be the matter of a few minutes to prepare your shaving water. I was not aware," said Webster in manly apology for having been found wanting, "that you intended rising so early."

"Webster," said Mr. Bennett, "I'm a dying man!"

"Indeed, sir?"

"A dying man!" repeated Mr. Bennett.

"Very good, sir. Which of your suits would you wish me to lay out?"

Mr. Bennett had the feeling that something was going wrong with the scene.

"Webster," he said, "this morning we had an unfortunate misunderstanding. I'm sorry."

"Pray don't mention it, sir."

"I was to blame. Webster, you have been a faithful servant! You have stuck to me, Webster, through thick and thin!" said Mr. Bennett, who had half persuaded himself by this time that the other had been in the family for years instead of having been engaged at a registry-office a little less than a month ago. "Through thick and thin!" repeated Mr. Bennett.

"I have endeavoured to give satisfaction, sir."

"I want to reward you, Webster."

"Thank you very much, sir."

"Take my trousers!"

Webster raised a deprecating hand.

"No, no, sir, thanking you exceedingly, I couldn't really! You will need them, sir, and I assure you I have an ample supply."

"Take my trousers," repeated Mr. Bennett, "and feel in the right-hand pocket. There is some money there."

"I'm sure I'm very much obliged, sir," said Webster, beginning for the first time to feel that there was a bright side. He embarked upon the treasure-hunt. "The sum is sixteen pounds eleven shillings and threepence, sir."

"Keep it!"

"Thank you very much, sir. Would there be anything further, sir?"

"Why, no," said Mr. Bennett, feeling dissatisfied nevertheless. There had been a lack of the deepest kind of emotion in the interview, and his yearning soul resented it. "Why, no."

"Good-night, sir."

"Stop a moment. Which is Mr. Mortimer's room?"

"Mr. Mortimer, senior, sir? It is at the further end of this passage, on the left facing the main staircase. Good-night, sir. I am extremely obliged. I will bring you your shaving-water when you ring."

Mr. Bennett, left alone, mused for awhile, then, rising from his bed, put on his dressing-gown, took his candle, and went down the passage.

In a less softened mood, the first thing Mr. Bennett would have done on crossing the threshold of the door facing the staircase would have been to notice resentfully that Mr. Mortimer, with his usual astuteness, had collared the best bedroom in the house. The soft carpet gave out no sound as Mr. Bennett approached the wide and luxurious bed. The light of the candle fell on the back of a semi-bald head. Mr. Mortimer was sleeping with his face buried in the pillow. It cannot have been good for him, but that was what he was doing. From the portion of the pillow in which his face was buried strange gurgles proceeded, like the distant rumble of an approaching train on the Underground.

"Mortimer," said Mr. Bennett.

The train stopped at a station to pick up passengers, and rumbled on again.

"Henry!" said Mr. Bennett, and nudged his sleeping friend in the small of the back.

"Leave it on the mat," mumbled Mr. Mortimer, stirring slightly and uncovering one corner of his mouth.

Mr. Bennett began to forget his remorse in a sense of injury. He felt like a man with a good story to tell who can get nobody to listen to him. He nudged the other again, more vehemently this time. Mr. Mortimer made a noise like a gramophone when the needle slips, moved restlessly for a moment, then sat up, staring at the candle.

"Rabbits! Rabbits! Rabbits!" said Mr. Mortimer, and sank back again. He had begun to rumble before he touched the pillow.

"What do you mean, rabbits?" said Mr. Bennett sharply.

The not unreasonable query fell on deaf ears. Mr. Mortimer was already entering a tunnel.

"Much too pink!" he murmured as the pillow engulfed him.

What steps Mr. Bennett would have taken at this juncture, one cannot say. Probably he would have given the thing up in despair and retired, for it is weary work forgiving a sleeping man. But, as he bent above his slumbering friend, a drop of warm grease detached itself from the candle and fell into Mr. Mortimer's exposed ear. The sleeper wakened.

"What? What? What?" he exclaimed, bounding up. "Who's that?"

"It's me—Rufus," said Mr. Bennett. "Henry, I'm dying!"

"Drying?"

"Dying!"

Mr. Mortimer yawned cavernously. The mists of sleep were engulfing him again.

"Eight rabbits sitting on the lawn," he muttered. "But too pink! Much too pink!"

And, as if considering he had borne his full share in the conversation and that no more could be expected of him, he snuggled down into the pillow again.

Mr. Bennett's sense of injury became more acute. For a moment he was strongly tempted to try the restorative effects of candle-grease once more, but, just as he was on the point of succumbing, a shooting pain, as if somebody had run a red-hot needle into his tongue, reminded him of his situation. A dying man cannot pass his last hours dropping candle-grease into people's ears. After all, it was perhaps a little late, and there would be plenty of time to become reconciled to Mr. Mortimer to-morrow. His task now was to seek out Bream and bring him the glad news of his renewed engagement.

He closed the door quietly, and proceeded upstairs. Bream's bedroom, he knew, was the one just off the next landing. He turned the handle quietly, and went in. Having done this, he coughed.

"Drop that pistol!" said the voice of Jane Hubbard immediately, with quiet severity. "I've got you covered!"

Mr. Bennett had no pistol, but he dropped the candle. It would have been a nice point to say whether he was more perturbed by the discovery that he had got into the wrong room, and that room a lady's, or by the fact that the lady whose wrong room it was had pointed what appeared to be a small cannon at him over the foot of the bed. It was not, as a matter of fact, a cannon but the elephant gun, which Miss Hubbard carried with her everywhere—a girl's best friend.

"My dear young lady!" he gasped.

On the five occasions during recent years on which men had entered her tent with the object of murdering her, Jane Hubbard had shot without making inquiries. What strange feminine weakness it was that had caused her to utter a challenge on this occasion, she could not have said. Probably it was due to the enervating effects of civilisation.

She was glad now that she had done so, for, being awake and in full possession of her faculties, she perceived that the intruder, whoever he was, had no evil intentions.

"Who is it?" she asked.

"I don't know how to apologise!"

"That's all right! Let's have a light." A match flared in the darkness. Miss Hubbard lit her candle, and gazed at Mr. Bennett with quiet curiosity. "Walking in your sleep?" she inquired.

"No, no!"

"Not so loud! You'll wake Mr. Hignett. He's next door. That's why I took this room, in case he was restless in the night."

"I want to see Bream Mortimer," said Mr. Bennett.

"He's in my old room, two doors along the passage. What do you want to see him about?"

"I wish to inform him that he may still consider himself engaged to my daughter."

"Oh, well, I don't suppose he'll mind being woken up to hear that. But what's the idea?"

"It's a long story."

"That's all right. Let's make a night of it."

"I am a dying man. I awoke an hour ago with a feeling of acute pain...."

Miss Hubbard listened to the story of his symptoms with interest but without excitement.

"What nonsense!" she said at the conclusion.

"I assure you...."

"I'd like to bet it's nothing serious at all."

"My dear young lady," said Mr. Bennett, piqued. "I have devoted a considerable part of my life to medical study...."

"I know. That's the trouble. People oughtn't to be allowed to read medical books."

"Well, we need not discuss it," said Mr. Bennett stiffly. He resented being dragged out of the valley of the shadow of death by the scruff of his neck like this. A dying man has his dignity to think of. "I will leave you now, and go and see young Mortimer." He clung to a hope that Bream Mortimer at least would receive him fittingly. "Good-night!"

"But wait a moment!"

Mr. Bennett left the room, unheeding. He was glad to go. Jane Hubbard irritated him.

His expectation of getting more satisfactory results from Bream was fulfilled. It took some time to rouse that young man from a slumber almost as deep as his father's; but, once roused, he showed a gratifying appreciation of the gravity of affairs. Joy at one half of his visitor's news competed with consternation and sympathy at the other half. He thanked Mr. Bennett profusely, showed a fitting concern on learning of his terrible situation, and evinced a practical desire to help by offering him a bottle of liniment which he had found useful for gnat-stings. Declining this, though not ungratefully, Mr. Bennett withdrew and made his way down the passage again with something approaching a glow in his heart. The glow lasted till he had almost reached the landing, when it was dissipated by a soft but compelling voice from the doorway of Miss Hubbard's room.

"Come here!" said Miss Hubbard. She had put on a blue bath-robe, and looked like a pugilist about to enter the ring.

"Well?" said Mr. Bennett coldly, coming nevertheless.

"I'm going to have a look at that tongue of yours," said Jane firmly. "It's my opinion that you're making a lot of fuss over nothing."

Mr. Bennett drew himself up as haughtily as a fat man in a dressing-gown can, but the effect was wasted on his companion, who had turned and gone into her room.

"Come in here," she said.

Tougher men than Mr. Bennett had found it impossible to resist the note of calm command in that voice, but for all that he reproached himself for his weakness in obeying.

"Sit down!" said Jane Hubbard.

She indicated a low stool beside the dressing-table.

"Put your tongue out!" she said, as Mr. Bennett, still under her strange influence, lowered himself on to the stool. "Further out! That's right. Keep it like that!"

"Ouch!" exclaimed Mr. Bennett, bounding up.

"Don't make such a noise! You'll wake Mr. Hignett. Sit down again!"

"I...."

"Sit down!"

Mr. Bennett sat down. Miss Hubbard extended once more the hand holding the needle which had caused his outcry. He winced away from it desperately.

"Baby!" said Miss Hubbard reprovingly. "Why, I once sewed eighteen stitches in a native bearer's head, and he didn't make half the fuss you're making. Now, keep quite still."

Mr. Bennett did—for perhaps the space of two seconds. Then he leaped from his seat once more. It was a tribute to the forceful personality of the fair surgeon, if one were needed, that the squeal he uttered was a subdued one. He was just about to speak—he had framed the opening words of a strong protest—when suddenly he became aware of something in his mouth, something small and hard. He removed it and examined it as it lay on his finger. It was a minute fragment of lobster-shell. And at the same time he became conscious of a marked improvement in the state of his tongue. The swelling had gone.

"I told you so!" said Jane Hubbard placidly. "What is it?"

"It—it appears to be a piece of...."

"Lobster-shell. And we had lobster for lunch. Good-night."

Half-way down the stairs, it suddenly occurred to Mr. Bennett that he wanted to sing. He wanted to sing very loud, and for quite some time. He restrained the impulse, and returned to bed. But relief such as his was too strong to keep bottled up. He wanted to tell someone all about it. He needed a confidant.

Webster, the valet, awakened once again by the ringing of his bell, sighed resignedly and made his way downstairs.

"Did you ring, sir?"

"Webster," cried Mr. Bennett, "it's all right! I'm not dying after all! I'm not dying after all, Webster!"

"Very good, sir," said Webster. "Will there be anything further?"

CHAPTER XII

The Lurid Past of Jno. Peters

"That's right!" said Sir Mallaby Marlowe. "Work while you're young, Sam, work while you're young." He regarded his son's bent head with affectionate approval. "What's the book to-day?"

"Widgery on Nisi Prius Evidence," said Sam, without looking up.

"Capital!" said Sir Mallaby. "Highly improving and as interesting as a novel—some novels. There's a splendid bit on, I think, page two hundred and fifty-four where the hero finds out all about Copyhold and Customary Estates. It's a wonderfully powerful situation. It appears—but I won't spoil it for you. Mind you don't skip to see how it all comes out in the end!" Sir Mallaby suspended conversation while he addressed an imaginary ball with the mashie which he had taken out of his golf-bag. For this was the day when he went down to Walton Heath for his weekly foursome with three old friends. His tubby form was clad in tweed of a violent nature, with knickerbockers and stockings. "Sam!"

"Well?"

"Sam, a man at the club showed me a new grip the other day. Instead of overlapping the little finger of the right hand.... Oh, by the way, Sam."

"Yes?"

"I should lock up the office to-day if I were you, or anxious clients will be coming in and asking for advice, and you'll find yourself in difficulties. I shall be gone, and Peters is away on his holiday. You'd better lock the outer door."

"All right," said Sam absently. He was finding Widgery stiff reading. He had just got to the bit about Raptu Haeredis, which—as of course you know, is a writ for taking away an heir holding in socage.

Sir Mallaby looked at his watch.

"Well, I'll have to be going. See you later, Sam."

"Good-bye."

Sir Mallaby went out, and Sam, placing both elbows on the desk and twining his fingers in his hair, returned with a frown of consternation to his grappling with Widgery. For perhaps ten minutes the struggle was an even one, then gradually Widgery got the upper hand. Sam's mind, numbed by constant batterings against the stony ramparts of legal phraseology, weakened, faltered, and dropped away; and a moment later his thoughts, as so often happened when he was alone, darted off and began to circle round the image of Billie Bennett.

Since they had last met, at Sir Mallaby's dinner-table, Sam had told himself perhaps a hundred times that he cared nothing about Billie, that she had gone out of his life and was dead to him; but unfortunately he did not believe it. A man takes a deal of convincing on a point like this, and Sam had never succeeded in convincing himself for more than two minutes at a time. It was useless to pretend that he did not still love Billie more than ever, because he knew he did; and now, as the truth swept over him for the hundred and first time, he groaned hollowly and gave himself up to the grey despair which is the almost inseparable companion of young men in his position.

So engrossed was he in his meditation that he did not hear the light footstep in the outer office, and it was only when it was followed by a tap on the door of the inner office that he awoke with a start to the fact that clients were in his midst. He wished that he had taken his father's advice and locked up the office. Probably this was some frightful bore who wanted to make his infernal will or something, and Sam had neither the ability nor the inclination to assist him.

Was it too late to escape? Perhaps if he did not answer the knock, the blighter might think there was nobody at home. But suppose he opened the door and peeped in? A spasm of Napoleonic strategy seized Sam. He dropped silently to the floor and concealed himself under the desk. Napoleon was always doing that sort of thing.

There was another tap. Then, as he had anticipated, the door opened. Sam, crouched like a hare in its form, held his breath. It seemed to him that he was going to bring this delicate operation off with success. He felt he had acted just as Napoleon would have done in a similar crisis. And so, no doubt, he had to a certain extent; only Napoleon would have seen to it that his boots and about eighteen inches of trousered legs were not sticking out, plainly visible to all who entered.

"Good morning," said a voice.

Sam thrilled from the top of his head to the soles of his feet. It was the voice which had been ringing in his ears through all his waking hours.

"Are you busy, Mr. Marlowe?" asked Billie, addressing the boots.

Sam wriggled out from under the desk like a disconcerted tortoise.

"Dropped my pen," he mumbled, as he rose to the surface.

He pulled himself together with an effort that was like a physical exercise. He stared at Billie dumbly. Then, recovering speech, he invited her to sit down, and seated himself at the desk.

"Dropped my pen!" he gurgled again.

"Yes?" said Billie.

"Fountain-pen," babbled Sam, "with a broad nib."

"Yes?"

"A broad *gold* nib," went on Sam, with the painful exactitude which comes only from embarrassment or the early stages of intoxication.

"Really?" said Billie, and Sam blinked and told himself resolutely that this would not do. He was not appearing to advantage. It suddenly occurred to him that his hair was standing on end as the result of his struggle with Widgery. He smoothed it down hastily, and felt a trifle more composed. The old fighting spirit of the Marlowes now began to assert itself to some extent. He must make an effort to appear as little of a fool as possible in this girl's eyes. And what eyes they were! Golly! Like stars! Like two bright planets in....

However, that was neither here nor there. He pulled down his waistcoat and became cold and business-like,—the dry young lawyer.

"Er—how do you do, Miss Bennett?" he said with a question in his voice, raising his eyebrows in a professional way. He modelled this performance on that of lawyers he had seen on the stage, and wished he had some snuff to take or something to tap against his front teeth. "Miss Bennett, I believe?"

The effect of the question upon Billie was disastrous. She had come to this office with beating heart, prepared to end all misunderstandings, to sob on her soul-mate's shoulder and generally make everything up; but at this inane exhibition the fighting spirit of the Bennetts—which was fully as militant as that of the Marlowes—became roused. She told herself that she had been mistaken in supposing that she still loved this man. She was a proud girl and refused to admit herself capable of loving any man who looked at her as if she was something that the cat had brought in. She drew herself up stiffly.

"Yes," she replied. "How clever of you to remember me."

"I have a good memory."

"How nice! So have I!"

There was a pause, during which Billie allowed her gaze to travel casually about the room. Sam occupied the intermission by staring furtively at her profile. He was by now in a thoroughly overwrought condition, and the thumping of his heart sounded to him as if workmen were mending the street outside. How beautiful she looked, with that red hair peeping out beneath her hat and.... However!

"Is there anything I can do for you?" he asked in the sort of voice Widgery might have used. Sam always pictured Widgery as a small man with bushy eyebrows, a thin face, and a voice like a rusty file.

"Well, I really wanted to see Sir Mallaby."

"My father has been called away on important business to Walton Heath. Cannot I act as his substitute?"

"Do you know anything about the law?"

"Do I know anything about the law!" echoed Sam, amazed. "Do I know——! Why, I was reading my Widgery on Nisi Prius Evidence when you came in."

"Oh, were you?" said Billie, interested. "Do you always read on the floor?"

"I told you I dropped my pen," said Sam coldly.

"And of course you couldn't read without that! Well, as a matter of fact, this has nothing to do with Nisi—what you said."

"I have not specialised exclusively on Nisi Prius Evidence. I know the law in all its branches."

"Then what would you do if a man insisted on playing the orchestrion when you wanted to get to sleep?"

"The orchestrion?"

"Yes."

"The orchestrion, eh? Ah! H'm!" said Sam.

"You still haven't made it quite clear," said Billie.

"I was thinking."

"Oh, if you want to *think*!"

"Tell me the facts," said Sam.

"Well, Mr. Mortimer and my father have taken a house together in the country...."

"I knew that."

"*What* a memory you have!" said Billie kindly. "Well, for some reason or other they have quarrelled, and now Mr. Mortimer is doing everything he can to make father uncomfortable. Yesterday afternoon father wanted to sleep, and Mr. Mortimer started this orchestrion just to annoy him."

"I think—I'm not quite sure—I think that's a tort," said Sam.

"A what?"

"Either a tort or a malfeasance."

"Why, you do know something about it after all!" cried Billie, startled into a sort of friendliness in spite of herself. And at the words and the sight of her quick smile Sam's professional composure reeled on its foundations.

He had half risen, with the purpose of springing up and babbling of the passion that consumed him, when the chill reflection came to him that this girl had once said that she considered him ridiculous. If he let himself go, would she not continue to think him ridiculous? He sagged back into his seat; and at that moment there came another tap on the door which, opening, revealed the sinister face of the holiday-making Peters.

"Good morning, Mr. Samuel," said Jno. Peters. "Good morning, Miss Milliken. Oh!"

He vanished as abruptly as he had appeared. He perceived that what he had taken at first glance for the stenographer was a client, and that the junior partner was engaged on a business conference. He left behind him a momentary silence.

"What a horrible-looking man!" said Billie, breaking it with a little gasp. Jno. Peters often affected the opposite sex like that at first sight.

"I beg your pardon?" said Sam absently.

"What a dreadful-looking man! He quite frightened me!"

For some moments Sam sat without speaking. If this had not been one of his Napoleonic mornings, no doubt the sudden arrival of his old friend, Mr. Peters, whom he had imagined at his home in Putney packing for his trip to America, would have suggested nothing to him. As it was, it suggested a great deal. He had had a brain-wave, and for fully a minute he sat tingling under its impact. He was not a young man who often had brain-waves, and, when they came, they made him rather dizzy.

"Who is he?" asked Billie. "He seemed to know you? And who," she demanded after a slight pause, "is Miss Milliken?"

Sam drew a deep breath.

"It's rather a sad story," he said. "His name is John Peters. He used to be clerk here."

"But he isn't any longer?"

"No." Sam shook his head. "We had to get rid of him."

"I don't wonder. A man looking like that...."

"It wasn't that so much," said Sam. "The thing that annoyed father was that he tried to shoot Miss Milliken."

Billie uttered a cry of horror.

"He tried to shoot Miss Milliken!"

"He *did* shoot her—the third time," said Sam, warming to his work. "Only in the arm, fortunately," he added. "But my father is rather a stern disciplinarian and he had to go. I mean, we couldn't keep him after that."

"Good gracious!"

"She used to be my father's stenographer, and she was thrown a good deal with Peters. It was quite natural that he should fall in love with her. She was a beautiful girl, with rather your own shade of hair. Peters is a man of volcanic passions, and, when, after she had given him to understand that his love was returned, she informed him one day that she was engaged to a fellow at Ealing West, he went right off his onion—I mean, he became completely distraught. I must say that he concealed it very effectively at first. We had no inkling of his condition till he came in with the pistol. And, after that ... well, as I say, we had to dismiss him. A great pity, for he was a good clerk. Still, it wouldn't do. It wasn't only that he tried to shoot Miss Milliken. The thing became an obsession with him, and we found that he had a fixed idea that every red-haired woman who came into the office was the girl who had deceived him. You can see how awkward that made it. Red hair is so fashionable now-a-days."

"My hair is red!" whispered Billie pallidly.

"Yes, I noticed it myself. I told you it was much the same shade as Miss Milliken's.

It's rather fortunate that I happened to be here with you when he came."

"But he may be lurking out there still!"

"I expect he is," said Sam carelessly. "Yes, I suppose he is. Would you like me to go and send him away? All right."

"But—but is it safe?"

Sam uttered a light laugh.

"I don't mind taking a risk or two for your sake," he said, and sauntered from the room, closing the door behind him. Billie followed him with worshipping eyes.

Jno. Peters rose politely from the chair in which he had seated himself for the more comfortable perusal of the copy of *Home Whispers* which he had brought with him to refresh his mind in the event of the firm being too busy to see him immediately. He was particularly interested in the series of chats with Young Mothers.

"Hullo, Peters," said Sam. "Want anything?"

"Very sorry to have disturbed you, Mr. Samuel. I just looked in to say good-bye. I sail on Saturday, and my time will be pretty fully taken up all the week. I have to go down to the country to get some final instructions from the client whose important papers I am taking over. I'm sorry to have missed your father, Mr. Samuel."

"Yes, this is his golf day. I'll tell him you looked in."

"Is there anything I can do before I go?"

"Do?"

"Well—"—Jno. Peters coughed tact-fully—"I see that you are engaged with a client, Mr. Samuel, and I was wondering if any little point of law had arisen with which you did not feel yourself quite capable of coping, in which case I might perhaps be of assistance."

"Oh, that lady," said Sam. "That was Miss Milliken's sister."

"Indeed? I didn't know Miss Milliken had a sister."

"No?" said Sam.

"She is not very like her in appearance."

"No. This one is the beauty of the family, I believe. A very bright, intelligent girl. I was telling her about your revolver just before you came in, and she was most interested. It's a pity you haven't got it with you now, to show to her."

"Oh, but I have it! I have, Mr. Samuel!" said Peters, opening a small handbag and taking out a hymn-book, half a pound of mixed chocolates, a tongue sandwich, and the pistol, in the order named. "I was on my way to the Rupert Street range for a little practice. I should be glad to show it to her."

"Well, wait here a minute or two," said Sam. "I'll have finished talking business in a moment."

He returned to the inner office.

"Well?" cried Billie.

"Eh? Oh, he's gone," said Sam. "I persuaded him to go away. He was a little excited, poor fellow. And now let us return to what we were talking about. You say...." He broke off with an exclamation, and glanced at his watch. "Good Heavens! I had no idea of the time. I promised to run up and see a man in one of the offices in the next court. He wants to consult me on some difficulty which has arisen with one of his clients. Rightly or wrongly he values my advice. Can you spare me for a short while? I shan't be more than ten minutes."

"Certainly."

"Here is something you may care to look at while I'm gone. I don't know if you have read it? Widgery on Nisi Prius Evidence. Most interesting."

He went out. Jno. Peters looked up from his *Home Whispers*.

"You can go in now," said Sam.

"Certainly, Mr. Samuel, certainly."

Sam took up the copy of *Home Whispers* and sat down with his feet on the desk. He turned to the serial story and began to read the synopsis.

In the inner room Billie, who had rejected the mental refreshment offered by Widgery and was engaged on making a tour of the office, looking at the portraits of whiskered men whom she took correctly to be the Thorpes, Prescotts, Winslows, and Applebys mentioned on the contents-bill outside, was surprised to hear the door open at her back. She had not expected Sam to return so instantaneously.

Nor had he done so. It was not Sam who entered. It was a man of repellent aspect whom she recognised instantly, for Jno. Peters was one of those men who, once seen, are not easily forgotten. He was smiling a cruel, cunning smile—at least, she thought he was; Mr. Peters himself was under the impression that his face was wreathed in a benevolent simper; and in his hand he bore the largest pistol ever seen outside a motion-picture studio.

"How do you do, Miss Milliken?" he said.

CHAPTER XIII

Shocks all Round

Billie had been standing near the wall, inspecting a portrait of the late Mr. Josiah Appleby, of which the kindest thing one can say is that one hopes it did not do him justice. She now shrank back against this wall, as if she were trying to get through it. The edge of the portrait's frame tilted her hat out of the straight, but in this supreme moment she did not even notice it.

"Er—how do you do?" she said.

If she had not been an exceedingly pretty girl, one would have said that she spoke squeakily. The fighting spirit of the Bennetts, though it was considerable fighting spirit, had not risen to this emergency. It had ebbed out of her, leaving in its place a cold panic. She had seen this sort of thing in the movies—there was one series of pictures, "The Dangers of Diana," where something of the kind had happened to the heroine in every reel—but she had not anticipated that it would ever happen to her; and consequently she had not thought out any plan for coping with such a situation. A grave error. In this world one should be prepared for everything, or where is one?

"I've brought the revolver," said Mr. Peters.

"So—so I see!" said Billie.

Mr. Peters nursed the weapon affectionately in his hand. He was rather a shy man with women as a rule, but what Sam had told him about her being interested in his revolver had made his heart warm to this girl.

"I was just on my way to have a little practice at the range," he said. "Then I thought I might as well look in here."

"I suppose—I suppose you're a good shot?" quavered Billie.

"I seldom miss," said Jno. Peters.

Billie shuddered. Then, reflecting that the longer she engaged this maniac in conversation, the more hope there was of Sam coming back in time to save her, she essayed further small-talk.

"It's—it's very ugly!"

"Oh, no!" said Mr. Peters, hurt.

Billie perceived that she had said the wrong thing.

"Very deadly-looking, I meant," she corrected herself hastily.

"It may have deadly work to do, Miss Milliken," said Mr. Peters.

Conversation languished again. Billie had no further remarks to make of immediate interest, and Mr. Peters was struggling with a return of the deplorable shyness which so handicapped him in his dealings with the other sex. After a few moments, he pulled himself together again, and, as his first act was to replace the pistol in the pocket of his coat, Billie became conscious of a faint stirring of relief.

"The great thing," said Jno. Peters, "is to learn to draw quickly. Like this!" he added producing the revolver with something of the smoothness and rapidity with which Billie, in happier moments, had seen Bream Mortimer take a bowl of gold fish out of a tall hat. "Everything depends on getting the first shot! The first shot, Miss Milliken, is vital."

Suddenly Billie had an inspiration. It was hopeless, she knew, to try to convince this poor demented creature, obsessed with his *idée fixe*, that she was not Miss Milliken. Denial would be a waste of time, and might even infuriate him into precipitating the tragedy. It was imperative that she should humour him. And, while she was humouring him, it suddenly occurred to her, why not do it thoroughly?

"Mr. Peters," she cried, "you are quite mistaken!"

"I beg your pardon," said Jno. Peters, with not a little asperity. "Nothing of the kind!"

"You are!"

"I assure you I am not. Quickness in the draw is essential...."

"You have been misinformed."

"Well, I had it direct from the man at the Rupert Street range," said Mr. Peters stiffly. "And if you have ever seen a picture called 'Two-Gun Thomas'...."

"Mr. Peters," cried Billie desperately. He was making her head swim with his meaningless ravings. "Mr. Peters, hear me! I am not married to a man at Ealing West!"

Mr. Peters betrayed no excitement at the information. This girl seemed for some reason to consider her situation an extraordinary one, but many women, he was aware, were in a similar position. In fact, he could not at the moment think of any of his feminine acquaintances who *were* married to men at Ealing West.

"Indeed?" he said politely.

"Won't you believe me?" exclaimed Billie wildly.

"Why, certainly, certainly," said Jno. Peters.

"Thank God!" said Billie. "I'm not even engaged! It's all been a terrible mistake!"

When two people in a small room are speaking on two distinct and different subjects and neither knows what on earth the other is driving at, there is bound to be a certain amount of mental confusion; but at this point Jno. Peters, though still not wholly equal to the intellectual pressure of the conversation, began to see a faint shimmer of light behind the clouds. In a nebulous kind of way he began to understand that the girl had come to consult the firm about a breach-of-promise action. Some unknown man at Ealing West had been trifling with her heart—hardened lawyer's clerk as he was, that poignant cry "I'm not even engaged!" had touched Mr. Peters—and she wished to start proceedings. Mr. Peters felt almost in his depth again. He put the revolver in his pocket, and drew out a note-book.

"I should be glad to hear the facts," he said with professional courtesy. "In the absence of the guv'nor ...."

"I have told you the facts!"

"This man at Ealing West," said Mr. Peters, moistening the point of his pencil, "he wrote you letters proposing marriage?"

"No, no, no!"

"At any rate," said Mr. Peters, disappointed but hopeful, "he made love to you before witnesses?"

"Never! Never! There is no man at Ealing West! There never was a man at Ealing West!"

It was at this point that Jno. Peters began for the first time to entertain serious doubts of the girl's mental balance. The most elementary acquaintance with the latest census told him that there were any number of men at Ealing West. The place was full of them. Would a sane woman have made an assertion to the contrary? He thought not, and he was glad that he had the revolver with him. She had done nothing as yet actively violent, but it was nice to feel prepared. He took it out and laid it nonchalantly in his lap.

The sight of the weapon acted on Billie electrically. She flung out her hands, in a gesture of passionate appeal, and played her last card.

"I love *you*!" she cried. She wished she could have remembered his first name. It would have rounded off the sentence neatly. In such a moment she could hardly call him "Mr. Peters." "You are the only man I love."

"My gracious goodness!" ejaculated Mr. Peters, and nearly fell over backwards. To a naturally shy man this sudden and wholly unexpected declaration was disconcerting; and the clerk was, moreover, engaged. He blushed violently. And yet, even in that moment of consternation, he could not check a certain thrill. No man thinks he is as plain as he really is, but Jno. Peters had always come fairly near to a correct estimate of his charms, and it had always seemed to him, that, in inducing his fiancée to accept him, he had gone some. He now began to wonder if he were not really rather a devil of a chap after all. There must be precious few men going about capable of inspiring devotion like this on the strength of about six and a half minutes casual conversation.

Calmer thoughts succeeded this little flicker of complacency. The girl was mad. That was the fact of the matter. He got up and began to edge towards the door. Mr. Samuel would be returning shortly, and he ought to be warned.

"So that's all right, isn't it!" said Billie.

"Oh, quite, quite!" said Mr. Peters. "Er—Thank you very much!"

"I thought you would be pleased," said Billie, relieved but puzzled. For a man of volcanic passions, as Sam Marlowe had described him, he seemed to be taking the thing very calmly. She had anticipated a strenuous scene.

"Oh, it's a great compliment!" Mr. Peters assured her.

At this point Sam came in, interrupting the conversation at a moment when it had reached a somewhat difficult stage. He had finished the instalment of the serial story in *Home Whispers*, and, looking at his watch, he fancied that he had allowed sufficient time to elapse for events to have matured along the lines which his imagination had indicated.

The atmosphere of the room seemed to him, as he entered, a little strained. Billie looked pale and agitated. Mr. Peters looked rather agitated, too. Sam caught Billie's eye. It had an unspoken appeal in it. He gave an imperceptible nod, a reassuring nod, the nod of a man who understood all and was prepared to handle the situation.

"Come, Peters," he said in a deep, firm, quiet voice, laying a hand on the clerk's arm. "It's time that you went."

"Yes, indeed, Mr. Samuel! Yes, yes, indeed!"

"I'll see you out," said Sam soothingly, and led him through the outer office and on to the landing outside. "Well, good luck, Peters," he said, as they stood at the head of the stairs. "I hope you have a pleasant trip. Why, what's the matter? You seem upset."

"That girl, Mr. Samuel! I really think— really, she cannot be quite right in her head."

"Nonsense, nonsense!" said Sam firmly. "She's all right! Well, good-bye."

"Good-bye, Mr. Samuel."

"When did you say you were sailing?"

"Next Saturday, Mr. Samuel. But I fear I shall have no opportunity of seeing you again before then. I have packing to do and I have to see this gentleman down in the country...."

"All right. Then we'll say good-bye now. Good-bye, Peters. Mind you have a good time in America. I'll tell my father you called."

Sam watched him out of sight down the stairs, then turned and made his way back to the inner office. Billie was sitting limply on the chair which Jno. Peters had occupied. She sprang to her feet.

"Has he really gone?"

"Yes. He's gone this time."

"Was he—was he violent?"

"A little," said Sam. "A little. But I calmed him down." He looked at her gravely. "Thank God I was in time!"

"Oh, you are the bravest man in the world!" cried Billie, and, burying her face in her hands, burst into tears.

"There, there!" said Sam. "There, there! Come, come! It's all right now! There, there, there!"

He knelt down beside her. He slipped one arm round her waist. He patted her hands.

"There, there, there!" he said.

I have tried to draw Samuel Marlowe so that he will live on the printed page. I have endeavoured to delineate his character so that it will be as an open book. And, if I have succeeded in my task, the reader will by now have become aware that he was a young man with the gall of an Army mule. His conscience, if he had ever had one, had become atrophied through long disuse. He had given this sensitive girl the worst fright she had had since a mouse had got into her bedroom at school. He had caused Jno. Peters to totter off to the Rupert Street range making low, bleating noises. And did he care? No! All he cared about was the fact that he had erased for ever from Billie's mind that undignified picture of himself as he had appeared on the boat, and substituted another which showed him brave, resourceful, gallant. All he cared about was the fact that Billie, so cold ten minutes before, had just allowed him to kiss her for the forty-second time. If you had asked him, he would have said that he had acted for the best, and that out of evil cometh good, or some sickening thing like that. That was the sort of man Samuel Marlowe was.

His face was very close to Billie's, who had cheered up wonderfully by this time, and he was whispering his degraded words of endearment into her ear, when there was a sort of explosion in the doorway.

"Great Godfrey!" exclaimed Mr. Rufus Bennett, gazing on the scene from this point of vantage and mopping with a large handkerchief a scarlet face, which, as the result of climbing three flights of stairs, had become slightly soluble. "Great Heavens above! Number four!"

CHAPTER XIV

Strong Remarks
by a Father

Mr. Bennett advanced shakily into the room, and supported himself with one hand on the desk, while with the other he still plied the handkerchief on his over-heated face. Much had occurred to disturb him this morning. On top of a broken night he had had an affecting reconciliation scene with Mr. Mortimer, at the conclusion of which he had decided to take the first train to London in the hope of intercepting Billie before she reached Sir Mallaby's office on her mission of war. The local train-service kept such indecently early hours that he had been compelled to bolt his breakfast, and, in the absence of Billie, the only member of the household who knew how to drive the car, to walk to the station, a distance of nearly two miles, the last hundred yards of which he had covered at a rapid gallop, under the erroneous impression that an express whose smoke he had seen in the distance was the train he had come to catch. Arrived on the platform, he had had a trying wait, followed by a slow journey to Waterloo. The cab which he had taken at Waterloo had kept him in a lively state of apprehension all the way to the Savoy, owing to an apparent desire to climb over motor-omnibuses when it could not get round them. At the Savoy he found that Billie had already left, which had involved another voyage through the London traffic under the auspices of a driver who appeared to be either blind or desirous of committing suicide. He had three flights of stairs to negotiate. And, finally, arriving at the office, he had found his daughter in the circumstances already described.

"Why, father!" said Billie. "I didn't expect you."

As an explanation of her behaviour this might, no doubt, have been considered sufficient, but as an excuse for it Mr. Bennett thought it inadequate and would have said so, had he had enough breath. This physical limitation caused him to remain speechless and to do the best he could in the way of stern fatherly reproof by puffing like a seal after a long dive in search of fish.

Having done this, he became aware that Sam Marlowe was moving towards him with outstretched hand. It took a lot to disconcert Sam, and he was the calmest person present. He gave evidence of this in a neat speech. He did not in so many words congratulate Mr. Bennett on the piece of luck which had befallen him, but he tried to make him understand by his manner that he was distinctly to be envied as the prospective father-in-law of such a one as himself.

"I am delighted to see you, Mr. Bennett," said Sam. "You could not have come at a more fortunate moment. You see for yourself how things are. There is no need for a long explanation. You came to find a daughter, Mr. Bennett, and you have found a son!"

And he would like to see the man, thought Sam, who could have put it more cleverly and pleasantly and tactfully than that.

"What are you talking about?" said Mr. Bennett, recovering breath. "I haven't got a son."

"I will be a son to you! I will be the prop of your declining years...."

"What the devil do you mean, my declining years?" demanded Mr. Bennett with asperity.

"He means when they do decline, father dear," said Billie.

"Of course, of course," said Sam. "When they do decline. Not till then, of course. I wouldn't dream of it. But, once they do decline, count on me! And I should like to say for my part," he went on handsomely, "what an honour I think it, to become the son-in-law of a man like Mr. Bennett. Bennett of New York!" he added spaciously, not so much because he knew what he meant, for he would have been the first to admit that he did not, but because it sounded well.

"Oh!" said Mr. Bennett. "You do, do you?"

Mr. Bennett sat down. He put away his handkerchief, which had certainly earned a rest. Then he fastened a baleful stare upon his newly-discovered son. It was not the sort of look a proud and happy father-in-law-to-be ought to have directed at a prospective relative. It was not, as a matter of fact, the sort of look which anyone ought to have directed at anybody, except possibly an exceptionally prudish judge at a criminal in the dock, convicted of a more than usually atrocious murder. Billie, not being in the actual line of fire, only caught the tail end of it, but it was enough to create a misgiving.

"Oh, father! You aren't angry!"

"Angry!"

"You *can't* be angry!"

"Why can't I be angry?" declared Mr. Bennett, with that sense of injury which comes to self-willed men when their whims are thwarted. "Why the devil shouldn't I be angry? I *am* angry! I come here and find you like—like this, and you seem to expect me to throw my hat in the air and give three rousing cheers! Of course I'm angry! You are engaged to be married to an excellent young man of the highest character, one of the finest young men I have ever known...."

"Oh, well!" said Sam, straightening his tie modestly. "It's awfully good of you...."

"But that's all over, father."

"What's all over?"

"You told me yourself that you had broken off my engagement to Bream."

"Well—er—yes, I did," said Mr. Bennett, a little taken aback. "That is—to a certain extent—so. But," he added, with restored firmness, "it's on again!"

"But I don't want to marry Bream!"

"Naturally!" said Sam. "Naturally! Quite out of the question. In a few days we'll all be roaring with laughter at the very idea."

"It doesn't matter what you want! A girl who gets engaged to a dozen men in three weeks...."

"It wasn't a dozen!"

"Well, four—five—six—you can't expect me not to lose count.... I say a girl who does that does not know what she wants, and older and more prudent heads must decide for her. You are going to marry Bream Mortimer!"

"All wrong! All wrong!" said Sam, with a reproving shake of the head. "All wrong! She's going to marry me."

Mr. Bennett scorched him with a look compared with which his earlier effort had been a loving glance.

"Wilhelmina," he said, "go into the outer office."

"But, father, Sam saved my life!"

"Go into the outer office and wait for me there."

"There was a lunatic in here...."

"There will be another if you don't go."

"He had a pistol."

"Go into the outer office!"

"I shall always love you, Sam!" said Billie, pausing mutinously at the door.

"I shall always love *you*!" said Sam cordially.

"Nobody can keep us apart!"

"They're wasting their time, trying."

"You're the most wonderful man in the world!"

"There never was another girl like you!"

"Get *out*!" bellowed Mr. Bennett, on whose equanimity this love-scene, which I think beautiful, was jarring profoundly. "Now, sir!" he said to Sam, as the door closed.

"Yes, let's talk it over calmly," said Sam.

"I will not talk it over calmly!"

"Oh, come! You can do it if you try. In the first place, whatever put this silly idea into your head about that sweet girl marrying Bream Mortimer?"

"Bream Mortimer is the son of Henry Mortimer."

"I know," said Sam. "And, while it is no doubt unfair to hold that against him, it's a point you can't afford to ignore. Henry Mortimer! You and I have Henry Mortimer's number. We know what Henry Mortimer is like! A man who spends his time thinking up ways of annoying you. You can't seriously want to have the Mortimer family linked to you by marriage."

"Henry Mortimer is my oldest friend."

"That makes it all the worse. Fancy a man who calls himself your friend treating you like that!"

"The misunderstanding to which you allude has been completely smoothed over. My relations with Mr. Mortimer are thoroughly cordial."

"Well, have it your own way. Personally, I wouldn't trust a man like that. And, as for letting my daughter marry his son...!"

"I have decided once and for all...."

"If you'll take my advice, you will break the thing off."

"I will not take your advice."

"I wouldn't expect to charge you for it," explained Sam reassuringly. "I give it you as a friend, not as a lawyer. Six-and-eightpence to others, free to you."

"Will you understand that my daughter is going to marry Bream Mortimer? What are you giggling about?"

"It sounds so silly. The idea of anyone marrying Bream Mortimer, I mean."

"Let me tell you he is a thoroughly estimable young man."

"And there you put the whole thing in a nutshell. Your daughter is a girl of spirit. She would hate to be tied for life to an estimable young man."

"She will do as I tell her."

Sam regarded him sternly.

"Have you no regard for her happiness?"

"I am the best judge of what is best for her."

"If you ask me," said Sam candidly, "I think you're a rotten judge."

"I did not come here to be insulted!"

"I like that! You have been insulting me ever since you arrived. What right have you to say that I'm not fit to marry your daughter?"

"I did not say that."

"You've implied it. And you've been looking at me as if I were a leper or something the Pure Food Committee had condemned. Why? That's what I ask you," said Sam, warming up. This he fancied, was the way Widgery would have tackled a troublesome client. "Why? Answer me that!"

"I...."

Sam rapped sharply on the desk.

"Be careful, sir. Be very careful!" He knew that this was what lawyers always said. Of course, there is a difference in position between a miscreant whom you suspect of an attempt at perjury and the father of the girl you love, whose consent to the match you wish to obtain, but Sam was in no mood for these nice distinctions. He only knew that lawyers told people to be very careful, so he told Mr. Bennett to be very careful.

"What do you mean, be very careful?" said Mr. Bennett.

"I'm dashed if I know," said Sam frankly. The question struck him as a mean attack. He wondered how Widgery would have met it. Probably by smiling quietly and polishing his spectacles. Sam had no spectacles. He endeavoured, however, to smile quietly.

"Don't laugh at me!" roared Mr. Bennett.

"I'm not laughing at you."

"You are!"

"I'm not! I'm smiling quietly."

"Well, don't then!" said Mr. Bennett. He glowered at his young companion. "I don't know why I'm wasting my time, talking to you. The position is clear to the meanest intelligence. I have no objection to you personally...."

"Come, this is better!" said Sam.

"I don't know you well enough to have any objection to you or any opinion of you at all. This is only the second time I have ever met you in my life."

"Mark you," said Sam, "I think I am one of those fellows who grow on people...."

"As far as I am concerned, you simply do not exist. You may be the noblest character in London or you may be wanted by the police. I don't know. And I don't care. It doesn't matter to me. You mean nothing in my life. I don't know you."

"You must persevere," said Sam. "You must buckle to and get to know me. Don't give the thing up in this half-hearted way. Everything has to have a beginning. Stick to it, and in a week or two you will find yourself knowing me quite well."

"I don't want to know you!"

"You say that now, but wait!"

"And thank goodness I have not got to!" exploded Mr. Bennett, ceasing to be calm and reasonable with a suddenness which affected Sam much as though half a pound of gunpowder had been touched off under his chair. "For the little I have seen of you has been quite enough! Kindly understand that my daughter is engaged to be married to another man, and that I do not wish to see or hear anything of you again! I shall try to forget your very existence, and I shall see to it that Wilhelmina does the same! You're an impudent scoundrel, sir! An impudent scoundrel! I don't like you! I don't wish to see you again! If you were the last man in the world I wouldn't allow my daughter to marry you! If that is quite clear, I will wish you good morning!"

Mr. Bennett thundered out of the room, and Sam, temporarily stunned by the outburst, remained where he was, gaping. A few minutes later life began to return to his palsied limbs. It occurred to him that Mr. Bennett had forgotten to kiss him good-bye, and he went into the outer office to tell him so. But the outer office was empty. Sam stood for a moment in thought, then he returned to the inner office, and, picking up a time-table, began to look out trains to the village of Windlehurst in Hampshire, the nearest station to his aunt Adeline's charming old-world house, Windles.

CHAPTER XV

Drama at a Country House

As I read over the last few chapters of this narrative, I see that I have been giving the reader rather too jumpy a time. To almost a painful degree I have excited his pity and terror; and, though that is what Aristotle says one ought to do, I feel that a little respite would not be out of order. The reader can stand having his emotions tortured up to a certain point; after that he wants to take it easy for a bit. It is with pleasure, therefore, that I turn now to depict a quiet, peaceful scene in domestic life. It won't last long—three minutes, perhaps, by a good stop-watch—but that is not my fault. My task is to record facts as they happened.

The morning sunlight fell pleasantly on the garden of Windles, turning it into the green and amber Paradise which Nature had intended it to be. A number of the local birds sang melodiously in the undergrowth at the end of the lawn, while others, more energetic, hopped about the grass in quest of worms. Bees, mercifully ignorant that, after they had worked themselves to the bone gathering honey, the proceeds of their labour would be collared and consumed by idle humans, buzzed industriously to and fro and dived head foremost into flowers. Winged insects danced sarabands in the sunshine. In a deck-chair under the cedar-tree Billie Bennett, with a sketching-block on her knee, was engaged in drawing a picture of the ruined castle. Beside her, curled up in a ball, lay her Pekinese dog, Pinky-Boodles. Beside Pinky-Boodles slept Smith, the bulldog. In the distant stable-yard, unseen but audible, a boy in shirt-sleeves was washing the car and singing as much as a treacherous memory would permit of a popular sentimental ballad.

You may think that was all. You may suppose that nothing could be added to deepen the atmosphere of peace and content. Not so. At this moment, Mr. Bennett emerged from the French windows of the drawing-room, clad in white flannels and buckskin shoes, supplying just the finishing touch that was needed.

Mr. Bennett crossed the lawn, and sat down beside his daughter. Smith, the bulldog, raising a sleepy head, breathed heavily; but Mr. Bennett did not quail. Since their last unfortunate meeting, relations of distant, but solid, friendship had come to exist between pursuer and pursued. Sceptical at first, Mr. Bennett had at length allowed himself to be persuaded of the mildness of the animal's nature and the essential purity of his motives; and now it was only when they encountered each other unexpectedly round sharp corners that he ever betrayed the slightest alarm. So now, while Smith slept on the grass, Mr. Bennett reclined in the chair. It was the nearest thing modern civilisation has seen to the lion lying down with the lamb.

"Sketching?" said Mr. Bennett.

"Yes," said Billie, for there were no secrets between this girl and her father.

At least, not many. She occasionally omitted to tell him some such trifle as that she had met Samuel Marlowe on the previous morning in a leafy lane, and intended to meet him again this afternoon, but apart from that her mind was an open book.

"It's a great morning," said Mr. Bennett.

"So peaceful," said Billie.

"The eggs you get in the country in England," said Mr. Bennett, suddenly striking a lyrical note, "are extraordinary. I had three for breakfast this morning which defied competition, simply defied competition. They were large and brown, and as fresh as new-mown hay!"

He mused for a while in a sort of ecstasy.

"And the hams!" he went on. "The ham I had for breakfast was what I call ham! I don't know when I've had ham like that. I suppose it's something they feed the pigs on!" he concluded, in soft meditation. And he gave a little sigh. Life was very beautiful.

Silence fell, broken only by the snoring of Smith. Billie was thinking of Sam, and of what Sam had said to her in the lane yesterday; of his clean-cut face, and the look in his eyes—so vastly superior to any look that ever came into the eyes of Bream Mortimer. She was telling herself that her relations with Sam were an idyll; for, being young and romantic, she enjoyed this freshet of surreptitious meetings which had come to enliven the stream of her life. It was pleasant to go warily into deep lanes where forbidden love lurked. She cast a swift side-glance at her father—the unconscious ogre in her fairy-story. What would he say if he knew? But Mr. Bennett did not know, and consequently continued to meditate peacefully on ham.

They had sat like this for perhaps a minute—two happy mortals lulled by the gentle beauty of the day—when from the window of the drawing-room there stepped out a white-capped maid. And one may just as well say at once—and have done with it—that this is the point where the quiet, peaceful scene in domestic life terminates with a jerk, and pity and terror resume work at the old stand.

The maid—her name, not that it matters, was Susan, and she was engaged to be married, though the point is of no importance, to the second assistant at Green's Grocery Stores in Windlehurst—approached Mr. Bennett.

"Please, sir, a gentleman to see you."

"Eh?" said Mr. Bennett, torn from a dream of large pink slices edged with bread-crumbed fat.

"A gentleman to see you, sir. In the drawing-room. He says you are expecting him."

"Of course, yes. To be sure."

Mr. Bennett heaved himself out of the deck-chair. Beyond the French windows he could see an indistinct form in a grey suit, and remembered that this was the morning on which Sir Mallaby Marlowe's clerk—who was taking those Schultz and Bowen papers for him to America—had written that he would call. To-day was Friday; no doubt the man was sailing from Southampton to-morrow.

He crossed the lawn, entered the drawing-room, and found Mr. Jno. Peters with an expression on his ill-favoured face, which looked like one of consternation, of uneasiness, even of alarm.

"Morning, Mr. Peters," said Mr. Bennett. "Very good of you to run down. Take a seat, and I'll just go through the few notes I have made about the matter."

"Mr. Bennett," exclaimed Jno. Peters. "May—may I speak?"

"What do you mean? Eh? What? Something to say? What is it?"

Mr. Peters cleared his throat awkwardly. He was feeling embarrassed at the unpleasantness of the duty which he had to perform, but it was a duty, and he did not intend to shrink from performing it.

Ever since, gazing appreciatively through the drawing-room windows at the charming scene outside, he had caught sight of the unforgettable form of Billie, seated in her chair with the sketching-block on her knee, he had realised that he could not go away in silence, leaving Mr. Bennett ignorant of what he was up against.

One almost inclines to fancy that there must have been a curse of some kind on this house of Windles. Certainly everybody who entered it seemed to leave his peace of mind behind him. Jno. Peters had been feeling notably happy during his journey in the train from London, and the subsequent walk from the station. The splendour of the morning had soothed his nerves, and the faint wind that blew inshore from the sea spoke to him hearteningly of adventure and romance. There was a jar of pot-pourri on the drawing-room table, and he had derived considerable pleasure from sniffing at it. In short, Jno. Peters was in the pink, without a care in the world, until he had looked out of the window and seen Billie.

"Mr. Bennett," he said, "I don't want to do anybody any harm, and, if you know all about it, and she suits you, well and good; but I think it is my duty to inform you that your stenographer is not quite right in her head. I don't say she's dangerous, but she isn't compos. She decidedly is *not* compos, Mr. Bennett!"

Mr. Bennett stared at his well-wisher dumbly for a moment. The thought crossed his mind that, if ever there was a case of the pot calling the kettle black, this was it. His opinion of Jno. Peters' sanity went down to zero.

"What are you talking about? My stenographer? What stenographer?"

It occurred to Mr. Peters that a man of the other's wealth and business connections might well have a troupe of these useful females. He particularised.

"I mean the young lady out in the garden there, to whom you were dictating just now. The young lady with the writing-pad on her knee."

"What! What!" Mr. Bennett spluttered. "Do you know who that is?" he exclaimed.

"Oh, yes, indeed!" said Jno. Peters. "I have only met her once, when she came into our office to see Mr. Samuel, but her personality and appearance stamped themselves so forcibly on my mind, that I know I am not mistaken. I am sure it is my duty to tell you exactly what happened when I was left alone with her in the office. We had hardly exchanged a dozen words, Mr. Bennett, when—"—here Jno. Peters, modest to the core, turned vividly pink—"when she told me—she told me that I was the only man she loved!"

Mr. Bennett uttered a loud cry.

"Sweet spirits of nitre! What!"

"Those were her exact words."

"Five!" ejaculated Mr. Bennett, in a strangled voice. "By the great horn spoon, number five!"

337

Mr. Peters could make nothing of this exclamation, and he was deterred from seeking light by the sudden action of his host, who, bounding from his seat with a vivacity of which one would not have believed him capable, charged to the French window and emitted a bellow.

"Wilhelmina!"

Billie looked up from her sketching-block with a start. It seemed to her that there was a note of anguish, of panic, in that voice. What her father could have found in the drawing-room to be frightened at, she did not know; but she dropped her block and hurried to his assistance.

"What is it, father?"

Mr. Bennett had retired within the room when she arrived; and, going in after him, she perceived at once what had caused his alarm. There before her, looking more sinister than ever, stood the lunatic Peters; and there was an ominous bulge in his right coat-pocket which to her excited senses betrayed the presence of the revolver. What Jno. Peters was, as a matter of fact, carrying in his right coat-pocket was a bag of mixed chocolates which he had purchased in Windlehurst. But Billie's eyes, though bright, had no X-ray quality. Her simple creed was that, if Jno. Peters bulged at any point, that bulge must be caused by a pistol. She screamed, and backed against the wall. Her whole acquaintance with Jno Peters had been one constant backing against walls.

"Don't shoot!" she cried, as Mr. Peters absent-mindedly dipped his hand into the pocket of his coat. "Oh, please don't shoot!"

"What the deuce do you mean?" said Mr. Bennett irritably. "Wilhelmina, this man says that you told him you loved him."

"Yes, I did, and I do. Really, really, Mr. Peters, I do!"

"Suffering cats!"

Mr. Bennett clutched at the back of his chair.

"But you've only met him once," he added almost pleadingly.

"You don't understand, father dear," said Billie desperately. "I'll explain the whole thing later, when...."

"Father!" ejaculated Jno. Peters feebly. "Did you say 'father?'"

"Of course I said 'father!'"

"This is my daughter, Mr. Peters."

"My daughter! I mean, your daughter! Are—are you sure?"

"Of course I'm sure. Do you think I don't know my own daughter?"

"But she called me Mr. Peters!"

"Well, it's your name, isn't it?"

"But, if she—if this young lady is your daughter, how did she know my name?"

The point seemed to strike Mr. Bennett. He turned to Billie.

"That's true. Tell me, Wilhelmina, when did you and Mr. Peters meet?"

"Why, in—in Sir Mallaby Marlowe's office, the morning you came there and found me when I was talking to Sam."

Mr. Peters uttered a subdued gargling sound. He was finding this scene oppressive to a not very robust intellect.

"He—Mr. Samuel—told me your name was Miss Milliken," he said dully.

Billie stared at him.

"Mr. Marlowe told you my name was Miss Milliken!" she repeated.

"He told me that you were the sister of the Miss Milliken who acts as stenographer for the guv'—for Sir Mallaby, and sent me in to show you my revolver, because he said you were interested and wanted to see it."

Billie uttered an exclamation. So did Mr. Bennett, who hated mysteries.

"What revolver? Which revolver? What's all this about a revolver? Have you a revolver?"

"Why, yes, Mr. Bennett. It is packed now in my trunk, but usually I carry it about with me everywhere in order to take a little practice at the Rupert Street range. I bought it when Sir Mallaby told me he was sending me to America, because I thought I ought to be prepared—because of the Underworld, you know."

A cold gleam had come into Billie's eyes. Her face was pale and hard. If Sam Marlowe—at that moment carolling blithely in his bedroom at the Blue Boar in Windlehurst, washing his hands preparatory to descending to the coffee-room for a bit of cold lunch—could have seen her, the song would have frozen on his lips. Which, one might mention, as showing that there is always a bright side, would have been much appreciated by the travelling gentleman in the adjoining room, who had had a wild night with some other travelling gentlemen, and was then nursing a rather severe headache, separated from

Sam's penetrating baritone only by the thickness of a wooden wall.

Billie knew all. And, terrible though the fact is as an indictment of the male sex, when a woman knows all, there is invariably trouble ahead for some man. There was trouble ahead for Samuel Marlowe. Billie, now in possession of the facts, had examined them and come to the conclusion that Sam had played a practical joke on her, and she was a girl who strongly disapproved of practical humour at her expense.

"That morning I met you at Sir Mallaby's office, Mr. Peters," she said in a frosty voice, "Mr. Marlowe had just finished telling me a long and convincing story to the effect that you were madly in love with a Miss Milliken, who had jilted you, and that this had driven you off your head, and that you spent your time going about with a pistol, trying to shoot every red-haired woman you saw, because you thought they were Miss Milliken. Naturally, when you came in and called me Miss Milliken, and brandished a revolver, I was very frightened. I thought it would be useless to tell you that I wasn't Miss Milliken, so I tried to persuade you that I was and hadn't jilted you after all."

"Good gracious!" said Mr. Peters, vastly relieved; and yet—for always there is bitter mixed with the sweet—a shade disappointed. "Then—er—you don't love me after all?"

"No!" said Billie. "I am engaged to Bream Mortimer, and I love him and nobody else in the world!"

The last portion of her observation was intended for the consumption of Mr. Bennett, rather than that of Mr. Peters, and he consumed it joyfully. He folded Billie in his ample embrace.

"I always thought you had a grain of sense hidden away somewhere," he said, paying her a striking tribute. "I hope now that we've heard the last of all this foolishness about that young hound Marlowe."

"You certainly have! I don't want ever to see him again! I hate him!"

"You couldn't do better, my dear," said Mr. Bennett, approvingly. "And now run away. Mr. Peters and I have some business to discuss."

A quarter of an hour later, Webster, the valet, sunning himself in the stable-yard, was aware of the daughter of his employer approaching him.

"Webster," said Billie. She was still pale. Her face was still hard, and her eyes still gleamed coldly.

"Miss?" said Webster politely, throwing away the cigarette with which he had been refreshing himself.

"Will you do something for me?"

"I should be more than delighted, miss."

Billie whisked into view an envelope which had been concealed in the recesses of her dress.

"Do you know the country about here well, Webster?"

"Within a certain radius, not unintimately, miss. I have been for several enjoyable rambles since the fine weather set in."

"Do you know the place where there is a road leading to Havant, and another to Cosham? It's about a mile down...."

"I know the spot well, miss."

"Well, straight in front of you when you get to the sign-post there is a little lane...."

"I know it, miss," said Webster, with a faint smile. Twice had he escorted Miss Trimblett, Billie's maid, thither. "A delightfully romantic spot. What with the overhanging trees, the wealth of blackberry bushes, the varied wild-flowers...."

"Yes, never mind about the wild-flowers now. I want you after lunch, to take this note to a gentleman you will find sitting on the gate at the bottom of the lane...."

"Sitting on the gate, miss. Yes, miss."

"Or leaning against it. You can't mistake him. He is rather tall and ... oh, well, there isn't likely to be anybody else there, so you can't make a mistake. Give him this, will you?"

"Certainly, miss. Er—any message?"

"Any what?"

"Any verbal message, miss?"

"No, certainly not! You won't forget, will you, Webster?"

"On no account whatever, miss. Shall I wait for an answer?"

"There won't be any answer," said Billie, setting her teeth for an instant. "Oh, Webster!"

"Miss?"

"I can rely on you to say nothing to anybody?"

"Most undoubtedly, miss. Most undoubtedly."

"Does anybody know anything about a feller named S. Marlowe?" inquired Webster, entering the kitchen. "Don't all speak at once! S. Marlowe. Ever heard of him?"

He paused for a reply, but nobody had any information to impart.

"Because there's something jolly well up! Our Miss B. is sending me with notes for him to the bottom of lanes."

"And her engaged to young Mr. Mortimer!" said the scullery-maid, shocked. "The way they go on. Chronic!" said the scullery-maid.

"Don't you go getting alarmed! And don't you," added Webster, "go shoving your oar in when your social superiors are talking! I've had to speak to you about that before. My remarks were addressed to Mrs. Withers here."

He indicated the cook with a respectful gesture.

"Yes, here's the note, Mrs. Withers. Of course, if you had a steamy kettle handy, in about half a moment we could ... but no, perhaps it's wiser not to risk it. And, come to that, I don't need to unstick the envelope to know what's inside here. It's the raspberry, ma'am, or I've lost all my power to read the human female countenance. Very cold and proud-looking she was! I don't know who this S. Marlowe is, but I do know one thing; in this hand I hold the instrument that's going to give it him in the neck, proper! Right in the neck, or my name isn't Montagu Webster!"

"Well!" said Mrs. Withers, comfortably, pausing for a moment from her labours. "Think of that!"

"The way I look at it," said Webster, "is that there's been some sort of understanding between our Miss B. and this S. Marlowe, and she's thought better of it and decided to stick to the man of her parent's choice. She's chosen wealth and made up her mind to hand the humble suitor the mitten. There was a rather similar situation in 'Cupid or Mammon,' that Nosegay Novelette I was reading in the train coming down here, only that ended different. For my part I'd be better pleased if our Miss B. would let the cash go, and obey the dictates of her own heart; but these modern girls are all alike! All out for the stuff, they are! Oh, well, it's none of my affair," said Webster, stifling a not unmanly sigh. For beneath that immaculate shirt-front there beat a warm heart. Montagu Webster was a sentimentalist.

CHAPTER XVI

Webster, Friend in Need

At half-past two that afternoon, full of optimism and cold beef, gaily unconscious that Webster with measured strides was approaching ever nearer with the note that was to give it him in the neck, proper, Samuel Marlowe dangled his feet from the top bar of the gate at the end of the lane, and smoked contentedly as he waited for Billie to make her appearance. He had had an excellent lunch; his pipe was drawing well, and all Nature smiled. The breeze from the sea across the meadows tickled pleasantly the back of his head, and sang a soothing song in the long grass and ragged-robins at his feet. He was looking forward with a roseate glow of anticipation to the moment when the white flutter of Billie's dress would break the green of the foreground. How eagerly he would jump from the gate! How lovingly he would....

The elegant figure of Webster interrupted his reverie. Sam had never seen Webster before, and it was with no pleasure that he saw him now. He had come to regard this lane as his own private property, and he resented trespassers. He tucked his legs under him, and scowled at Webster under the brim of his hat.

The valet advanced towards him with the air of an affable executioner stepping daintily to the block.

"Mr. Marlowe, sir?" he inquired politely.

Sam was startled. He could making nothing of this.

"Eh? What?"

"Have I the pleasure of addressing Mr. S. Marlowe?"

"Yes, that's my name."

"Mine is Webster, sir. I am Mr. Bennett's personal gentleman's gentleman. Miss Bennett entrusted me with this note to deliver to you, sir."

Sam began to grasp the position. For some reason or other, the dear girl had been prevented from coming this afternoon, and she had written to explain and relieve his anxiety. It was like her. It was just the sweet, thoughtful thing he would have expected her to do. His contentment with the existing scheme of things returned. The sun shone out again, and he found himself amiably disposed towards the messenger.

"Fine day," he said, as he took the note.

"Extremely, sir," said Webster, outwardly unemotional, inwardly full of a grave pity.

It was plain to him that there had been no previous little rift to prepare the young man for the cervical operation which awaited him, and he edged a little nearer, in order to be handy to catch Sam if the shock knocked him off the gate.

As it happened, it did not. Having read the opening words of the note, Sam rocked violently; but his feet were twined about the lower bars and this saved him from overbalancing. Webster stepped back, relieved.

The note fluttered to the ground. Webster, picking it up and handing it back, was enabled to get a glimpse of the first two sentences. They confirmed his suspicions. The note was hot stuff. Assuming that it continued as it began, it was about the warmest thing of its kind that pen had ever written. Webster had received one or two heated epistles from the sex in his time—your man of gallantry can hardly hope to escape these unpleasantnesses—but none had got off the mark quite so swiftly, and with quite so much frigid violence as this.

"Thanks," said Sam mechanically.

"Not at all, sir. You are very welcome."

Sam resumed his reading. A cold perspiration broke out on his forehead. His toes curled, and something seemed to be crawling down the small of his back. His heart had moved from its proper place and was now beating in his throat. He swallowed once or twice to remove the obstruction, but without success. A kind of pall had descended on the landscape, blotting out the sun.

Of all the rotten sensations in this world, the worst is the realisation that a thousand-to-one chance has come off, and caused our wrong-doing to be detected. There had seemed no possibility of that little ruse of his being discovered, and yet here was Billie in full possession of the facts. It almost made the thing worse that she did not say how she had come into possession of them. This gave Sam that feeling of self-pity, that sense of having been ill-used by Fate, which makes the bringing home of crime so particularly poignant.

"Fine day!" he muttered. He had a sort of subconscious feeling that it was imperative to keep engaging Webster in light conversation.

"Yes, sir. Weather still keeps up," agreed the valet suavely.

Sam frowned over the note. He felt injured. Sending a fellow notes didn't give him a chance. If she had come in person and denounced him it would not have been an agreeable experience, but at least it would have been possible then to have pleaded and cajoled and—and all that sort of thing. But what could he do now? It seemed to him that his only possible course was to write a note in reply, begging her to see him. He explored his pockets and found a pencil and a scrap of paper. For some moments he scribbled desperately. Then he folded the note.

"Will you take this to Miss Bennett?" he said, holding it out.

Webster took the missive, because he wanted to read it later at his leisure; but he shook his head.

"Useless, I fear, sir," he said gravely.

"What do you mean?"

"I am afraid it would effect little or nothing, sir, sending our Miss B. notes.

She is not in the proper frame of mind to appreciate them. I saw her face when she handed me the letter you have just read, and I assure you, sir, she is not in a malleable mood."

"You seem to know a lot about it!"

"I have studied the sex, sir," said Webster modestly.

"I mean, about my business, confound it! You seem to know all about it!"

"Why, yes, sir, I think I may say that I have grasped the position of affairs. And, if you will permit me to say so, sir, you have my respectful sympathy."

Dignity is a sensitive plant which nourishes only under the fairest conditions. Sam's had perished in the bleak east wind of Billie's note. In other circumstances he might have resented this intrusion of a stranger into his most intimate concerns. His only emotion now, was one of dull but distinct gratitude. The four winds of Heaven blew chilly upon his raw and unprotected soul, and he wanted to wrap it up in a mantle of sympathy, careless of the source from which he borrowed that mantle. If Webster felt disposed, as he seemed to indicate, to comfort him, let the thing go on. At that moment Sam would have accepted condolences from a coal-heaver.

"I was reading a story—one of the Nosegay Novelettes; I do not know if you are familiar with the series, sir?—in which much the same situation occurred. It was entitled 'Cupid or Mammon.' The heroine, Lady Blanche Trefusis, forced by her parents to wed a wealthy suitor, despatches a note to her humble lover, informing him it cannot be. I believe it often happens like that, sir."

"You're all wrong," said Sam. "It's not that at all."

"Indeed, sir? I supposed it was."

"Nothing like it! I—I——."

Sam's dignity, on its death-bed, made a last effort to assert itself.

"I don't know what it's got to do with you!"

"Precisely, sir!" said Webster, with dignity. "Just as you say! Good afternoon, sir!"

He swayed gracefully, conveying a suggestion of departure without moving his feet. The action was enough for Sam. Dignity gave an expiring gurgle, and passed away, regretted by all.

"Don't go!" he cried.

The idea of being left alone in this infernal lane, without human support, overpowered him. Moreover, Webster had personality. He exuded it. Already Sam had begun to cling to him in spirit, and rely on his support.

"Don't go!"

"Certainly not, if you do not wish it, sir."

Webster coughed gently, to show his appreciation of the delicate nature of the conversation. He was consumed with curiosity, and his threatened departure had been but a pretence. A team of horses could not have moved Webster at that moment.

"Might I ask, then, what...?"

"There's been a misunderstanding," said Sam. "At least, there was, but now there isn't, if you see what I mean."

"I fear I have not quite grasped your meaning, sir."

"Well, I—I—played a sort of—you might almost call it a sort of trick on Miss Bennett. With the best motives, of course!"

"Of course, sir!"

"And she's found out! I don't know how she's found out, but she has! So there you are!"

"Of what nature would the trick be, sir? A species of ruse, sir,—some kind of innocent deception?"

"Well, it was like this."

It was a complicated story to tell, and Sam, a prey to conflicting emotions, told it badly; but such was the almost superhuman intelligence of Webster, that he succeeded in grasping the salient points. Indeed, he said that it reminded him of something of much the same kind in the Nosegay Novelette, "All for Her," where the hero, anxious to win the esteem of the lady of his heart, had bribed a tramp to simulate an attack upon her in a lonely road.

"The principle's the same," said Webster.

"Well, what did he do when she found out?"

"She did not find out, sir. All ended happily, and never had the wedding-bells in the old village church rung out a blither peal than they did at the subsequent union."

Sam was thoughtful.

"Bribed a tramp to attack her, did he?"

"Yes, sir. She had never thought much of him till that moment, sir. Very cold and haughty she had been, his social status being considerably inferior to her own. But, when she cried for help, and he dashed out from behind a hedge, well, it made all the difference."

"I wonder where I could get a good tramp," said Sam, meditatively.

Webster shook his head.

"I really would hardly recommend such a procedure, sir."

"No, it would be difficult to make a tramp understand what you wanted."

Sam brightened.

"I've got it! *You* pretend to attack her, and I'll...."

"I couldn't, sir! I couldn't, really! I should jeopardise my situation."

"Oh, come. Be a man!"

"No, sir, I fear not. There's a difference between handing in your resignation—I was compelled to do that only recently, owing to a few words I had with the guv'nor, though subsequently prevailed upon to withdraw it—I say there's a difference between handing in your resignation and being given the sack, and that's what would happen—without a character, what's more, and lucky if it didn't mean a prison cell! No, sir, I could not contemplate such a thing."

"Then I don't see that there's anything to be done," said Sam, morosely.

"Oh, I shouldn't say that, sir," said Webster encouragingly. "It's simply a matter of finding the way. The problem confronting us—you, I should say...."

"Us," said Sam. "Most decidedly us."

"Thank you very much, sir. I would not have presumed, but if you say so.... The problem confronting us, as I envisage it, resolves itself into this. You have offended our Miss B. and she has expressed a disinclination ever to see you again. How, then, is it possible, in spite of her attitude, to recapture her esteem?"

"Exactly," said Sam.

"There are several methods which occur to one...."

"They don't occur to *me*!"

"Well, for example, you might rescue her from a burning building, as in 'True As Steel'...."

"Set fire to the house, eh?" said Sam reflectively. "Yes, there might be something in that."

"I would hardly advise such a thing," said Webster, a little hastily—flattered at the readiness with which his disciple was taking his advice, yet acutely alive to the fact that he slept at the top of the house himself. "A little drastic, if I may say so. It might be better to save her from drowning, as in 'The Earl's Secret.'"

"Ah, but where could she drown?"

"Well, there is a lake in the grounds...."

"Excellent!" said Sam. "Terrific! I knew I could rely on you. Say no more! The whole thing's settled. You take her out rowing on the lake, and upset the boat. I plunge in.... I suppose you can swim?"

"No, sir."

"Oh? Well, never mind. You'll manage somehow, I expect. Cling to the upturned boat or something, I shouldn't wonder. There's always a way. Yes, that's the plan. When is the earliest you could arrange this?"

"I fear such a course must be considered out of the question, sir. It really wouldn't do."

"I can't see a flaw in it."

"Well, in the first place, it would certainly jeopardise my situation...."

"Oh, hang your situation! You talk as if you were Prime Minister or something. You can easily get another situation.

A valuable man like you," said Sam ingratiatingly.

"No, sir," said Webster firmly. "From boyhood up I've always had a regular horror of the water. I can't so much as go paddling without an uneasy feeling."

The image of Webster paddling was arresting enough to occupy Sam's thoughts for a moment. It was an inspiring picture, and for an instant uplifted his spirits. Then they fell again.

"Well, I don't see what there *is* to be done," he said, gloomily. "It's no good my making suggestions, if you have some frivolous objection to all of them."

"My idea," said Webster, "would be something which did not involve my own personal and active co-operation, sir. If it is all the same to you, I should prefer to limit my assistance to advice and sympathy. I am anxious to help, but I am a man of regular habits, which I do not wish to disturb. Did you ever read 'Footpaths of Fate,' in the Nosegay series, sir? I've only just remembered it, and it contains the most helpful suggestion of the lot. There had been a misunderstanding between the heroine and the hero—their names have slipped my mind, though I fancy his was Cyril—and she had told him to hop it...."

"To what?"

"To leave her for ever, sir. And what do you think he did?"

"How the deuce do I know?"

"He kidnapped her little brother, sir, to whom she was devoted, kept him hidden for a bit, and then returned him, and in her gratitude all was forgotten and forgiven, and never...."

"I know. Never had the bells of the old village church...."

"Rung out a blither peal. Exactly, sir. Well, there, if you will allow me to say so, you are, sir! You need seek no further for a plan of action."

"Miss Bennett hasn't got a little brother."

"No, sir. But she has a dog, and is greatly attached to it."

Sam stared. From the expression on his face it was evident that Webster imagined himself to have made a suggestion of exceptional intelligence. It struck Sam as the silliest he had ever heard.

"You mean I ought to steal her dog?"

"Precisely, sir."

"But, good heavens! Have you seen that dog?"

"The one to which I allude is a small brown animal with a fluffy tail."

"Yes, and a bark like a steam-siren, and, in addition to that, about eighty-five teeth, all sharper than razors. I couldn't get within ten feet of that dog without its lifting the roof off, and, if I did, it would chew me into small pieces."

"I had anticipated that difficulty, sir. In 'Footpaths of Fate' there was a nurse who assisted the hero by drugging the child."

"By Jove!" said Sam, impressed.

"He rewarded her," said Webster, allowing his gaze to stray nonchalantly over the countryside, "liberally, very liberally."

"If you mean that you expect me to reward you if you drug the dog," said Sam, "don't worry. Let me bring this thing off, and you can have all I've got, and my cuff-links as well. Come now, this is really beginning to look like something. Speak to me more of this matter. Where do we go from here?"

"I beg your pardon, sir?"

"I mean, what's the next step in the scheme? Oh, Lord!" Sam's face fell. The light of hope died out of his eyes. "It's all off! It can't be done! How could I possibly get into the house? I take it that the little brute sleeps in the house?"

"That need constitute no obstacle, sir, no obstacle at all. The animal sleeps in a basket in the hall.... Perhaps you are familiar with the interior of the house, sir?"

"I haven't been inside it since I was at school. I'm Mr. Hignett's cousin, you know."

"Indeed, sir? I wasn't aware. Mr. Hignett has the mumps, poor gentleman."

"Has he?" said Sam, not particularly interested. "I used to stay with him," he went on, "during the holidays sometimes, but I've practically forgotten what the place is like inside. I remember the hall vaguely. Fireplace at one side, one or two suits of armour standing about, a sort of window-ledge near the front door...."

"Precisely, sir. It is close beside that window-ledge that the animal's basket is situated. If I administer a slight soporific...."

"Yes, but you haven't explained yet how I am to get into the house in the first place."

"Quite easily, sir. I can admit you through the drawing-room windows while dinner is in progress."

"Fine!"

"You can then secrete yourself in the cupboard in the drawing-room. Perhaps you recollect the cupboard to which I refer, sir?"

"No, I don't remember any cupboard. As a matter of fact, when I used to stay at the house the drawing-room was barred. Mrs. Hignett wouldn't let us inside it for fear we should smash her china. Is there a cupboard?"

"Immediately behind the piano, sir. A nice, roomy cupboard. I was glancing into it myself in a spirit of idle curiosity only the other day. It contains nothing except a few knick-knacks on an upper shelf. You could lock yourself in from the interior, and be quite comfortably seated on the floor till the household retired to bed."

"When would that be?"

"They retire quite early, sir, as a rule. By half-past ten the coast is generally clear. At that time I would suggest that I came down and knocked on the cupboard door to notify you that all was well."

Sam was glowing with frank approval.

"You know, you're a master-mind!" he said, enthusiastically.

"You're very kind, sir!"

"One of the lads, by Jove!" said Sam. "And not the worst of them! I don't want to flatter you, but there's a future for you in crime, if you cared to go in for it."

"I am glad that you appreciate my poor efforts, sir. Then we will regard the scheme as passed and approved?"

"I should say we would! It's a bird!"

"Very good, sir."

"I'll be round at about a quarter to eight. Will that be right?"

"Admirable, sir."

"And, I say, about that soporific.... Don't overdo it. Don't go killing the little beast."

"Oh, no, sir."

"Well," said Sam, "you can't say it's not a temptation. And you know what you Napoleons of the Underworld are!"

CHAPTER XVII

A Crowded Night

§ 1

If there is one thing more than another which weighs upon the mind of a story-teller as he chronicles the events which he has set out to describe, it is the thought that the reader may be growing impatient with him for straying from the main channel of his tale and devoting himself to what are, after all, minor developments. This story, for instance, opened with Mrs. Horace Hignett, the world-famous writer on Theosophy, going over to America to begin a lecturing-tour; and no one realises more keenly than I do that I have left Mrs. Hignett flat. I have thrust that great thinker into the background and concentrated my attention on the affairs of one who is both her mental and her moral inferior, Samuel Marlowe. I seem at this point to see the reader—a great brute of a fellow with beetling eyebrows and a jaw like the ram of a battleship, the sort of fellow who is full of determination and will stand no nonsense—rising to remark that he doesn't care what happened to Samuel Marlowe and that what he wants to know is, how Mrs. Hignett made out on her lecturing-tour. Did she go big in Buffalo? Did she have 'em tearing up the seats in Schenectady? Was she a riot in Chicago and a cyclone in St. Louis? Those are the points on which he desires information, or give him his money back.

I cannot supply the information. And, before you condemn me, let me hastily add that the fault is not mine but that of Mrs. Hignett herself. The fact is, she never went to Buffalo. Schenectady saw nothing of her. She did not get within a thousand miles of Chicago, nor did she penetrate to St. Louis. For the very morning after her son Eustace sailed for England in the liner "Atlantic," she happened to read in the paper one of those abridged passenger-lists which the journals of New York are in the habit of printing, and got a nasty shock when she saw that, among those whose society Eustace would enjoy during the voyage, was "Miss Wilhelmina Bennett, daughter of J. Rufus Bennett of Bennett, Mandelbaum and Co.". And within five minutes of digesting this information, she was at her desk writing out telegrams cancelling all her engagements. Iron-souled as this woman was, her fingers trembled as she wrote. She had a vision of Eustace and the daughter of J. Rufus Bennett strolling together on moonlit decks, leaning over rails damp with sea-spray and, in short, generally starting the whole trouble all over again.

In the height of the tourist season it is not always possible for one who wishes to leave America to spring on to the next boat. A long morning's telephoning to the offices of the Cunard and the White Star brought Mrs. Hignett the depressing information that it would be a full week before she could sail for England. That meant that the inflammable Eustace would have over two weeks to conduct an uninterrupted wooing, and Mrs. Hignett's heart sank, till suddenly she remembered that so poor a sailor as her son was not likely to have had leisure for any strolling on the deck during the voyage on the "Atlantic."

Having realised this, she became calmer and went about her preparations for departure with an easier mind. The danger was still great, but there was a good chance that she might be in time to intervene. She wound up her affairs in New York, and on the following Wednesday, boarded the "Nuronia" bound for Southampton.

The "Nuronia" is one of the slowest of the Cunard boats. It was built at a time when delirious crowds used to swoon on the dock if an ocean liner broke the record by getting across in nine days. It rolled over to Cherbourg, dallied at that picturesque port for some hours, then sauntered across the Channel and strolled into Southampton Water in the evening of the day on which Samuel Marlowe had sat in the lane plotting with Webster, the valet. At almost the exact moment when Sam, sidling through the windows of the drawing-room, slid into the cupboard behind the piano, Mrs. Hignett was standing at the Customs barrier telling the officials that she had nothing to declare.

Mrs. Hignett was a general who believed in forced marches. A lesser woman might have taken the boat-train to London and proceeded to Windles at her ease on the following afternoon. Mrs. Hignett was made of sterner stuff. Having fortified herself with a late dinner, she hired a car and set out on the cross-country journey. It was only when the car, a genuine antique, had broken down three times in the first ten miles, that she directed the driver to take her instead to the "Blue Boar" in Windlehurst, where she arrived, tired but thankful to have reached it at all, at about eleven o'clock.

At this point many, indeed most, women would have gone to bed; but the familiar Hampshire air and the knowledge that half an hour's walking would take her to her beloved home acted on Mrs. Hignett like a restorative. One glimpse of Windles she felt that she must have before she retired for the night, if only to assure herself that it was still there. She had a cup of coffee and a sandwich brought to her by the night-porter whom she had roused from sleep, for bedtime is early in Windlehurst, and then informed him that she was going for a short walk and would ring when she returned.

Her heart leaped joyfully as she turned in at the drive gates of her home and felt the well-remembered gravel crunching under her feet. The silhouette of the ruined castle against the summer sky gave her the feeling which all returning wanderers know. And, when she stepped on to the lawn and looked at the black bulk of the house, indistinct and shadowy with its backing of trees, tears came into her eyes. She experienced a rush of emotion which made her feel quite faint, and which lasted until, on tiptoeing nearer to the house in order to gloat more adequately upon it, she perceived that the French windows of the drawing-room were standing ajar. Sam had left them like this in order to facilitate departure, if a hurried departure should by any mischance be rendered necessary, and drawn curtains had kept the household from noticing the fact.

All the proprietor in Mrs. Hignett was roused. This, she felt indignantly, was the sort of thing she had been afraid would happen the moment her back was turned. Evidently laxity—one might almost say anarchy—had set in directly she had removed the eye of authority. She marched to the window and pushed it open. She had now completely abandoned her kindly scheme of refraining from rousing the sleeping house and spending the night at the inn. She stepped into the drawing-room with the single-minded purpose of routing Eustace out of his sleep and giving him a good talking-to for having failed to maintain her own standard of efficiency among the domestic staff. If there was one thing on which Mrs. Horace Hignett had always insisted it was that every window in the house must be closed at lights-out.

She pushed the curtains apart with a rattle and, at the same moment, from the direction of the door there came a low but distinct gasp which made her resolute heart jump and flutter. It was too dark to see anything distinctly, but, in the instant before it turned and fled, she caught sight of a shadowy male figure, and knew that her worst fears had been realised. The figure was too tall to be Eustace, and Eustace, she knew, was the only man in the house. Male figures, therefore, that went flitting about Windles, must be the figures of burglars.

Mrs. Hignett, bold woman though she was, stood for an instant spell-bound, and for one moment of not unpardonable panic tried to tell herself that she had been mistaken. Almost immediately, however, there came from the direction of the hall a dull chunky sound as though something soft had been kicked, followed by a low gurgle and the noise of staggering feet. Unless he were dancing a *pas seul* out of sheer lightness of heart, the nocturnal visitor must have tripped over something.

The latter theory was the correct one. Montagu Webster was a man who, at many a subscription ball, had shaken a gifted dancing-pump, and nothing in the proper circumstances pleased him better than to exercise the skill which had become his as the result of twelve private lessons at half-a-crown a visit; but he recognised the truth of the scriptural adage that there is a time for dancing, and that this was not it. His only desire when, stealing into the drawing-room he had been confronted through the curtains by a female figure, was to get back to his bedroom undetected. He supposed that one of the feminine members of the house-party must have been taking a stroll in the grounds, and he did not wish to stay and be compelled to make laborious explanations of his presence there in the dark. He decided to postpone the knocking on the cupboard door, which had been the signal arranged between himself and Sam, until a more suitable occasion. In the meantime he bounded silently out into the hall, and instantaneously tripped over the portly form of Smith, the bulldog, who, roused from a light sleep to the knowledge that something was going on, and being a dog who always liked to be in the centre of the maelstrom of events, had waddled out to investigate.

By the time Mrs. Hignett had pulled herself together sufficiently to feel brave enough to venture into the hall, Webster's presence of mind and Smith's gregariousness had combined to restore that part of the house to its normal nocturnal condition of emptiness. Webster's stagger had carried him almost up to the green baize door leading to the servants' staircase, and he proceeded to pass through it without checking his momentum, closely followed by Smith who, now convinced that interesting events were in progress which might possibly culminate in cake, had abandoned the idea of sleep, and meant to see the thing through. He gambolled in Webster's wake up the stairs and along the passage leading to the latter's room, and only paused when the door was brusquely shut in his face. Upon which he sat down to think the thing over. He was in no hurry. The night was before him, promising, as far as he could judge from the way it had opened, excellent entertainment.

Mrs. Hignett had listened fearfully to the uncouth noises from the hall. The burglars—she had now discovered that there were at least two of them—appeared to be actually romping. The situation had grown beyond her handling. If this troupe of terpsichorean marauders was to be dislodged she must have assistance. It was man's work. She made a brave dash through the hall mercifully unmolested; found the stairs; raced up them; and fell through the doorway of her son Eustace's bedroom like a spent Marathon runner staggering past the winning-post.

§ 2

At about the moment when Mrs. Hignett was crunching the gravel of the drive, Eustace was lying in bed, listening to Jane Hubbard as she told the story of how an alligator had once got into her tent while she was camping on the banks of the Issawassi River in Central Africa. Ever since he had become ill, it had been the large-hearted girl's kindly practice to soothe him to rest with some such narrative from her energetic past.

"And what happened then?" asked Eustace, breathlessly.

He had raised himself on one elbow in his bed. His eyes shone excitedly from a face which was almost the exact shape of an Association football; for he had reached the stage of mumps when the patient begins to swell as though somebody were inflating him with a bicycle-pump.

"Oh, I jabbed him in the eye with a pair of nail-scissors, and he went away!" said Jane Hubbard.

"You know, you're wonderful!" cried Eustace. "Simply wonderful!"

Jane Hubbard flushed a little beneath her tan. She loved his pretty enthusiasm. He was so genuinely stirred by what were to her the merest commonplaces of life.

"Why, if an alligator got into *my* tent," said Eustace, "I simply wouldn't know what to do! I should be nonplussed."

"Oh, it's just a knack," said Jane, carelessly. "You soon pick it up."

"Nail-scissors!"

"It ruined them, unfortunately. They were never any use again. For the rest of the trip I had to manicure myself with a hunting-spear."

"You're a marvel!"

Eustace lay back in bed and gave himself up to meditation. He had admired Jane Hubbard before, but the intimacy of the sick-room and the stories which she had told him to relieve the tedium of his invalid state had set the seal on his devotion. It has always been like this since Othello wooed Desdemona. For three days Jane Hubbard had been weaving her spell about Eustace Hignett, and now she monopolised his entire horizon. She had spoken, like Othello, of antres vast and deserts idle, rough quarries, rocks and hills whose heads touched heaven, and of the cannibals that each other eat, the Anthropophagi, and men whose heads do grow beneath their shoulders. This to hear would Eustace Hignett seriously incline, and swore, in faith, 'twas strange, 'twas passing strange, 'twas pitiful, 'twas wondrous pitiful. He loved her for the dangers she had passed, and she loved him that he did pity them. In fact, one would have said that it was all over except buying the licence, had it not been for the fact that his very admiration served to keep Eustace from pouring out his heart. It seemed incredible to him that the queen of her sex, a girl who had chatted in terms of equality with African head-hunters and who swatted alligators as though they were flies, could ever lower herself to care for a man who looked like the "after-taking" advertisement of a patent food.

But even those whom Nature has destined to be mates may misunderstand each other, and Jane, who was as modest as she was brave, had come recently to place a different interpretation on his silence. In the last few days of the voyage she had quite made up her mind that Eustace Hignett loved her and would shortly intimate as much in the usual manner; but, since coming to Windles, she had begun to have doubts. She was not blind to the fact that Billie Bennett was distinctly prettier than herself and far more the type to which the ordinary man is attracted. And, much as she loathed the weakness and despised herself for yielding to it, she had become distinctly jealous of her. True, Billie was officially engaged to Bream Mortimer, but she had had experience of the brittleness of Miss Bennett's engagements, and she could by no means regard Eustace as immune.

"Do you suppose they will be happy?" she asked.

"Eh? Who?" said Eustace, excusably puzzled, for they had only just finished talking about alligators. But there had been a pause since his last remark, and Jane's thoughts had flitted back to the subject that usually occupied them.

"Billie and Bream Mortimer."

"Oh!" said Eustace. "Yes, I suppose so."

"She's a delightful girl."

"Yes," said Eustace without much animation.

"And, of course, it's nice their fathers being so keen on the match. It doesn't often happen that way."

"No. People's people generally want people to marry people people don't want to marry," said Eustace, clothing in words a profound truth which from the earliest days of civilisation has deeply affected the youth of every country.

"I suppose your mother has got somebody picked out for you to marry?" said Jane casually.

"Mother doesn't want me to marry anybody," said Eustace with gloom. It was another obstacle to his romance.

"What, never?"

"No."

"Why ever not?"

"As far as I can make out, if I marry, I get this house and mother has to clear out. Silly business!"

"Well, you wouldn't let your mother stand in the way if you ever really fell in love?" said Jane.

"It isn't so much a question of *letting* her stand in the way. The tough job would be preventing her. You've never met my mother!"

"No, I'm looking forward to it!"

"You're looking forward...!" Eustace eyed her with honest amazement.

"But what could your mother do? I mean, supposing you had made up your mind to marry somebody."

"What could she do? Why, there isn't anything she wouldn't do. Why, once...." Eustace broke off. The anecdote which he had been about to tell contained information which, on reflection, he did not wish to reveal.

"Once—...?" said Jane.

"Oh, well, I was just going to show you what mother is like. I—I was going out to lunch with a man, and—and—" Eustace was not a ready improvisator—"and she didn't want me to go, so she stole all my trousers!"

Jane Hubbard started, as if, wandering through one of her favourite jungles, she had perceived a snake in her path. She was thinking hard. That story which Billie had told her on the boat about the man to whom she had been engaged, whose mother had stolen his trousers on the wedding morning ... it all came back to her with a topical significance which it had never had before. It had lingered in her memory, as stories will, but it had been a detached episode, having no personal meaning for her. But now.... "She did that just to stop you going out to lunch with a man?" she said slowly.

"Yes, rotten thing to do, wasn't it?"

Jane Hubbard moved to the foot of the bed, and her forceful gaze, shooting across the intervening counterpane, pinned Eustace to the pillow. She was in the mood which had caused spines in Somaliland to curl like withered leaves.

"Were you ever engaged to Billie Bennett?" she demanded.

Eustace Hignett licked dry lips. His face looked like a hunted melon. The flannel bandage, draped around it by loving hands, hardly supported his sagging jaw.

"Why—er—"

"*Were* you?" cried Jane, stamping an imperious foot. There was that in her eye before which warriors of the lower Congo had become as chewed blotting-paper. Eustace Hignett shrivelled in the blaze. He was filled with an unendurable sense of guilt.

"Well—er—yes," he mumbled weakly.

Jane Hubbard buried her face in her hands and burst into tears. She might know what to do when alligators started exploring her tent, but she was a woman.

This sudden solution of steely strength into liquid weakness had on Eustace

Hignett the stunning effects which the absence of the last stair has on the returning reveller creeping up to bed in the dark. It was as though his spiritual foot had come down hard on empty space and caused him to bite his tongue. Jane Hubbard had always been to him a rock of support. And now the rock had melted away and left him wallowing in a deep pool.

He wallowed gratefully. It had only needed this to brace him to the point of declaring his love. His awe of this girl had momentarily vanished. He felt strong and dashing. He scrambled down the bed and peered over the foot of it at her huddled form.

"Have some barley-water," he urged. "Try a little barley-water."

It was all he had to offer her except the medicine which, by the doctor's instructions, he took three times a day in a quarter of a glass of water.

"Go away!" sobbed Jane Hubbard.

The unreasonableness of this struck Eustace.

"But I can't. I'm in bed. Where could I go?"

"I hate you!"

"Oh, don't say that!"

"You're still in love with her!"

"Nonsense! I never was in love with her."

"Then why were you going to marry her?"

"Oh, I don't know. It seemed a good idea at the time."

"Oh! Oh! Oh!"

Eustace bent a little further over the end of the bed and patted her hair.

"Do have some barley-water," he said. "Just a sip!"

"You *are* in love with her!" sobbed Jane.

"I'm *not*! I love *you*!"

"You don't!"

"Pardon *me*!" said Eustace firmly. "I've loved you ever since you gave me that extraordinary drink with Worcester sauce in it on the boat."

"They why didn't you say so before?"

"I hadn't the nerve. You always seemed so—I don't know how to put it—I always seemed such a worm. I was just trying to get the courage to propose when I caught the mumps, and that seemed to me to finish it. No girl could love a man with three times the proper amount of face."

"As if that could make any difference! What does your outside matter? I have seen your inside!"

"I beg your pardon?"

"I mean...."

Eustace fondled her back hair.

"Jane! Queen of my soul! Do you really love me?"

"I've loved you ever since we met on the Subway." She raised a tear-stained face. "If only I could be sure that you really loved me!"

"I can prove it!" said Eustace proudly. "You know how scared I am of my mother. Well, for your sake I overcame my fear, and did something which, if she ever found out about it, would make her sorer than a sunburned neck! This house. She absolutely refused to let it to old Bennett and old Mortimer. They kept after her about it, but she wouldn't hear of it. Well, you told me on the boat that Wilhelmina Bennett had invited you to spend the summer with her, and I knew that, if they didn't come to Windles, they would take some other place, and that meant I wouldn't see you. So I hunted up old Mortimer, and let it to him on the quiet, without telling my mother anything about it!"

"Why, you darling angel child," cried Jane Hubbard joyfully. "Did you really do that for my sake? Now I know you love me!"

"Of course, if mother ever got to hear of it...!"

Jane Hubbard pushed him gently into the nest of bedclothes, and tucked him in with strong, calm hands. She was a very different person from the girl who so short a while before had sobbed on the carpet. Love is a wonderful thing.

"You mustn't excite yourself," she said. "You'll be getting a temperature. Lie down and try to get to sleep." She kissed his bulbous face. "You have made me so happy, Eustace darling."

"That's good," said Eustace cordially. "But it's going to be an awful jar for mother!"

"Don't you worry about that. I'll break the news to your mother. I'm sure she will be quite reasonable about it."

Eustace opened his mouth to speak, then closed it again.

"Lie back quite comfortably, and don't worry," said Jane Hubbard. "I'm going to my room to get a book to read you to sleep. I shan't be five minutes. And forget about your mother. I'll look after her."

Eustace closed his eyes. After all, this girl had fought lions, tigers, pumas, cannibals, and alligators in her time with a good deal of success. There might be a sporting chance of victory for her when she moved a step up in the animal kingdom and tackled his mother. He was not unduly optimistic, for he thought she was going out of her class; but he felt faintly hopeful. He allowed himself to drift into pleasant meditation.

There was a scrambling sound outside the door. The handle turned.

"Hullo! Back already?" said Eustace, opening his eyes.

The next moment he opened them wider. His mouth gaped slowly like a hole in a sliding cliff. Mrs. Horace Hignett was standing at his bedside.

§ 3

In the moment which elapsed before either of the two could calm their agitated brains to speech, Eustace became aware, as never before, of the truth of that well-known line—"Peace, perfect peace, with loved ones far away." There was certainly little hope of peace with loved ones in his bedroom. Dully, he realised that in a few minutes Jane Hubbard would be returning with her book, but his imagination refused to envisage the scene which would then occur.

"Eustace!"

Mrs. Hignett gasped, hand on heart.

"Eustace!" For the first time Mrs. Hignett seemed to become aware that it was a changed face that confronted hers. "Good gracious! How stout you've grown!"

"It's mumps."

"Mumps!"

"Yes, I've got mumps."

Mrs. Hignett's mind was too fully occupied with other matters to allow her to dwell on this subject.

"Eustace, there are men in the house!"

This fact was just what Eustace had been wondering how to break to her.

"I know," he said uneasily.

"You know!" Mrs. Hignett stared. "Did you hear them?"

"Hear them?" said Eustace, puzzled.

"The drawing-room window was left open, and there are two burglars in the hall!"

"Oh, I say, no! That's rather rotten!" said Eustace.

"I saw them and heard them! I—oh!" Mrs. Hignett's sentence trailed off into a suppressed shriek, as the door opened and Jane Hubbard came in.

Jane Hubbard was a girl who by nature and training was well adapted to bear shocks. Her guiding motto in life was that helpful line of Horace—*Aequam memento rebus in arduis servare mentem.* (For the benefit of those who have not, like myself, enjoyed an expensive classical education,—memento—Take my tip—servare—preserve—aequam— an unruffled—mentem—mind—rebus in arduis—in every crisis). She had only been out of the room a few minutes, and in that brief period a middle-aged lady of commanding aspect had apparently come up through a trap. It would have been enough to upset most girls, but Jane Hubbard bore it calmly. All through her vivid life her bedroom had been a sort of cosy corner for murderers, alligators, tarantulas, scorpions, and every variety of snake, so she accepted the middle-aged lady without comment.

"Good evening," she said placidly.

Mrs. Hignett, having rallied from her moment of weakness, glared at the new arrival dumbly. She could not place Jane. From the airy way in which she had strolled into the room, she appeared to be some sort of a nurse; but she wore no nurse's uniform.

"Who are you?" she asked stiffly.

"Who are *you*?" asked Jane.

"I," said Mrs. Hignett portentously, "am the owner of this house, and I should be glad to know what you are doing in it. I am Mrs. Horace Hignett."

A charming smile spread itself over Jane's finely-cut face.

"I'm so glad to meet you," she said. "I have heard so much about you."

"Indeed?" said Mrs. Hignett coldly. "And now I should like to hear a little about you."

"I've read all your books," said Jane. "I think they're wonderful."

In spite of herself, in spite of a feeling that this young woman was straying from the point, Mrs. Hignett could not check a slight influx of amiability. She was an authoress who received a good deal of incense from admirers, but she could always do with a bit more. Besides, most of the incense came by post. Living a quiet and retired life in the country, it was rarely that she got it handed to her face to face. She melted quite perceptibly. She did not cease to look like a basilisk, but she began to look like a basilisk who has had a good lunch.

"My favourite," said Jane, who for a week had been sitting daily in a chair in the drawing-room adjoining the table on which the authoress's complete works were assembled, "is 'The Spreading Light.' I *do* like 'The Spreading Light!'"

"It was written some years ago," said Mrs. Hignett with something approaching cordiality, "and I have since revised some of the views I state in it, but I still consider it quite a good text-book."

"Of course, I can see that 'What of the Morrow?' is more profound," said Jane. "But I read 'The Spreading Light' first, and of course that makes a difference."

"I can quite see that it would," agreed Mrs. Hignett. "One's first step across the threshold of a new mind, one's first glimpse...."

"Yes, it makes you feel...."

"Like some watcher of the skies," said Mrs. Hignett, "when a new planet swims into his ken, or like...."

"Yes, doesn't it!" said Jane.

Eustace, who had been listening to the conversation with every muscle tense, in much the same mental attitude as that of a peaceful citizen in a Wild West Saloon who holds himself in readiness to dive under a table directly the shooting begins, began to relax. What he had shrinkingly anticipated would be the biggest thing since the Dempsey-Carpentier fight seemed to be turning into a pleasant social and literary evening not unlike what he imagined a meeting of old Girton students must be. For the first time since his mother had come into the room he indulged in the luxury of a deep breath.

"But what are you doing here?" asked Mrs. Hignett, returning almost reluctantly to the main issue.

Eustace perceived that he had breathed too soon. In an unobtrusive way he subsided into the bed and softly pulled the sheets over his head, following the excellent tactics of the great Duke of Wellington in his Peninsular campaign. "When in doubt," the Duke used to say, "retire and dig yourself in."

"I'm nursing dear Eustace," said Jane.

Mrs. Hignett quivered, and cast an eye on the hump in the bedclothes which represented dear Eustace. A cold fear had come upon her.

"'Dear Eustace!'" she repeated mechanically.

"We're engaged," said Jane.

"Engaged! Eustace, is this true?"

"Yes," said a muffled voice from the interior of the bed.

"And poor Eustace is so worried," continued Jane, "about the house." She went on quickly. "He doesn't want to deprive you of it, because he knows what it means to you. So he is hoping—we are both hoping—that you will accept it as a present when we are married. We really shan't want it, you know. We are going to live in London. So you will take it, won't you—to please us?"

We all of us, even the greatest of us, have our moments of weakness. Only a short while back, in this very room, we have seen Jane Hubbard, that indomitable girl, sobbing brokenly on the carpet. Let us then not express any surprise at the sudden collapse of one of the world's greatest female thinkers. As the meaning of this speech smote on Mrs. Horace Hignett's understanding, she sank weeping into a chair. The ever-present fear that had haunted her had been exorcised. Windles was hers in perpetuity. The relief was too great. She sat in her chair and gulped; and Eustace, greatly encouraged, emerged slowly from the bedclothes like a worm after a thunderstorm.

How long this poignant scene would have lasted, one cannot say. It is a pity that it was cut short, for I should have liked to dwell upon it. But at this moment, from the regions downstairs, there suddenly burst upon the silent night such a whirlwind of sound as effectually dissipated the tense emotion in the room. Somebody appeared to have touched off the orchestrion in the drawing-room, and that willing instrument had begun again in the middle of a bar at the point where Jane Hubbard had switched it off four afternoons ago. Its wailing lament for the passing of Summer filled the whole house.

"That's too bad!" said Jane, a little annoyed. "At this time of night!"

"It's the burglars!" quavered Mrs. Hignett. In the stress of recent events she had completely forgotten the existence of those enemies of Society. "They were dancing in the hall when I arrived, and now they're playing the orchestrion!"

"Light-hearted chaps!" said Eustace, admiring the sang-froid of the criminal world. "Full of spirits!"

"This won't do," said Jane Hubbard, shaking her head. "We can't have this sort of thing. I'll go and fetch my gun."

"They'll murder you, dear!" panted Mrs. Hignett, clinging to her arm.

Jane Hubbard laughed.

"Murder *me*!" she said amusedly. "I'd like to catch them at it!"

Mrs. Hignett stood staring at the door as Jane closed it softly behind her.

"Eustace," she said solemnly, "that is a wonderful girl!"

"Yes! She once killed a panther—or a puma, I forget which—with a hat-pin!" said Eustace with enthusiasm.

"I could wish you no better wife!" said Mrs. Hignett.

She broke off with a sharp wail. Out in the passage something like a battery of artillery had roared.

The door opened and Jane Hubbard appeared, slipping a fresh cartridge into the elephant-gun.

"One of them was popping about outside here," she announced. "I took a shot at him, but I'm afraid I missed. The visibility was bad. At any rate he went away."

In this last statement she was perfectly accurate. Bream Mortimer, who had been aroused by the orchestrion and who had come out to see what was the matter, had gone away at the rate of fifty miles an hour. He had been creeping down the passage when he found himself suddenly confronted by a dim figure which, without a word, had attempted to slay him with an enormous gun. The shot had whistled past his ears and gone singing down the corridor. This was enough for Bream. He had returned to his room in three strides, and was now under the bed. The burglars might take everything in the house and welcome, so that they did not molest his privacy. That was the way Bream looked at it. And very sensible of him, too, I consider.

"We'd better go downstairs," said Jane. "Bring the candle. Not you, Eustace darling. You stay where you are or you may catch a chill. Don't stir out of bed!"

"I won't," said Eustace obediently.

§ 4

Of all the leisured pursuits, there are few less attractive to the thinking man than sitting in a dark cupboard waiting for a house-party to go to bed; and Sam, who had established himself in the one behind the piano at a quarter to eight, soon began to feel as if he had been there for an eternity. He could dimly remember a previous existence in which he had not been sitting in his present position, but it seemed so long ago that it was shadowy and unreal to him. The ordeal of spending the evening in this retreat had not appeared formidable when he had contemplated it that afternoon in the lane; but, now that he was actually undergoing it, it was extraordinary how many disadvantages it had.

Cupboards, as a class, are badly ventilated, and this one seemed to contain no air at all; and the warmth of the night, combined with the cupboard's natural stuffiness, had soon begun to reduce Sam to a condition of pulp. He seemed to himself to be sagging like an ice-cream in front of a fire. The darkness, too, weighed upon him. He was abominably thirsty. Also he wanted to smoke. In addition to this, the small of his back tickled, and he more than suspected the cupboard of harbouring mice. Not once or twice but many hundred times he wished that the ingenious Webster had thought of something simpler.

His was a position which would just have suited one of those Indian mystics who sit perfectly still for twenty years, contemplating the Infinite, but it reduced Sam to an almost imbecile state of boredom. He tried counting sheep. He tried going over his past life in his mind from the earliest moment he could recollect, and thought he had never encountered a duller series of episodes. He found a temporary solace by playing a succession of mental golf-games over all the courses he could remember, and he was just teeing up for the sixteenth at Muirfield, after playing Hoylake, St. Andrew's, Westward Ho, Hanger Hill, Mid-Surrey, Walton Heath, and Sandwich, when the light ceased to shine through the crack under the door, and he awoke with a sense of dull incredulity to the realisation that the occupants of the drawing-room had called it a day and that his vigil was over.

But was it? Once more alert, Sam became cautious. True, the light seemed to be off, but did that mean anything in a country-house, where people had the habit of going and strolling about the garden to all hours? Probably they were still popping about all over the place. At any rate, it was not worth risking coming out of his lair. He remembered that Webster had promised to come and knock an all-clear signal on the door. It would be safer to wait for that.

But the moments went by, and there was no knock. Sam began to grow impatient. The last few minutes of waiting in a cupboard are always the hardest. Time seemed to stretch out again interminably. Once he thought he heard footsteps but they led to nothing. Eventually, having strained his ears and finding everything still, he decided to take a chance. He fished in his pocket for the key, cautiously unlocked the door, opened it by slow inches, and peered out.

The room was in blackness. The house was still. All was well. With the feeling of a life-prisoner emerging from the Bastille, he began to crawl stiffly forward; and it was just then that the first of the disturbing events occurred which were to make this night memorable to him. Something like a rattlesnake suddenly went off with a whirr, and his head, jerking up, collided with the piano. It was only the cuckoo-clock, which now, having cleared its throat as was its custom before striking, proceeded to cuck eleven times in rapid succession before subsiding with another rattle; but to Sam it sounded like the end of the world.

He sat in the darkness, massaging his bruised skull. His hours of imprisonment in the cupboard had had a bad effect on his nervous system, and he vacillated between tears of weakness and a militant desire to get at the cuckoo-clock with a hatchet. He felt that it had done it on purpose and was now chuckling to itself in fancied security. For quite a minute he raged silently, and any cuckoo-clock which had strayed within his reach would have had a bad time of it. Then his attention was diverted.

So concentrated was Sam on his private vendetta with the clock that no ordinary happening would have had the power to distract him. What occurred now was by no means ordinary, and it distracted him like an electric shock. As he sat on the floor, passing a tender hand over the egg-shaped bump which had already begun to manifest itself beneath his hair, something cold and wet touched his face, and paralysed him so completely both physically and mentally that he did not move a muscle but just congealed where he sat into a solid block of ice. He felt vaguely that this was the end. His heart had stopped beating and he simply could not imagine it ever starting again, and, if your heart refuses to beat, what hope is there for you?

At this moment something heavy and solid struck him squarely in the chest, rolling him over. Something gurgled asthmatically in the darkness. Something began to lick his eyes, ears, and chin in a sort of ecstasy; and, clutching out, he found his arms full of totally unexpected bulldog.

"Get out!" whispered Sam tensely, recovering his faculties with a jerk. "Go away!"

Smith took the opportunity of Sam's lips having opened to lick the roof of his mouth. Smith's attitude in the matter was that Providence in its all-seeing wisdom had sent him a human being at a moment when he had reluctantly been compelled to reconcile himself to a total absence of such indispensable adjuncts to a good time. He had just trotted downstairs in rather a disconsolate frame of mind after waiting with no result in front of Webster's bedroom door, and it was a real treat to him to meet a man, especially one seated in such a jolly and sociable manner on the floor. He welcomed Sam like a long-lost friend.

Between Smith and the humans who provided him with dog-biscuits and occasionally with sweet cakes there had always existed a state of misunderstanding which no words could remove. The position of the humans was quite clear; they had elected Smith to his present position on a straight watch-dog ticket. They expected him to be one of those dogs who rouse the house and save the spoons. They looked to him to pin burglars by the leg and hold on till the police arrived. Smith simply could not grasp such an attitude of mind. He regarded Windles not as a private house but as a social club, and was utterly unable to see any difference between the human beings he knew and the strangers who dropped in for a late chat after the place was locked up. He had no intention of biting Sam. The idea never entered his head. At the present moment what he felt about Sam was that he was one of the best fellows he had ever met and that he loved him like a brother.

Sam, in his unnerved state, could not bring himself to share these amiable sentiments. He was thinking bitterly that Webster might have had the intelligence to warn him of bulldogs on the premises. It was just the sort of woollen-headed thing fellows did, forgetting facts like that. He scrambled stiffly to his feet and tried to pierce the darkness that hemmed him in. He ignored Smith, who snuffled sportively about his ankles, and made for the slightly less black oblong which he took to be the door leading into the hall. He moved warily, but not warily enough to prevent his cannoning into and almost upsetting a small table with a vase on it. The table rocked and the vase jumped, and the first bit of luck that had come to Sam that night was when he reached out at a venture and caught it just as it was about to bound on to the carpet.

He stood there, shaking. The narrowness of the escape turned him cold. If he had been an instant later, there would have been a crash loud enough to wake a dozen sleeping houses. This sort of thing could not go on. He must have light. It might be a risk; there might be a chance of somebody upstairs seeing it and coming down to investigate; but it was a risk that must be taken. He declined to go on stumbling about in this darkness any longer. He groped his way with infinite care to the door, on the wall adjoining which, he presumed, the electric-light switch would be. It was nearly ten years since he had last been inside Windles, and it never occurred to him that in this progressive age even a woman like his Aunt Adeline, of whom he could believe almost anything, would still be using candles and oil-lamps as a means of illumination. His only doubt was whether the switch was where it was in most houses, near the door.

It is odd to reflect that, as his searching fingers touched the knob, a delicious feeling of relief came to Samuel Marlowe. This misguided young man actually felt at that moment that his troubles were over. He positively smiled as he placed a thumb on the knob and shoved.

He shoved strongly and sharply, and instantaneously there leaped at him out of the darkness a blare of music which appeared to his disordered mind quite solid. It seemed to wrap itself round him. It was all over the place. In a single instant the world had become one vast bellow of Tosti's "Good-bye."

How long he stood there, frozen, he did not know; nor can one say how long he would have stood there had nothing further come to invite his notice elsewhere. But, suddenly, drowning even the impromptu concert, there came from somewhere upstairs the roar of a gun; and, when he heard that, Sam's rigid limbs relaxed and a violent activity descended upon him. He bounded out into the hall, looking to right and to left for a hiding-place. One of the suits of armour which had been familiar to him in his boyhood loomed up in front of him, and with the sight came the recollection of how, when a mere child on his first visit to Windles, playing hide and seek with his cousin Eustace, he had concealed himself inside this very suit, and had not only baffled Eustace through a long summer evening but had wound up by almost scaring him into a decline by booing at him through the vizor of the helmet. Happy days, happy days! He leaped at the suit of armour. Having grown since he was last inside it, he found the helmet a tight fit, but he managed to get his head into it at last, and the body of the thing was quite roomy.

"Thank heaven!" said Sam.

He was not comfortable, but comfort just then was not his primary need.

Smith the bulldog, well satisfied with the way the entertainment had opened, sat down, wheezing slightly, to await developments.

§ 5

He had not long to wait. In a few minutes the hall had filled up nicely. There was Mr. Mortimer in his shirt-sleeves, Mr. Bennett in blue pyjamas and a dressing-gown, Mrs. Hignett in a travelling costume, Jane Hubbard with her elephant-gun, and Billie in a dinner dress. Smith welcomed them all impartially.

Somebody lit a lamp, and Mrs. Hignett stared speechlessly at the mob.

"Mr. Bennett! Mr. Mortimer!"

"Mrs. Hignett! What are you doing here?"

Mrs. Hignett drew herself up stiffly.

"What an odd question, Mr. Mortimer! I am in my own house!"

"But you rented it to me for the summer. At least, your son did."

"Eustace let you Windles for the summer!" said Mrs. Hignett incredulously.

Jane Hubbard returned from the drawing-room, where she had been switching off the orchestrion.

"Let us talk all that over cosily to-morrow," she said. "The point now is that there are burglars in the house."

"Burglars!" cried Mr. Bennett aghast. "I thought it was you playing that infernal instrument, Mortimer."

"What on earth should I play it for at this time of night?" said Mr. Mortimer irritably.

"It woke me up," said Mr. Bennett complainingly. "And I had had great difficulty in dropping off to sleep. I was in considerable pain. I believe I've caught the mumps from young Hignett."

"Nonsense! You're always imagining yourself ill," snapped Mr. Mortimer.

"My face hurts," persisted Mr. Bennett.

"You can't expect a face like that not to hurt," said Mr. Mortimer.

It appeared only too evident that the two old friends were again on the verge of one of their distressing fallings-out; but Jane Hubbard intervened once more. This practical-minded girl disliked the introducing of side-issues into the conversation. She was there to talk about burglars, and she intended to do so.

"For goodness sake stop it!" she said, almost petulantly for one usually so superior to emotion. "There'll be lots of time for quarrelling to-morrow. Just now we've got to catch these...."

"I'm not quarrelling," said Mr. Bennett.

"Yes, you are," said Mr. Mortimer.

"I'm not!"

"You are!"

"Don't argue!"

"I'm not arguing!"

"You are!"

"I'm not!"

Jane Hubbard had practically every noble quality which a woman can possess with the exception of patience. A patient woman would have stood by, shrinking from interrupting the dialogue. Jane Hubbard's robuster course was to raise the elephant-gun, point it at the front door, and pull the trigger.

"I thought that would stop you," she said complacently, as the echoes died away and Mr. Bennett had finished leaping into the air. She inserted a fresh cartridge, and sloped arms. "Now, the question is...."

"You made me bite my tongue!" said Mr. Bennett, deeply aggrieved.

"Serve you right!" said Jane placidly. "Now, the question is, have the fellows got away or are they hiding somewhere in the house? I think they're still in the house."

"The police!" exclaimed Mr. Bennett, forgetting his lacerated tongue and his other grievances. "We must summon the police!"

"Obviously!" said Mrs. Hignett, withdrawing her fascinated gaze from the ragged hole in the front door, the cost of repairing which she had been mentally assessing. "We must send for the police at once."

"We don't really need them, you know," said Jane. "If you'll all go to bed and just leave me to potter round with my gun...."

"And blow the whole house to pieces!" said Mrs. Hignett tartly. She had begun to revise her original estimate of this girl. To her, Windles was sacred, and anyone who went about shooting holes in it forfeited her esteem.

"Shall I go for the police?" said Billie. "I could bring them back in ten minutes in the car."

"Certainly not!" said Mr. Bennett. "My daughter gadding about all over the countryside in an automobile at this time of night!"

"If you think I ought not to go alone, I could take Bream."

"Where *is* Bream?" said Mr. Mortimer.

The odd fact that Bream was not among those present suddenly presented itself to the company.

"Where can he be?" said Billie.

Jane Hubbard laughed the wholesome, indulgent laugh of one who is broad-minded enough to see the humour of the situation even when the joke is at her expense.

"What a silly girl I am!" she said. "I do believe that was Bream I shot at upstairs. How foolish of me making a mistake like that!"

"You shot my only son!" cried Mr. Mortimer.

"I shot *at* him," said Jane. "My belief is that I missed him. Though how I came to do it beats me. I don't suppose I've missed a sitter like that since I was a child in the nursery. Of course," she proceeded, looking on the reasonable side, "the visibility wasn't good, but it's no use saying I oughtn't at least to have winged him, because I ought." She shook her head with a touch of self-reproach. "I shall get chaffed about this if it comes out," she said regretfully.

"The poor boy must be in his room," said Mr. Mortimer.

"Under the bed, if you ask me," said Jane, blowing on the barrel of her gun and polishing it with the side of her hand. "*He's* all right! Leave him alone, and the housemaid will sweep him up in the morning."

"Oh, he can't be!" cried Billie, revolted.

A girl of high spirit, it seemed to her repellent that the man she was engaged to marry should be displaying such a craven spirit. At that moment she despised and hated Bream Mortimer. I think she was wrong, mind you. It is not my place to criticise the little group of people whose simple annals I am relating—my position is merely that of a reporter—; but personally I think highly of Bream's sturdy common-sense. If somebody loosed off an elephant-gun at me in a dark corridor, I would climb on to the roof and pull it up after me. Still, rightly or wrongly, that was how Billie felt; and it flashed across her mind that Samuel Marlowe, scoundrel though he was, would not have behaved like this. And for a moment a certain wistfulness added itself to the varied emotions then engaging her mind.

"I'll go and look, if you like," said Jane agreeably. "You amuse yourselves somehow till I come back."

She ran easily up the stairs, three at a time. Mr. Mortimer turned to Mr. Bennett.

"It's all very well your saying Wilhelmina mustn't go, but, if she doesn't, how can we get the police? The house isn't on the 'phone, and nobody else can drive the car."

"That's true," said Mr. Bennett, wavering.

"Of course, we could drop them a post-card first thing to-morrow morning," said Mr. Mortimer in his nasty sarcastic way.

"I'm going," said Billie resolutely. It occurred to her, as it has occurred to so many women before her, how helpless men are in a crisis. The temporary withdrawal of Jane Hubbard had had the effect which the removal of the rudder has on a boat. "It's the only thing to do. I shall be back in no time."

She stepped firmly to the coat-rack, and began to put on her motoring-cloak. And just then Jane Hubbard came downstairs, shepherding before her a pale and glassy-eyed Bream.

"Right under the bed," she announced cheerfully, "making a noise like a piece of fluff in order to deceive burglars."

Billie cast a scornful look at her fiancé. Absolutely unjustified, in my opinion, but nevertheless she cast it. But it had no effect at all. Terror had stunned Bream Mortimer's perceptions. His was what the doctors call a penumbral mental condition.

"Bream," said Billie, "I want you to come in the car with me to fetch the police."

"All right," said Bream.

"Get your coat."

"All right," said Bream.

"And cap."

"All right," said Bream.

He followed Billie in a docile manner out through the front door, and they made their way to the garage at the back of the house, both silent. The only difference between their respective silences was that Billie's was thoughtful, while Bream's was just the silence of a man who has unhitched his brain and is getting along as well as he can without it.

In the hall they had left, Jane Hubbard once more took command of affairs.

"Well, that's something done," she said, scratching Smith's broad back with the muzzle of her weapon. "Something accomplished, something done, has earned a night's repose. Not that we're going to get it yet. I think those fellows are hiding somewhere, and we ought to search the house and rout them out. It's a pity Smith isn't a bloodhound. He's a good cake-hound, but as a watch-dog he doesn't finish in the first ten."

The cake-hound, charmed at the compliment, frisked about her feet like a young elephant.

"The first thing to do," continued Jane, "is to go through the ground-floor rooms...." She paused to strike a match against the suit of armour nearest to her, a proceeding which elicited a sharp cry of protest from Mrs. Hignett, and lit a cigarette. "I'll go first, as I've got a gun...." She blew a cloud of smoke. "I shall want somebody with me to carry a light, and...."

"Tchoo!"

"What?" said Jane.

"I didn't speak," said Mr. Mortimer. "Who am I to speak?" he went on bitterly. "Who am I that it should be supposed that I have anything sensible to suggest?"

"Somebody spoke," said Jane. "I...."

"Achoo!"

"Do you feel a draught, Mr. Bennett?" cried Jane sharply, wheeling round on him.

"There *is* a draught," began Mr. Bennett.

"Well, finish sneezing and I'll go on."

"I didn't sneeze!"

"Somebody sneezed."

"It seemed to come from just behind you," said Mrs. Hignett nervously.

"It couldn't have come from just behind me," said Jane, "because there isn't anything behind me from which it could have...." She stopped suddenly, in her eyes the light of understanding, on her face the set expression which was wont to come to it on the eve of action. "Oh!" she said in a different voice, a voice which was cold and tense and sinister. "Oh, I see!" She raised her gun, and placed a muscular forefinger on the trigger. "Come out of that!" she said. "Come out of that suit of armour and let's have a look at you!"

"I can explain everything," said a muffled voice through the vizor of the helmet. "I can—*achoo!*" The smoke of the cigarette tickled Sam's nostrils again, and he suspended his remarks.

"I shall count three," said Jane Hubbard, "One—two—"

"I'm coming! I'm coming!" said Sam petulantly.

"You'd better!" said Jane.

"I can't get this dashed helmet off!"

"If you don't come quick, I'll blow it off."

Sam stepped out into the hall, a picturesque figure which combined the costumes of two widely separated centuries. Modern as far as the neck, he slipped back at that point to the Middle Ages.

"Hands up!" commanded Jane Hubbard.

"My hands *are* up!" retorted Sam querulously, as he wrenched at his unbecoming head-wear.

"Never mind trying to raise your hat," said Jane. "If you've lost the combination, we'll dispense with the formalities. What we're anxious to hear is what you're doing in the house at this time of night, and who your pals are. Come along, my lad, make a clean breast of it and perhaps you'll get off easier. Are you a gang?"

"Do I look like a gang?"

"If you ask me what you look like...."

"My name is Marlowe ... Samuel Marlowe...."

"Alias what?"

"Alias nothing! I say my name is Samuel Marlowe...."

An explosive roar burst from Mr. Bennett.

"The scoundrel! I know him! I forbade him the house, and...."

"And by what right did you forbid people my house, Mr. Bennett?" said Mrs. Hignett with acerbity.

"I've rented the house, Mortimer and I rented it from your son...."

"Yes, yes, yes," said Jane Hubbard. "Never mind about that. So you know this fellow, do you?"

"I don't know him!"

"You said you did."

"I refuse to know him!" went on Mr. Bennett. "I won't know him! I decline to have anything to do with him!"

"But you identify him?"

"If he says he's Samuel Marlowe," assented Mr. Bennett grudgingly, "I suppose he is. I can't imagine anybody saying he was Samuel Marlowe if he didn't know it could be proved against him."

"Are you my nephew Samuel?" said Mrs. Hignett.

"Yes," said Sam.

"Well, what are you doing in my house?"

"It's *my* house," said Mr. Bennett, "for the summer, Henry Mortimer's and mine. Isn't that right, Henry?"

"Dead right," said Mr. Mortimer.

"There!" said Mr. Bennett. "You hear? And when Henry Mortimer says a thing, it's so. There's nobody's word I'd take before Henry Mortimer's."

"When Rufus Bennett makes an assertion," said Mr. Mortimer, highly flattered by these kind words, "you can bank on it. Rufus Bennett's word is his bond. Rufus Bennett is a white man!"

The two old friends, reconciled once more, clasped hands with a good deal of feeling.

"I am not disputing Mr. Bennett's claim to belong to the Caucasian race," said Mrs. Hignett testily. "I merely maintain that this house is m...."

"Yes, yes, yes, yes!" interrupted Jane. "You can thresh all that out some other time. The point is, if this fellow is your nephew, I don't see what we can do. We'll have to let him go."

"I came to this house," said Sam, raising his vizor to facilitate speech, "to make a social call...."

"At this hour of the night!" snapped Mrs. Hignett. "You always were an inconsiderate boy, Samuel."

"I came to inquire after poor Eustace's mumps. I've only just heard that the poor chap was ill."

"He's getting along quite well," said Jane, melting. "If I had known you were so fond of Eustace...."

"All right, is he?" said Sam.

"Well, not quite all right, but he's going on very nicely."

"Fine!"

"Eustace and I are engaged, you know!"

"No, really? Splendid! I can't see you very distinctly—how those Johnnies in the old days ever contrived to put up a scrap with things like this on their heads beats me—but you sound a good sort. I hope you'll be very happy."

"Thank you ever so much, Mr. Marlowe. I'm sure we shall."

"Eustace is one of the best."

"How nice of you to say so."

"All this," interrupted Mrs. Hignett, who had been a chaffing auditor of this interchange of courtesies, "is beside the point. Why did you dance in the hall, Samuel, and play the orchestrion?"

"Yes," said Mr. Bennett, reminded of his grievance, "waking people up."

"Scaring us all to death!" complained Mr. Mortimer.

"I remember you as a boy, Samuel," said Mrs. Hignett, "lamentably lacking in consideration for others and concentrated only on your selfish pleasures. You seem to have altered very little."

"Don't ballyrag the poor man," said Jane Hubbard. "Be human! Lend him a sardine opener!"

"I shall do nothing of the sort," said Mrs. Hignett. "I never liked him and I dislike him now. He has got himself into this trouble through his own wrong-headedness."

"It's not his fault his head's the wrong size," said Jane.

"He must get himself out as best he can," said Mrs. Hignett.

"Very well," said Sam with bitter dignity. "Then I will not trespass further on your hospitality, Aunt Adeline. I have no doubt the local blacksmith will be able to get this damned thing off me. I shall go to him now. I will let you have the helmet back by parcel-post at the earliest opportunity. Good-night!" He walked coldly to the front door. "And there are people," he remarked sardonically, "who

say that blood is thicker than water! I'll
bet they never had any aunts!"

He tripped over the mat and withdrew.

§ 6

Billie meanwhile, with Bream trotting
docilely at her heels, had reached the
garage and started the car. Like all cars
which have been spending a considerable
time in secluded inaction, it did not start
readily. At each application of Billie's
foot on the self-starter, it emitted a
tinny and reproachful sound and then
seemed to go to sleep again. Eventually,
however, the engines began to revolve
and the machine moved reluctantly out
into the drive.

"The battery must be run down," said
Billie.

"All right," said Bream.

Billie cast a glance of contempt at
him out of the corner of her eyes. She
hardly knew why she had spoken to him
except that, as all motorists are aware,

the impulse to say rude things about their battery is almost irresistible. To a motorist the art of conversation consists in rapping out scathing remarks either about the battery or the oiling-system.

Billie switched on the head-lights and turned the car down the dark drive. She was feeling thoroughly upset. Her idealistic nature had received a painful shock on the discovery of the yellow streak in Bream. To call it a yellow streak was to understate the facts. It was a great belt of saffron encircling his whole soul. That she, Wilhelmina Bennett, who had gone through the world seeking a Galahad, should finish her career as the wife of a man who hid under beds simply because people shot at him with elephant guns was abhorrent to her. Why, Samuel Marlowe would have perished rather than do such a thing. You might say what you liked about Samuel Marlowe—and, of course, his habit of playing practical jokes put him beyond the pale—but nobody could question his courage. Look at the way he had dived overboard that time in the harbour at

New York! Billie found herself thinking wistfully about Samuel Marlowe.

There are only a few makes of car in which you can think about anything except the actual driving without stalling the engines, and Mr. Bennett's Twin-Six Complex was not one of them. It stopped as if it had been waiting for the signal.... The noise of the engine died away. The wheels ceased to revolve. The car did everything except lie down. It was a particularly pig-headed car and right from the start it had been unable to see the sense in this midnight expedition. It seemed now to have the idea that if it just lay low and did nothing, presently it would be taken back to its cosy garage.

Billie trod on the self-starter. Nothing happened.

"You'll have to get down and crank her," she said curtly.

"All right," said Bream.

"Well, go on," said Billie impatiently.

"Eh?"

"Get out and crank her."

Bream emerged for an instant from his trance.

"All right," he said.

The art of cranking a car is one that is not given to all men. Some of our greatest and wisest stand helpless before the task. It is a job towards the consummation of which a noble soul and a fine brain help not at all. A man may have all the other gifts and yet be unable to accomplish a task which the fellow at the garage does with one quiet flick of the wrist without even bothering to remove his chewing gum. This being so, it was not only unkind but foolish of Billie to grow impatient as Bream's repeated efforts failed of their object. It was wrong of her to click her tongue, and certainly she ought not to have told Bream that he was not fit to churn butter. But women are an emotional sex and must be forgiven much in moments of mental stress.

"Give it a good sharp twist," she said.

"All right," said Bream.

"Here, let me do it," cried Billie.

She jumped down and snatched the thingummy from his hand. With bent brows and set teeth she wrenched it round. The engine gave a faint protesting mutter, like a dog that has been disturbed in its sleep, and was still once more.

"May I help?"

It was not Bream who spoke but a strange voice—a sepulchral voice, the sort of voice someone would have used in one of Edgar Allen Poe's cheerful little tales if he had been buried alive and were speaking from the family vault. Coming suddenly out of the night it affected Bream painfully. He uttered a sharp exclamation and gave a bound which, if he had been a Russian dancer would undoubtedly have caused the management to raise his salary. He was in no frame of mind to bear up under sudden sepulchral voices.

Billie, on the other hand, was pleased. The high-spirited girl was just beginning to fear that she was unequal to the task which she had chided Bream for being unable to perform and this was mortifying her.

"Oh, would you mind? Thank you so much. The self-starter has gone wrong."

Into the glare of the headlights there stepped a strange figure, strange, that is to say, in these tame modern times. In the Middle Ages he would have excited no comment at all. Passers by would simply have said to themselves, "Ah, another of those knights off after the dragons!" and would have gone on their way with a civil greeting. But in the present age it is always somewhat startling to see a helmeted head pop up in front of your motor car. At any rate, it startled Bream. I will go further. It gave Bream the shock of a lifetime. He had had shocks already that night, but none to be compared with this. Or perhaps it was that this shock, coming on top of those shocks, affected him more disastrously than it would have done if it had been the first of the series instead of the last. One may express the thing briefly by saying that, as far as Bream was concerned, Sam's unconventional appearance put the lid on it. He did not hesitate. He did not pause to make comments or ask questions. With a single cat-like screech which took years off the lives of the abruptly wakened birds roosting in the neighbouring trees, he dashed away towards the house and, reaching his room, locked the door and pushed the bed, the chest of drawers, two chairs, the towel stand, and three pairs of boots against it.

Out on the drive Billie was staring at the man in armour who had now, with a masterful wrench which informed the car right away that he would stand no nonsense, set the engine going again.

"Why—why," she stammered, "why are you wearing that thing on your head?"

"Because I can't get it off."

Hollow as the voice was, Billie recognised it.

"S—Mr. Marlowe!" she exclaimed.

"Get in," said Sam. He had seated himself at the steering wheel. "Where can I take you?"

"Go away!" said Billie.

"Get in!"

"I don't want to talk to you."

"I want to talk to *you*! Get in!"

"I won't."

Sam bent over the side of the car, put his hands under her arms, lifted her like a kitten, and deposited her on the seat beside him. Then throwing in the clutch, he drove at an ever-increasing speed down the drive and out into the silent road. Strange creatures of the night came and went in the golden glow of the head-lights.

§ 7

"Put me down," said Billie.

"You'd get hurt if I did, travelling at this pace."

"What are you going to do?"

"Drive about till you promise to marry me."

"You'll have to drive a long time."

"Right ho!" said Sam.

The car took a corner and purred down a lane. Billie reached out a hand and grabbed at the steering wheel.

"Of course, if you *want* to smash up in a ditch!" said Sam, righting the car with a wrench.

"You're a brute!" said Billie.

"Caveman stuff," explained Sam, "I ought to have tried it before."

"I don't know what you expect to gain by this."

"That's all right," said Sam, "I know what I'm about."

"I'm glad to hear it."

"I thought you would be."

"I'm not going to talk to you."

"All right. Lean back and doze off. We've the whole night before us."

"What do you mean?" cried Billie, sitting up with a jerk.

"Have you ever been to Scotland?"

"What do you mean?"

"I thought we might push up there. We've got to go somewhere and, oddly enough, I've never been to Scotland."

Billie regarded him blankly.

"Are you crazy?"

"I'm crazy about you. If you knew what I've gone through to-night for your sake you'd be more sympathetic. I love you," said Sam, swerving to avoid a rabbit. "And what's more, you know it."

"I don't care."

"You will!" said Sam confidently. "How about North Wales? I've heard people speak well of North Wales. Shall we head for North Wales?"

"I'm engaged to Bream Mortimer."

"Oh no, that's all off," Sam assured her.

"It's not!"

"Right off!" said Sam firmly. "You could never bring yourself to marry a man who dashed away like that and deserted you in your hour of need. Why, for all he knew, I might have tried to murder you. And he ran away! No, no, we eliminate Bream Mortimer once and for all. He won't do!"

This was so exactly what Billie was feeling herself that she could not bring herself to dispute it.

"Anyway, I hate *you*!" she said, giving the conversation another turn.

"Why? In the name of goodness, why?"

"How dared you make a fool of me in your father's office that morning?"

"It was a sudden inspiration. I had to do something to make you think well of me, and I thought it might meet the case if I saved you from a lunatic with a pistol. It wasn't my fault that you found out."

"I shall never forgive you!"

"Why not Cornwall?" said Sam. "The Riviera of England! Let's go to Cornwall. I beg your pardon. What were you saying?"

"I said I should never forgive you and I won't."

"Well, I hope you're fond of motoring," said Sam, "because we're going on till you do."

"Very well! Go on, then!"

"I intend to. Of course, it's all right now while it's dark. But have you considered what is going to happen when the sun gets up? We shall have a sort of triumphal procession. How the small boys will laugh when they see a man in a helmet go by in a car! I shan't notice them myself because it's a little difficult to notice anything from inside this thing, but I'm afraid it will be rather unpleasant for you.... I know what we'll do. We'll go to London and drive up and down Piccadilly! That will be fun!"

There was a long silence.

"Is my helmet on straight?" said Sam.

Billie made no reply. She was looking before her down the hedge-bordered road. Always a girl of sudden impulses, she had just made a curious discovery, to wit that she was enjoying herself. There was something so novel and exhilarating about this midnight ride that imperceptibly her dismay and resentment had ebbed away. She found herself struggling with a desire to laugh.

"Lochinvar!" said Sam suddenly. "That's the name of the chap I've been trying to think of! Did you ever read about Lochinvar? 'Young Lochinvar' the poet calls him rather familiarly. He did just what I'm doing now, and everybody thought very highly of him. I suppose in those days a helmet was just an ordinary part of what the well-dressed man should wear. Odd how fashions change!"

Till now dignity and wrath combined had kept Billie from making any inquiries into a matter which had excited in her a quite painful curiosity. In her new mood she resisted the impulse no longer.

"*Why* are you wearing that thing?"

"I told you. Purely and simply because I can't get it off. You don't suppose I'm trying to set a new style in gents' head-wear, do you?"

"But why did you ever put it on?"

"Well, it was this way. After I came out of the cupboard in the drawing-room...."

"What!"

"Didn't I tell you about that? Oh yes, I was sitting in the cupboard in the drawing-room from dinner-time onwards. After that I came out and started cannoning about among Aunt Adeline's china, so I thought I'd better switch the light on. Unfortunately I switched on some sort of musical instrument instead. And then somebody started shooting. So, what with one thing and another, I thought it would be best to hide somewhere. I hid in one of the suits of armour in the hall."

"Were you inside there all the time we were...?"

"Yes. I say, that was funny about Bream, wasn't it? Getting under the bed, I mean."

"Don't let's talk about Bream."

"That's the right spirit! I like to see it! All right, we won't. Let's get back to the main issue. Will you marry me?"

"But why did you come to the house at all?"

"To see you."

"To see me! At that time of night?"

"Well, perhaps not actually to see you." Sam was a little perplexed for a moment. Something told him that it would be injudicious to reveal his true motive and thereby risk disturbing the harmony which he felt had begun to exist between them. "To be near you! To be in the same house with you!" he went on vehemently feeling that he had struck the right note. "You don't know the anguish I went through after I read that letter of yours. I was mad! I was ... well, to return to the point, will you marry me?"

Billie sat looking straight before her. The car, now on the main road, moved smoothly on.

"Will you marry me?"

Billie rested her hand on her chin and searched the darkness with thoughtful eyes.

"Will you marry me?"

The car raced on.

"Will you marry me?" said Sam. "Will you marry me? Will you marry me?"

"Oh, don't talk like a parrot," cried Billie. "It reminds me of Bream."

"But will you?"

"Yes," said Billie.

Sam brought the car to a standstill with a jerk, probably very bad for the tyres.

"Did you say 'yes'?"

"Yes!"

"Darling!" said Sam, leaning towards her. "Oh, curse this helmet!"

"Why?"

"Well, I rather wanted to kiss you and it hampers me."

"Let me try and get it off. Bend down!"

"Ouch!" said Sam.

"It's coming. There! How helpless men are!"

"We need a woman's tender care," said Sam depositing the helmet on the floor of the car and rubbing his smarting ears. "Billie!"

"Sam!"

"You angel!"

"You're rather a darling after all," said Billie. "But you want keeping in order," she added severely.

"You will do that when we're married. When we're married!" he repeated luxuriously. "How splendid it sounds!"

"The only trouble is," said Billie, "father won't hear of it."

"No, he won't. Not till it is all over," said Sam.

He started the car again.

"What are you going to do?" said Billie. "Where are you going?"

"To London," said Sam. "It may be news to you but the old lawyer like myself knows that, by going to Doctors' Commons or the Court of Arches or somewhere or by routing the Archbishop of Canterbury out of bed or something, you can get a special licence and be married almost before you know where you are. My scheme—roughly—is to dig this special licence out of whoever keeps such things, have a bit of breakfast, and then get married at our leisure before lunch at a registrar's."

"Oh, not a registrar's!" said Billie.

"No?"

"I should hate a registrar's."

"Very well, angel. Just as you say. We'll go to a church. There are millions of churches in London. I've seen them all over the place." He mused for a moment. "Yes, you're quite right," he said. "A church is the thing. It'll please Webster."

"Webster?"

"Yes, he's rather keen on the church bells never having rung out so blithe a peal before. And we must consider Webster's feelings. After all, he brought us together."

"Webster? How?"

"Oh, I'll tell you all about that some other time," said Sam. "Just for the moment I want to sit quite still and think. Are you comfortable? Fine! Then off we go."

The birds in the trees fringing the road stirred and twittered grumpily as the noise of the engine disturbed their slumbers. But, if they had only known it, they were in luck. At any rate, the worst had not befallen them, for Sam was too happy to sing.

THE END.

CPSIA information can be obtained at www.ICGtesting.com

226865LV00001B/10/A

9 788189 952914